CELESTIAL DANCE

JOYCE WELLS

Celestial Dance

This book is printed in the U.S. by Peace Seeker Books
With the exception of quotes used in reviews, this book may
not be reproduced or used in whole or in part by any means
existing without written permission

Contact information: jwellsfam@yahoo.com

This book is a work of fiction. Any resemblance to persons, living
or dead, or places, events and locales is purely coincidental. Names,
places, incidents, and characters are either the products of the
author's imagination or used fictitiously.

ISBN: 0615600255
ISBN 13: 9780615600253.

WHAT CRITICS SAID ABOUT THE PEACE SEEKERS

"Wow, this is a fun story!.... If you love a good heart-pounding, edgy, suspense story along with a good triumph over evil theme, and wonderfully creative psychic powers, then you'll enjoy this story!"

—Fallen Angel Reviews, 5 Angels

"Satisfying action, suspense-filled days, and mysterious characters make this story a good one to get involved in....Joyce developed a believable plot, filled it with the right characters, and brought the story to a satisfying end. A story a few notches above a real good tale."

—Alternative Read Reviews

This book is dedicated to Spirit, source of all knowledge, comfort and initiative, with special thanks to angels David and Davon, a spritely pair who never let me down.

Also dedicated to husband, Ben, who endures my occasional fits of uncontrolled creativity and productivity with kindness and devotion.

Acknowledgments

Special Thanks To:

Karen Dean Benson and Brenda Pierce, critique partners extraordinaire, and others too numerous to mention, but who nevertheless occupy a place in this book and in my heart.

About The Author

An independent literary consultant and an instructor for
Writer's Digest University online classes in, among others,
Fundamentals of Fiction, Advanced Novel Writing, and
Advanced Poetry Writing, Joyce Wells earned a BA and MA
in Developmental Psychology from Oakland University
in Rochester, Michigan, where she volunteered as a peer
counselor. After marrying and raising a son and daughter, and
while working for an executive office group, she returned to
her love of writing and received an award in a national short
story competition.

She has published poems, essays, and stories in antholo-
gies, newsletters, newspapers, and national magazines. She
belongs to Romance Writers of America and Detroit Working
Writers. She also serves as a judge for a national self-published
mainstream novel writing competition.

Joyce divides her time between the Midwest and Florida,
where she indulges her passion for golf and swimming. When
she isn't on the links, she's studying parapsychology and the
connection between the present and the past, the physical, and
the spiritual.

CELESTIAL DANCE is a sequel to her acclaimed debut
novel *THE PEACE SEEKERS*, Jasmine-Jade Enterprises, LLC.

Trademarks & Acknowledgments:

Penny Bears:
The Penny Bear Company,
a nonprofit all-volunteer organization,
www.pennybear.org

Gold's Gym
Band Aid, registered trademark
Mamma Mia! The Musical
www.mamma-mia.com

Chapter One

"Do you know where you are?"

Cassie opened her eyes and peered at the man who leaned on the table beside her. *A bartender. Maybe she should order an iced tea or cola.* She blinked.

"Cassie, do you know where you are?"

She looked around the room, trying to focus her eyes. The walls were a softly muted taupe. The patterned curtain beside her bed matched the wall color. *Bed.* She blinked again. "A hotel?" she asked.

The man smiled. "You're in the hospital."

"Oh." She noticed the TV hanging from the wall, the bulletin board that told the day of the week and date. Her mind cleared a little. She recalled being taken by ambulance from her condo to the nearby suburban hospital.

"You were sedated so your wounds could be cleaned out. Would you like something to eat?"

"What time is it?" She lifted her head. A clock on the wall indicated eight o'clock. *Was it a.m. or p.m.? It didn't matter.* "I don't want anything."

"I'll bring you juice and crackers."

She raised her arm, felt a sharp pain. "What happened?"

"You were hit with scatter pellets from a shotgun. Nothing serious. We picked some of them out. You'll be as good as new in a few days."

She laid a bandaged hand over her heart and turned her head away from the man she now realized was a male nurse. *The shotgun blast, Nate bleeding, EMS. Dead.*

"I'll check your vitals now, and I'll bring a snack later."

The next time Cassie opened her eyes, Seth Hawthorne, his wheat-colored shock of hair in disarray and deep shadows circling his startling blue eyes, stood at the end of her hospital bed.

"Nate's gone," he said. His distress was a solid thing that she wanted to grab and hold in her hands, as if by gripping it she could dispel its power. "Cassie, I'm sorry."

She stared at her bandages. "So am I." Her entire body was numb. Nate couldn't possibly be dead. She couldn't go on without him. She studied Seth, the charming U.S. Senate candidate, with dislike. *Go away.*

He jumped as though her thought had a force of its own. "We need each other, Cassie. It's just the two of us now."

She sighed. Because of their shared talent of sub-vocal communication, even her deepest thoughts were open to him. She would need strength to get through the coming days.

"The doctor wants to keep you overnight for observation."

She shook her head. "No."

He glanced at her bandages. "Apparently you threw your arms in front of your face. The police told me not to talk about the shooting until they take your statement. They want an accounting of everything that happened tonight, and Nate's

2

background as well as yours."

"I have nothing to say."

"And don't bring up the Peace Seekers unless he mentions them."

"No." She forced the word through stiff lips.

He paced a few steps and then returned to the end of her bed. "I hope to be with you when you're questioned. Would you like that?"

"I don't want to stay here."

"Of course, I wouldn't tell you what to say or not say."

"I want to go home." She stumbled over the last word.

"Cassie, I'm sorry." He spread his arms in front of him. "You can't go back to your condo. It's a crime scene."

Red filled her vision. When it cleared, she saw Nate lying on the floor in a pool of blood.

"I'll arrange to have your things picked up." He moved toward her and placed his hand on her arm. His soothing touch brought tears to her eyes, and she nearly lost her tight hold on her emotions.

He continued, "The sooner you join the Peace Seeker community, the better."

"I can't do that."

"You can, Cassie. We'll drive there in the morning. I think it's better if you stay here overnight."

Seth's persuasive voice revealed a softer side to his personality, but she still wanted to leave.

"Cassie, think about it. I have *known you* for years, through many *lifetimes*. Wouldn't you rather be questioned in a hospital bed instead of police headquarters?"

She let the image sink in. "You might be right." Considering her confused state, a night in the hospital sounded better than a session at a police station. If she stayed overnight she'd be questioned with Seth in all his splendor standing near the bed.

"I'll stay," she said.

"Good. Did you pack anything to take to Peace Lake?"

"No." Her voice fell to a whisper. "We'd just arrived." She remembered the sound of men trashing her condo. "I don't know…"

"I'll see to it."

"Do you need my keys?" Confusion set in with the smallest amount of mental effort. "And I need my purse." She pressed her hand to her forehead. "I might have a concussion."

"They mentioned that, and shock."

"What else did they say?"

"Slight injuries." He glanced at her bandages. "Some flesh gone from your hands and forearms. Nothing to worry about."

His smile, meant to comfort, only increased her resentment that he was here and not Nate. Even though Seth had nothing to do with their friend's death, she couldn't stand his practiced smile. She watched him stiffen and she sighed again, knowing he'd read her thoughts.

"Sorry," she murmured.

"You're traumatized. A lot of people who knew Nate were shocked. We never thought he would be careless. He knew better."

Her eyes filled with tears. Her fault, all of it. She had met her angel and destroyed him.

"You're not to blame."

"Don't read my mind!" she yelled at him. "Don't!"

Seth moved to her shoulder and placed his hand on her head, stroking her hair lightly. "Shh, Cassie. Quiet. None of this was your fault."

A fresh wave of anguish tore through her. Nate had been her true love, her soul mate, and now she would never see him again. "I am to blame. Don't you see?" A muffled cry escaped her lips, followed by a sob. "It's my fault." Tears splashed down her cheeks. "All my fault!" she said, her voice shrill.

His gaze shifted to the doorway, and he pressed a firm hand over her mouth. *"Quiet."*

She jerked in surprise. The whispered word sounded like a shout to her. She stiffened, tears drying on her cheeks.

Seth's hand left her mouth. "Don't tell anyone you're responsible for Nate's death, not even the nurse. I want you questioned and released as soon as possible so we can continue on to Peace Lake. Your life might depend upon it."

A nurse appeared at the door. "Everything all right in here?" She looked at Cassie, and then around the room. She stopped at Seth, and her eyes narrowed. "The detective will be here in a minute, sir. Please step out while I check her vitals."

Seth looked down his nose at the nurse and left the room.

The woman stood beside Cassie and took a pulse reading at her carotid. "Are you okay?" She adjusted the IV drip and checked the blood pressure monitor. "If you need help of any kind, just ask one of us."

Cassie nodded. If she opened her mouth, she didn't know whether a sob or a scream would emerge.

Seth had stopped her shriek with a hand over her mouth, but when Nate wanted to quiet her, he would press a spot on the back of her neck. "Goodnight, Cassie," he'd say, effectively stopping her questions by putting her in a light trance. When she awoke, her misgivings returned, but learning about the Peace Seekers' psychic talents and their goal to create a more peaceful life on the planet was the balm that soothed her anger and allowed her to stay with him. Perhaps Seth hadn't time for Nate's subtlety.

The nurse left the room and a strange man entered,

followed by Seth.

Cassie stared at the newcomer. He wore glasses, and his tweed jacket was rumpled and too tight in the shoulders.

"Cassandra West?" He gave her a respectful nod. "I'm Detective Mike Riley of the Northfield Police Department. Are you up to some questions?"

She nodded.

"You're entitled to legal representation," Detective Riley said. "Perhaps Mr. Hawthorne is—"

"An attorney, exactly," Seth said. "I see no reason for Cassie to avoid questioning and, if necessary, I'll give her any legal advice she might need."

Detective Riley rubbed his cheek. "Okay with you, Ms. West?"

"Yes," she said in a voice void of emotion.

"I want to tape this interview if it's all right with you." He took out a pocket-sized recorder and set it on the bedside table.

She glanced at Seth, who nodded. "Okay," she said.

Riley turned on the recorder. "You were with the deceased, Nathan Chambray, when he was murdered?"

Seth interrupted, "My aide, yes."

"I'm sorry, Mr. Hawthorne, but Ms. West needs to answer directly."

"Of course." Seth turned his back on the detective and walked away from the bed.

Calmed by Detective Riley's soft eyes and clear aura that seemed somehow familiar, Cassie asked, "Would you like to sit down?"

He pulled a chair nearer her bed. "Thanks, I will." He took out a notebook. "Just some quick notes. It's easier than listening to a tape. How long have you known Mr. Chambray?"

"A week or two." They'd spent those weeks running from

mysterious men who were pursuing them, so Nate had said.

"Where did you meet Nate?"

"On Mackinac Island. At my mother's cottage. Nate and Mr. Hawthorne," she looked at Seth who straightened at hearing his name, "were at a political fund raiser."

"I see. And how did Nate happen to be at your condo tonight?"

"We returned today. My mother died unexpectedly, and we had attended her memorial service on the island." Eudora had been murdered like Nate, although the police called it accidental. She blinked hard.

"Your mother died? What happened?"

"She fell down a high bluff to the rocks below." She paused as grief swept through her. *Oh, Eudora.* "She died in the hospital within a week."

"Could the two deaths be connected?"

"No." But she knew they were. She shuddered and looked down at her bandages.

He shifted in his chair. "What happened tonight?" he asked in a softer tone.

She took a deep breath and continued. "We were fixing dinner when two men came in." She pressed her lips together.

"Was the door locked?"

"I'm not sure. Everything happened so fast. The door usually locks when it shuts."

"Did you know the men?"

She shook her head. "No, but two other men rode up with us in the elevator. They got out at a lower floor."

"Do you remember which floor?"

With difficulty, she visualized the scene. "Two women also rode up with us, and they left the elevator before we did." She tried to visualize it, but saw only red. "I can't remember anything else."

"Could you identify any of them if I showed you pictures?"

"I could try. I remember one of the women had red hair. But my mind's not…working well. Everything seems blurred."

He nodded. "You were sedated earlier. Did Nate seem to know the men who broke into your place?"

"I don't think he did. It was so unexpected. One moment my condo door flew open, two men entered, and…next, the blast." She covered her face with her bandaged hands and took a shaky breath.

"Did Nate ever mention any enemies?"

She lowered her hands. "No." The lie stuck in her throat. Her mind reeled with remembering what Nate had said about the men who had followed them. Dark forces, he'd said, who profited from crime and wanted chaos to cover the earth. These people ruthlessly kept track of their opposition. And now they'd struck down Nate.

Mistaken identity. She looked at Seth. Had he spoken aloud? "It could be mistaken identity," she said. "I've no enemies, or any reason to be attacked. You can ask my employers at the Northfield library. I live quietly." Or had, until she met Nate.

Seth cleared his throat, and she glanced at him. Was he reading her thoughts, or merely disagreeing with her statement?

"And Nate? What kind of life did he live?"

"I couldn't say. I didn't know him well." Yet she'd promised to marry him less than a week ago.

"You were in the car with him enough hours to drive from Mackinac to your condo. Can you give us his friends' names?"

She shook her head. She'd met Willie, Nate's assistant. Better not mention him as he was connected to the Peace Seekers. "Only Mr. Hawthorne."

"What did he do for a living?"

Seth stirred. "He was my campaign manager. I thought you understood that. I can tell you anything you need to know—"

"I want to hear what Ms. West has to say." The detective's expression was patient as he waited for her to shed light on Nate's life.

He probably read the pain in her eyes. Did he suspect she loved Nate? "I didn't know anything about his personal life. He was a friend of my mother and Seth, a family friend. Because of that connection, I trusted him."

Another lie. She hadn't trusted him. She loved him, but she'd hated the way he'd taken over her life from the moment they met. She even ran away from him once, but the police didn't need to know that either.

"What about his family?"

She shook her head. "Mr. Hawthorne is right. There's not much more I can tell you."

"What about yourself? How do you spend your days?"

She closed her eyes briefly. "I'm a research librarian at the Northfield library, and three nights a week I work out at Gold's Gym." She paused.

Riley nodded, and his gaze softened. "I've been there. Great trainers."

She felt the comfort of a common bond with him. "Yes."

"What nights are you there?"

Seth cleared his throat again.

The detective glanced at him and then continued. "Uh, what else do you do?"

"I'm a literacy volunteer. I help kids in a Pontiac school with their reading."

"And your family?"

"My mother was my last living relative." She lowered her

eyes, and tears blurred her vision. "I have no one else." The hurt was nearly unbearable. She was alone now, completely alone.

The room grew quiet. Detective Riley closed his notebook, slid it into a pocket, and turned off his tape recorder. "You're sure you never saw those guys before, and you have no idea why they'd want to kill either of you?"

She swallowed around a lump in her throat.

"Mistaken identity?" he asked, looking deep into her eyes.

"Yes." She lowered her head and whispered in a tiny voice.

"Okay." He stood up, looking as if he might have a hundred different questions he wanted to ask but knew her answers would remain vague. "That about does it for now."

She was truly sorry for her lies and evasions. She hadn't realized she could be so dishonest. "Please find Nate's killer."

"We'll do our best." He hesitated, and Cassie thought he might want to say something more, but he turned away. "Are you available now, Mr. Hawthorne, to give a statement?"

"Ready and willing, Detective Riley."

She bet the politician in Seth never forgot a name.

"I'll meet you in the room at the end of the hall." Detective Riley glanced at Cassie. "You'll need to stay in town for questioning if needed."

"Okay." She couldn't wait for these two men to leave so she could cry into her pillow.

After the detective left, Seth brushed a strand of hair off her forehead. "Try and get some sleep, Cassie."

Her control broke. "Are you crazy? What kind of a man are you? Do you really think I'm going to sleep on the night Nate was murdered?"

He held up a hand. "Okay, okay. I'll be here in the morning when you're discharged."

10

Part of her wanted to run away as fast as she could, but another part wanted to lean on someone. "Seth, I'm sorry. I can't help myself right now."

"Forget it. I'm here for you."

Chapter Two

At Kootenay Lake, British Columbia, Patrick Cardenas sat rooted to the swivel chair in front of his computer. Encoded news from the worldwide cartel blasted from the screen until, finally, Cardenas lips spread into a grin. Here was the message he wanted to see:

"Objective accomplished. Both problems extinguished. Need instructions for the third. Probably not a good time to try another shipment. Pressure building. Need to shut down, conserve energy."

"Mr. Cardenas?" His servant drew him out of his euphoria. Reluctantly, he turned to see a glass filled with ice and a bottle of Scotch whiskey on the circular counter in the middle of the room.

Cardenas removed his computer glasses and rubbed his eyes. "Ah, Manuel. I thought I heard the security code beep. Is it that late then?" He stretched and checked the time on his screen. "Midnight in the Eastern Time Zone."

"Yes, sir. Your toddy."

Cardenas wished he had someone else to talk to rather than this ignorant servant who understood English better than he could speak it. "And Manuel, I have news for you." He slapped the console with the palm of his hand. "We're leaving for Michigan soon."

"Yes, sir."

He waved expansively. "Bring that drink here."

While Cardenas watched, Manuel poured a double portion of whiskey over the ice, filling the glass. Then the servant raised the glass to his lips and took a long sip. "Very good, sir. You won't have no trouble from it."

Cardenas exploded with a hacking laugh. "As long as you don't drop dead in the next ten seconds."

The servant smiled and bobbed. "Yes, sir." He approached the console with the glass and set it on a cocktail napkin at Cardenas's side.

Cardenas lifted it and drew a long drink.

With his employer busy, Manuel glanced at the message on the monitor.

"What you are doing?" Cardenas stared at the younger man. "Never look at this screen while I am working." He pointed a crooked finger at Manuel. "Do you understand, you ignorant son of a dog?"

Manuel stepped backward. "Sorry, sir. I saw nothing, only waiting for you to finish."

"Nosy employees do not live long," Cardenas grumbled and turned his back.

"No, sir."

"Give me my cell phone and then get out."

Cardenas watched as Manuel walked over and found the cell in its holder on the same console table where the monitors sat. With eyes lowered, he handed it to his employer.

Cardenas took the cell and then slurped from the glass of Scotch. Its smoky tang stung his throat and washed some of the acid taste from his mouth. He punched in a single number, waited, and then hooted a loud greeting. "Geon, good news. Wait…"

He turned toward Manuel who was standing near the door. "Get out!" He waited until the door closed and then lifted the cell to his ear. "You got those bastards. Both dead. Ha! No, don't worry about the big guy. The Feds would be too interested. We'll take care of him later."

When Seth picked up Cassie in the morning, she still struggled to believe Nate was dead. Seth sat in the backseat with her while Willie, his assistant, drove the black SUV with dark windows that hid the passengers from curious eyes.

In Detective Riley's cubicle at police headquarters, Cassie reviewed screen after screen of pictures of men and women until they spun in her head. "I can't tell them apart any longer," she said. "The doctor says it's a concussion."

Riley gently took the computer mouse out of her hands. "Don't worry about it. You can go over these when you're feeling better."

Seth cleared his throat. "I understand our lawyer spoke to you about Cassie going to Ohio for a short time so she can be taken care of properly."

"I don't have a problem with that as long as you give us her new address and both of you sign that she will return to Michigan when she's needed for help with the case, such as identification of suspects." He pushed a legal form across the desk toward Seth.

Seth glanced at it and then took a pen from the detective's desk and signed. He passed the paper to Cassie. "Sign here," he instructed and pointed to the proper line.

She glanced at the printed form and then wrote her name.

Riley took the paper, examined it, and stood. "Since you signed your statements earlier, and with this waiver, I guess you're free to leave." He looked at the purse before him on the desk. "You'll want your purse back, Cassie."

She smiled weakly and took it from him. "Thanks for getting it."

"The officer said it was in the living room, in a duffel bag."

She nodded. "I packed it that way for the trip home."

Riley leaned toward her. "We examined everything in the purse, and also retained your cell and computer for further investigation. We'll get them back to you as soon as our investigation is finished."

She nodded. "I understand."

"Okay then." Riley walked around the desk and led them toward the hallway. He patted Cassie awkwardly on the shoulder. "We appreciate your cooperation, and I hope you heal well."

⊕   ⊕   ⊕

Although Seth sat with her in the backseat on the way to Peace Lake, he talked constantly on his cell phone. She was certain he kept his voice low to hide his conversation—not that she wanted to hear what he said. However, when he mentioned Nate, she paid attention.

"Yes," he murmured. "The police said they'll call when they're through with him. You can pick him up at the morgue and take him to your place."

Through with him. Morgue. Tears filled Cassie's eyes.

"His parents will come in from Connecticut for the burial," Seth said. "Yes, quiet. They'll hold a memorial service later."

Cassie missed some of the words, but then she heard

"Peace Lake. We'll hold one there also."

She closed her eyes and leaned her forehead against the cold window. A single tear slid down her cheek, and her thoughts turned to the statement she'd made to the detective. Except for one or two important omissions, she had told the truth. She didn't know the men who entered her condo, killed Nate, and wounded her. But then she swore she had no enemies—hadn't known Nate well enough to know if he had enemies. That lie bothered her.

For Seth, lying seemed easier. She'd heard him vouch for Nate, his aide. He said violence happened daily in the Detroit metropolitan area. Drugs, crimes of all sorts. Living in any big city held risks. Whether in Michigan or Montana, life wasn't easy these days. Perhaps it never had been.

That's why, Nate had told her, the Peace Seekers existed, the reason for men like Nate and Seth, and women like Liz and Sarah and their other Peace Seeker friends in Northern Michigan. They reincarnated for the specific purpose of raising the vibration of the world's consciousness to reduce violence.

Of course, she hadn't said any of this to the detectives. They would have laughed, or labeled her mentally disturbed. She recalled her earlier flight with Nate from their pursuers— the killers. He had said even the police couldn't be trusted, another reason for her silence.

And now Nate was gone—lost forever to the Peace Seekers, and to her.

Not forever, Cassie. She thought she heard his voice. Perhaps it was him. She had so much to learn, or remember, as he liked to say.

Nate was home now, Seth had told her. The reincarnated Peace Seekers spoke of death as a relief and a return home to a loving spiritual plane where they were co-creators with the great universal spirit.

She should have known all this. She might have if only she hadn't been separated as a baby from her Peace Seeker parents when they'd died in a cabin fire. Her mother was supposed to teach her all the knowledge that was handed down from mother to daughter generation after generation. Instead, she'd been raised by Eudora and Charles. Good people, but if only she hadn't forgotten all she knew at birth. If only—such regrets were useless.

Yet, she couldn't help wondering what awaited her at Peace Lake.

CHAPTER THREE

Seth and the community of Peace Seekers at Peace Lake Village in Ohio would help her remember. What sort of thing had she been drawn into?

They had traveled in the SUV for hours without a break, and she had dozed lightly from the effects of her injuries, lack of sleep, and the mild sedative she'd been given that morning. She'd been awake all night trying to memorize Nate's face. Now his features came to her plainly, and with the memory, a rush of pain squeezed her chest.

"It isn't far now," Seth said, apparently sensing her mental state.

"Good."

She needed to guard against his mind reading. Peace Seekers possessed psychic talents. Among other things, they read thoughts and emotions. She mustn't let down her guard.

From childhood she had known she was different. Her psychic abilities set her apart from others. They frightened Eudora and in turn scared Cassie. And now when she'd discovered she wasn't alone in the world, she should be glad. But she wasn't. She was suspicious of what awaited her.

Her psychic talents helped her understand what the Peace Seekers believed about "going home" and "peaceful co-creation." In the past, she had projected her mind into other times and other places. Why not the ability to reincarnate?

Many of earth's greatest minds believed in reincarnation. Still, there should be some kind of proof, some memory of past lives.

A glance through the window showed Ohio's farmland giving way to rolling hills and dense woods. It didn't matter. She didn't care where she was.

"Here we are," Seth said quietly. The SUV slowed for a right turn and bumped over metal plates in the road. "Cattle guard," he answered her unspoken query.

The SUV bounced and rattled its way down a narrow rutted lane. They passed wire fences along rows of trees and vegetation bordering cultivated fields. The fields were smaller here than in central Ohio. They looked as if individual farmers tended them rather than large agri-businesses.

"This is the back way in," Seth said.

As if she cared. Nate was gone.

"You'd be impressed by the front entrance."

"I'm sure."

He glanced at her with amusement. "Sarcasm?"

"No, the truth. I'm sure I would be impressed. You people never cease to amaze me."

"You're one of us, Cassie."

"As you say." She gazed at him, surprised that in the midst of her despair she was aware of his startling good looks. He was robust and athletically built. "You're a powerful man, aren't you, Seth?"

"That's the idea."

"Idea?"

"That's why we're here after all—power."

"I see." She paused. "I thought it was altruism. To help others."

"Thus, power. It takes power to change things. Every organization understands that."

A flicker of anger stirred in her icy interior. "Then what about Mother Teresa, Mahatma Gandhi, Martin Luther King Jr.?"

"All people who believed in the power of nonviolent opposition, but you're too kind with your comparisons."

Her anger bubbled up. "I'm not comparing you to them!"

"Thought you were." His eyes shimmered with good humor as if he were teasing her.

With that realization, her heat faded. "It's too soon after Nate. I can't—"

He stroked her bandaged hand with his, the same hand that had covered her mouth in the hospital. "I understand." The lines around his eyes softened. "You'll soon let him go."

This man—she looked down at her bandaged hand folded into his—was not what he seemed on the surface. She must not be fooled by his attractive exterior and kind words. Overcome with loss, she turned away. "I'll never get over Nate. We are soul mates."

"Yes, you are. But you're soul mates with all of us."

She raised her chin. "No, I'm not." She felt like a child arguing just because she didn't like Seth. The truth was she hated feeling alone, hated feeling helpless with no family and no memory of the many lifetimes these Peace Seekers accepted so easily.

"You'll soon believe the truth about yourself."

"That we're all soul mates? I doubt it."

"Why are you angry, Cassie? Why so angry with me?" He

waited. "I didn't kill Nate."

She shook her head. "That's not what bothers me."

"What then?"

"Well for starters, you read minds, and you've read mine too many times." She held hers purposefully blank.

"That's not what's bothering you, Cassie. Give it up a little."

"Give it up? Two men attacked us with a shotgun." She held up her bandaged hands and arms. "And Nate," she stumbled over his name. "Nate was murdered—shot in cold blood—and you tell me to give it up?" Her voice rose. "No, you give it up! Give up trying to convince me that soon I'm going to be all right."

She continued, "I may have a concussion, but I know your role in what happened over these past weeks. I know you encouraged Nate to recruit me for whatever scheme you had in mind. And I know if he hadn't been killed, you'd still be pushing him to bring me on board." Her voice broke.

"Cassie." He touched her bandaged hand again, but she jerked it away. He said, "No matter what you think of me, don't blame Nate for any of this. He loved you. We both love you."

She sniffed, wrapped her arms around her chest and willed back her tears. But she refused to look at him.

"Okay?" he pleaded.

She knew from his voice that he was probably smiling his ever-present smile considered charming by most of the women in the state. His looks alone would get him elected to any office. Her anger eased with the realization that he wasn't using his personal power as a weapon against her individually. He was merely a well-trained, public personality.

"Okay. I know Nate loved me. I wouldn't want to live if I didn't believe it."

"And me?"

"You are who you are. I accept that for whatever it means to you."

His warm smile washed over her. "You're a stubborn woman, Cassie."

"I need to be." Regret ran so strong within her, she tasted it. These two men, Nate and Seth, had disrupted the neat safe life she'd created for herself. She'd let it happen. Now she was on her way to their community—their supposedly co-creative community. She had wanted to refuse, but she remembered the light in Nate's eyes when he spoke of the Peace Seekers. And she remembered her cousin Liz's eyes and Sarah's, the women she'd met in Northern Michigan. These Peace Seekers healed using spiritual power. They were healers and educators, and they carried the power of love within them.

Were the Peace Seekers all about power, as Seth said? She would make it her business to find out. Then she realized that was precisely what Nate and Seth wanted.

Willie slowed the SUV to make another turn. "That's odd. The gate to the institute is open," he said over his shoulder.

"Guess they knew we were coming," Seth answered with a laugh.

"I'd be surprised if they didn't," she said. A pulse pounded in her neck. "You people seem to know everything." Over the slight rise of a hill, a water tower loomed toward the sky. As the car topped the hill, a community of houses and shops appeared, and a group of earth-colored buildings spread out in a pleasant campus-like arrangement.

"We're home." Willie's voice held a note of pleasure.

Cassie glanced at Seth. He was unusually quiet.

"I don't come here often," he said. "I live in Michigan, at least I will until after the national election when I hope to move to DC."

At the thought he'd soon be gone, her tension eased.

"You'll have to get accustomed to our being together at some time."

"I suppose." Once again she reminded herself to guard her thoughts.

Unexpectedly, he placed his hand in a gentle caress on her knee. She stiffened under his touch. "Don't forget me, Cassie, while I'm away campaigning."

Her pulse tripped faster.

"I'm going to think of you constantly," Seth said. "I'll call you as often as I can."

She stared out the window and then felt a brief squeeze, a disconcerting press of fingers on her knee. She pulled her leg away.

"Here we are, boss." At the note of pleasure in Willie's voice, Cassie caught a look at him in the rearview mirror. He grinned from ear to ear. "Wish to hell Nate was with us."

She raised her chin. At least one Peace Seeker missed Nate's presence.

"Don't start again," Seth told Willie.

"Can't help thinking about him."

"Nate did what he had to do and now he's gone. We'll manage without him."

"I wonder what her ladyship will have to say about his passing."

"What can she say? He's gone." Seth stared at Cassie. "He should never have stopped in Northfield."

She lowered her gaze and studied the SUV's carpeting. Seth's remark stung. She knew he was annoyed with Willie, but he'd directed his cruel comment at her. His lapse was a very human failing. Seth had his faults, as she knew too well. Nate had said that although Peace Seekers were reincarnated souls, they were fully human in every way. And he had proved it. Her eyes moistened with the memory of his lovemaking.

Willie brought the vehicle to a stop in a parking lot beside one of the dark, low-slung buildings. Seth pulled the back door open and offered her a hand.

She let him take her elbow as she slid down from the SUV. Seth's gaze lowered to the opening of her blouse.

Annoyed, she gave him a challenging look and flung his hurtful words back in his face. "Don't let me distract you. It could be fatal."

He laughed and tossed his head. His sandy hair danced in the light summer breeze. "Hell, Cassie, I've been distracted by people more dangerous than you and survived the experience."

"I bet you have." She believed him. Seth was earthy. He showed none of the ethereal qualities that had attracted her to Nate.

He steered her forward. "Come and meet the Cat Woman."

"Cat Woman?" Beyond Seth's shoulder, Willie's expression registered disapproval.

"Or her ladyship. Our illustrious leader."

The middle-aged woman who greeted them at the curb was anything but feline. She was of medium build and height, with graying, simply styled hair falling in natural waves to her shoulders. Cassie noticed as the woman approached that her loosely draped outfit was made of linen and cotton in lovely muted colors of beige and tan.

"This is Ann Marie Stewart, our director," Seth said.

"Dear Cassie, so glad you're here." Ann Marie spread her arms and Cassie walked into a welcoming hug. "We hope you'll be happy with us." The woman's throaty voice was rich with affection.

Cassie, thinking of Seth's characterization of her as Cat

Woman, embraced Ann Marie as best she could with her bandaged hands and arms. "I'm glad to meet you," she said with honesty.

"You must be tired. And your arms. I'm sorry about your injuries. How terrible the entire experience was for you." She wrapped an arm around Cassie's waist and led her toward the brick building. "Losing Nate the way you did, right in front of your eyes, must have been extremely difficult."

"Yes." Here was a Peace Seeker who acknowledged the trauma she'd been through. Was Seth the only one who didn't see Nate's passing as a terrible loss?

"I'll show you to your room, and you can rest before our evening meal."

A double-seated golf cart was parked outside the front door. Ann Marie slid behind the wheel and motioned Cassie into the front seat beside her. "Willie, you can put Cassie's things in back."

Except for her purse, she had nothing but flip-flops and the clothes on her back, which Seth's assistant, Vicki, had purchased for her and left at the hospital that morning. The police had sealed Cassie's condo. Instead of luggage, Seth climbed into the back seat.

Ann Marie looked over her shoulder at him. "Seth, you're free to do as you like. We'll see you at dinner."

"I'll go with you," Seth said. "I want to see Cassie settled."

Ann Marie hesitated, clearly not happy with him. "She's quite all right with us now."

"I'm sure she is. Nevertheless, I'll go along."

Cassie thought she detected a flush on Ann Marie's cheeks, and then buried the thought. Could Peace Seekers read every thought or was sub-vocalization only possible with an effort? She wondered how she could tell if someone was monitoring her thoughts. Perhaps Ann Marie could help later with that question.

She was surprised when they left the main campus, and Ann Marie guided the cart down a gravel lane toward a farmhouse standing on the edge of the settlement, far away from the rest of the buildings.

"Rupert and Lucille King are caretakers of this house," Ann Marie said. "They're a loving couple who often take in strays like you." Her warm smile took any sting from her words.

"Are they part of the colony? I thought I'd be living with a group."

"They're very much part of the colony, or institution as we like to call ourselves."

"They're busybodies," Seth said from the rear seat, "who like to mess in everyone's business."

"Seth, for goodness sake, you'll have Cassie thinking poorly of the Kings before she's even met them."

"Just speaking the truth."

Ann Marie bristled. "I can't agree. The Kings are nurturing people. I'm sure Cassie will find them just like parents."

"And just as restricting," Seth said.

Cassie glanced over her shoulder at him. "Why would you say that? Previous experience?"

He ignored her question. "Cassie's a professional woman who's been on her own for years, Ann Marie. She hardly needs parenting."

"My information was she lost her parents at an early age. And we're never too old for a little coddling." She pulled the golf cart to a stop near the rear door of the farmhouse.

The entrance was rather plain, Cassie noted, with nothing to signify it was part of the Peace Seekers community. A clump of lilac bushes stood to one side, slightly withered by the summer heat. Cassie imagined she could still smell their spring-like fragrance.

Seth led the way to the door. He knocked once, called "Rupert? Lucille?" then pulled the screen door open and stepped inside onto a back landing.

Cassie followed Seth through the door. Straight ahead were an open flight of stairs that she noticed went straight down into a dark and damp-smelling basement. To the left, a few steps up brought her into a large old-fashioned kitchen. She heard footsteps behind her. An older, balding man climbed the basement stairs.

"Make yourself at home," he said to Cassie. "Hi, Ann Marie." He hugged the director. Hugs were apparently her official form of greeting, Cassie thought, although Ann Marie had not extended the privilege to Seth.

"Good to see you again, Seth." Rupert shook Seth's hand. "Lucille's getting Cassie's room ready." He went to the second-story stairs. "She's here, Lucille," he called. "Come on down and say hello." He turned to Cassie. "She would polish wood until the sun went down and still not be satisfied."

"You'll take your evening meal at the lodge tonight, Rupert?"

"Yep, we will, Ann Marie."

"Good." She turned as if to leave. "We'll see you then." She touched Seth's elbow but he ignored her.

Lucille hurried into the room, a wide smile on her round face. "Cassie, oh Cassie, we're so glad you're here." Lucille seemed carried away with enthusiasm for her new charge and enveloped Cassie in a warm, smothering embrace.

Cassie gently disengaged herself from the woman's grasp. "Nice to meet you."

"Your bandages," Lucille exclaimed. "We'll need to see to

them, Ann Marie."

Cassie said, "I brought the discharge instructions from the hospital. But the injuries are nothing, really. I don't know why I need all this wrapping." Images of Nate's crumpled form lying in her kitchen archway filled her mind. *Red, red everywhere.*

"We'll take the doctor's orders with us to the clinic tomorrow," Ann Marie said. "And now we'll leave you with the Kings."

"Which room is hers?" Seth asked.

"Would you like to see it, Cassie?" Lucille asked. "Right this way. It's lovely," she said over her shoulder. "Gets the morning sun, cool in the afternoon. No air conditioning needed."

Conscious of Seth behind her, Cassie followed Lucille up the stairs. Ann Marie followed behind Seth.

"Here we go," he mumbled, "this ought to be charming, no A/C. They've stuck you away in the middle of nowhere."

Cassie reached the top of the stairs and paused in the hallway. She looked back and gave Seth a quick look, and then caught Ann Marie's gaze over his shoulder. "It's fine," Cassie muttered to Seth. All she wanted was to be alone.

"Damn stupid to have you in this house," he muttered close to her ear. "I'll move you out as soon as I can."

She felt a surprising tug of appreciation for the man crowded next to her in the narrow hallway. He obviously was concerned about her and cared that she had no air conditioning, and had been relegated to this worn, rather primitive farmhouse.

But she wasn't certain Seth actually cared. His indignation could be a power play against Ann Marie, or a pretense aimed at gaining Cassie's trust. She glanced at him. In response he squeezed her shoulder gently.

Cassie peeked into the bedroom where Lucille waited. The furnishings were sparse. The narrow metal bed was painted white and covered by a patchwork quilt. Beside it was a walnut rocker. On the opposite wall stood an old oak dresser with a framed mirror on its top. Gauzy white curtains fluttered from an open window. Cassie's gaze lingered on a ceramic ewer and bowl sitting on a battered washstand.

"Of course, those are just for show," Lucille said. "Your bathroom is in here." She opened a creaking door. "Shower too," she said proudly.

"Nice," Cassie said, giving the bathroom a quick glance.

Seth sat on the bed. The thin mattress sagged under his muscular build. He bounced on it a couple of times. "Needs new springs."

Lucille's eyes widened.

Any other time Cassie would have laughed, but yesterday's terror robbed her of any humor.

"You're going to ruin my bed." She touched Seth's shoulder and he rose and stood beside her. His masculine bulk felt soothing, even pleasant. Her perception of him must have softened. Even if the truce were temporary, it was calming to know someone cared about her, even if that person was Seth. He might be an ally—if she didn't cross him. She had seen his other side.

"Dinner's at six," Ann Marie said as she left the room. "I'll send a cart for you."

"Thanks," Cassie said.

Seth halted Cassie's attempt to follow the women down the stairs. "Wait." He guided her back to the bedroom and gathered her in, pressing her head against the curve of his neck. "You'll be all right, don't worry," he whispered. He patted her back. "Don't pay any attention to what I said. They're good people, all of them. They mean well."

Despite her dislike for him, she found a certain peace in

his arms. He had a scent and aura similar to Nate's. No. It was wishful thinking. She thought she saw Nate and heard his voice and smelled him everywhere.

"I'm driving back to Lansing early tomorrow," Seth said. "I've a heavy schedule until the election, but I'll call you. Have them move you out of here. That bed's not worth shit."

She stirred but didn't move out of his embrace. "It's all right for now."

"And Rupert and Lucille?" Seth said. "They're a pair out of a bad TV show."

She shook her head against his shoulder. If she closed her eyes, she would fall asleep from pure emotional fatigue.

"And you need a computer and a new cell phone. We need to keep in touch."

"The police took my old one." She heard footsteps on the stairs and broke away.

"Ask Ann Marie to make arrangements as soon as possible for new ones. If she gives you any trouble, I'll ship them myself."

"Seth, are you coming down?" Ann Marie called.

"Your keeper," he mumbled.

"We'll be right down," Cassie called. She shook her head at Seth and tried to read what he was thinking, but couldn't. "You don't like her, do you?"

"She's okay but she can be an interfering bitch when she wants."

Cassie raised her brows.

"She wants to run everything." When Cassie didn't comment, Seth continued. "Nate didn't like her either. He thought she needed a husband and children. Too late now."

"She'll hear you," she whispered.

"It doesn't matter. She knows how I feel."

31

"I suppose she does. You're about as subtle as a cold shower."

"Cassie." Ann Marie had climbed to the hallway and poked her head into the bedroom. "I'm leaving you here now. Seth, if you want a ride back, you'd better come with me. Otherwise, you'll have to walk."

"Or fly."

Ann Marie's eyes narrowed. "Not here, you won't." She left the room in a huff.

"See, I told you she has a mean streak."

Cassie listened to Ann Marie's footsteps clatter down the stairs. "I thought all Peace Seekers would get along."

"We do, some of us more than others." He called out, "Wait up, Ann Marie." He bent low and startled Cassie with a light kiss on her lips. "We're in this together. Now that Nate's gone, it's the two of us. You've got to help me." He paused until he captured Cassie's gaze with a searching look. "I need you, Cassie. I'm counting on you."

Alone in the world, she found she didn't mind the thought that someone needed her. "Just don't try to control me." She followed him down the stairs.

"Whatever you say."

Cassie walked out with him into the late afternoon sun. Insects buzzed in the tall grasses surrounding the gravel driveway.

As Seth climbed into the golf cart beside Ann Marie, he asked Cassie "Now do you understand the conflict going on in the village? Among all of us here?"

Surprised that Seth would speak so openly in front of the community director, Cassie nodded. It was control, she thought. A power struggle. Each person wanted to control the others. They all thought they knew best. Except for her. She knew nothing. She only knew Nate was gone. Her future, her love, the man she'd waited for and had given up praying for, had at long last walked into her life. He had taken it over and made Cassie his woman. And then he was taken away from her.

A pity, she could almost hear her mother, Eudora, say. Cassie called it a tragedy of the worst sort. Yet, in the sweltering summer afternoon, watching Ann Marie's golf cart carry Seth Hawthorne away, she felt a faint flicker of hope within her.

Chapter Four

"What do you mean you've lost track of him?" In British Columbia, Cardenas stared at the swarthy face on the computer screen.

"We holed up overnight and now we can't find Hawthorne anywhere."

"You fool!" Spit flew from Cardenas's mouth. "I told you never to use names."

The face grimaced. "Okay, the hawk has flown."

"How can he disappear? He's a public figure."

"All I know is we've been watching him by satellite, but he's gone off the grid."

"He's to be tracked twenty-four/seven. You know that."

"We're doing our best. As soon as he surfaces, we'll be on him like leeches."

"You have ten minutes before we leave for dinner," Lucille said as she stuck her head into Cassie's bedroom.

"Thanks, Lucille." She stumbled into the tiny bathroom and cleaned up as well as possible considering her injuries. At

the hospital that morning, the nurse had changed the dressings on her hands and arms and said they would last until
tomorrow. She wondered how her skin looked under the bandages. At least her pain was being controlled with the help of
mild analgesics.

Lucille and Rupert kept a rusting blue and white pickup
truck in a weather-beaten garage with a door that didn't close.
Cassie could see it from her bedroom window. Earlier, after
Seth left, she went to her room pleading fatigue, and flopped
on the sagging mattress he'd ridiculed. A nap was impossible.
Sorrow over Nate's cold-blooded murder washed over her. She
fought giving in to her grief. Instead she focused on recalling
Nate's voice and remembering first his serenity and then his
agony as he struggled with his love for her.

He had told her marriage was discouraged, if not forbidden, to Peace Seekers except for practical reasons. Like Lucille
and Rupert, she thought. They most likely were married. Seth
had said Ann Marie didn't have a husband. Seth and Nate had
talked about Cassie's marrying Seth. Fortunately, Nate had
fallen in love with her and insisted her future was with him.

The life of each Peace Seeker was apparently preordained.
It was up to each person to remember, recall, and recognize—
she struggled with the thought—his or her purpose for reincarnating. In the birth process, memories of past lives were
forgotten, but intentions were recaptured. Perhaps Ann Marie
would teach her that process.

In the bathroom mirror, she looked at her unruly silver-
blonde hair and set to work with the brush and comb Lucille
had provided. Her makeup was in her purse that Detective
Riley had given back to her. She patted some pressed powder
on her face and brushed on some lipstick. The police had gone
through the purse's contents, but she was permitted to keep

them. Too bad she hadn't been as lucky with her cell phone.

Truthfully, the morning was a blur. She'd taken a cleansing shower at the hospital and then put on the clean clothes Seth's assistant had brought. In the last twenty-four hours, he had helped her in many ways. He'd taken care of her as a father might look after his child.

She was thankful for his help. That was a new start between them. Gratitude, she supposed, was the basis for a lot of mediocre marriages. What had made her think about marriage? She would never marry Seth. Although the three of them—Seth, Nate, and she—had planned it in another lifetime, that plan was discarded when she and Nate fell in love.

She went downstairs and stepped outside into the late afternoon sunshine. Her body was numb, but she couldn't help feeling anxious about having dinner with the Peace Seeker community. These people were strangers. She had no idea what they would think of her.

Rupert and Lucille were waiting by the truck. Rupert helped the two women into the pickup and drove them to the middle of the community. He pulled into a parking space at the side of a building. "Are you okay to walk from here? I can drop you off at the door if you're feeling weak."

"I'm fine," Cassie said, "please don't treat me as if I'm ill." Despite her protest her knees trembled when she climbed down from the truck. Any kind of weakness was a new sensation to her. She'd never had a serious injury in her life. Even now, with all she'd gone through, she only had a slight concussion. The doctor had told her to take it easy for a day or two.

"I should have dropped you two off at the door," he mumbled.

"Don't fuss, we're here now," Lucille said. She linked her arm with Cassie's.

From the stream of people entering the building, Cassie thought it was probably a community center.

Inside, Lucille led her into a dining room and past a cafeteria line toward a series of closed doors. "We have private dining rooms for special guests. Ann Marie's expecting you."

Lucille opened the door and stepped aside for Cassie to enter. She took one tentative step into the room and noticed two walnut tables set side by side, forming a table large enough to accommodate twelve people.

"Cassie." Ann Marie motioned toward an empty chair beside hers. "I'm glad you feel well enough to join us."

She hadn't been given a choice, had she? Conscious of her bandages, she took her courage in hand and sat on the chair offered.

Ann Marie nodded to a young woman standing nearby. "You may serve now, Kathy."

The door to the hallway opened. Seth stepped inside and looked around. "Is there room for one more?"

Ann Marie stiffened. "I'm afraid we weren't expecting you, Seth. We thought you'd eat with your campaign committee down the hall."

"I met with them late this afternoon." He grabbed a folding chair from against the wall and dragged it toward Cassie. "Can I fit in here?" he asked the woman on the other side of her.

Cassie shook her head at Seth's continuing effort to ruin Ann Marie's attempt to keep them apart. For whatever reason, Cassie found his slightly rebellious attitude interesting. Was he only rebellious toward Ann Marie, or did he rebel against the entire organization? She'd have to find out. Perhaps that was what Nate had liked about Seth, his freewheeling attitude. Perhaps that was a part of Seth's personality she found hard to appreciate.

Seth nudged her elbow as he crowded in next to her. She watched while those sitting closest moved their chairs to make room for him.

"There will be one more for dinner, Kathy," Ann Marie instructed with a sigh.

"You're not getting bigger, are you, Seth?" asked one of the men at the table.

Seth laughed good-naturedly. "I hope not, with the election coming up."

"You want to project an appearance of the health-conscious American," another said.

Cassie found the reaction toward Seth interesting. How would he deal with these Peace Seekers?

"How is the campaign coming?" a woman across the table asked.

"Better than I'd hoped," Seth said. "Nate was away a lot during these past weeks."

"Do you like your new campaign manager?" the woman continued.

"Yes, Vicki's doing a fine job. Thanks for your help in finding her."

The strained silence was relieved when a young man carried in a laden tray while Kathy, the server, wheeled a cart in behind him.

"We'll ask a short blessing," Ann Marie said.

Cassie bowed her head and let Ann Marie's soothing voice flow over her. Her own thoughts and worries blocked out the prayer. She had distracted Nate, as Seth hinted earlier, drawing him away from the campaign. She kept Nate away with her stubborn insistence, and disbelief in what he'd told her was his plain duty.

Not your fault, she thought she heard Seth say quietly beside her. Or had she imagined it?

Wondering when the prayer would end, she looked sideways and found Seth studying her. A sense of relief moved through her. She sighed with the knowledge Nate had followed his own heart. She wasn't responsible in any way for his death.

Or was she?

"Not your fault." This time she knew she heard the whispered words.

"You said earlier, I distracted him." She kept her voice faint, merely a murmur, to shield her words from other ears, and not to interrupt Ann Marie's lengthy prayer.

Beneath the table, Seth's hand groped for hers and found it. His careful touch set her fingers tingling beneath the bandages. "I was wrong to say that."

She found strength in his touch. "But you said—"

Seth's gaze moved beyond her to Ann Marie. "Forget what I said. I was wrong."

"Amen." Ann Marie's resonant voice rang throughout the room. She turned to Cassie. "Did you rest this afternoon?"

She felt compelled to give the woman her attention, but drawing her gaze from Seth's was impossible. As if sensing her dilemma, he looked away.

She turned to Ann Marie. "I rested, but my mind wouldn't be quiet."

Ann Marie nodded wisely. "We'll take care of that."

"Meditation 101," Seth murmured.

"What was that, Seth?" Ann Marie asked.

She had the impression the woman heard Seth perfectly. Apparently battle lines were being drawn. At that moment, the server set a plate of steaming food in front of Cassie and she thankfully turned her attention to eating. The scent of roasted turkey drifted up from the plate.

A sharp pain, like a piercing arrow, passed through her heart at the thought of never again sharing a meal with Nate. She drew a deep breath and willed the thought away. Still, the forkful of food nearly gagged her.

She sipped her glass of water and let her gaze slide over the others seated at the table. They seemed to be an even mixture of men and women of various ages. Many displayed youthful energy while others, with graying hair, seemed closer to retirement age.

The one characteristic distinguishing them was their overall appearance of happiness. Their demeanor demonstrated more than contentment. Their faces fairly glowed.

She glanced from one to another. Their eyes were clear and sparkling, their faces lit from within by a special light that each possessed in various degrees. It was the same light she'd seen upon Seth's face, and Nate's. These Peace Seekers were a happy lot. She had no belief that she would ever feel contented again.

Seth placed a gentle hand on her shoulder, and she wondered if he had once more read her thoughts.

"Food all right?" he asked.

She glanced at him, saw nothing unusual in his face, nothing to indicate he knew what she was thinking. Heavy grief settled on her shoulders. "I can't eat."

"Too much excitement."

"And more," she murmured.

"The grief will pass, Cassie."

"Will it? But then, I don't want it gone." She faced him and spoke in a ragged voice filled with sorrow. "I don't want to ever forget Nate."

"No, not forget him, but you will eventually let him go."

She shook her head.

"You will. Believe me."

His voice moved over her in healing waves. She hadn't noticed the kindness in his voice. Worse, she had been too busy hating Seth, fighting his and Nate's plans for her future to notice what a balm Seth's voice could be to the pain inside her.

"Just eat what you want, Cassie," Ann Marie said. "The Kings will have a snack for you later."

"Thanks." She toyed with the mashed potatoes and gravy that shared her plate with roast turkey and stuffing. "It seems I've left my appetite in Michigan."

"After dinner we'll talk for a while, and then I'll drive you over to the farmhouse," Ann Marie said.

"I'll see Cassie back to the house," Seth said. "I need to discuss things with her."

"You don't have transportation unless I okay it," Ann Marie said.

A silence fell over the group.

"Hey, Annie," Seth's voice, rough now, carried through the room, "you forget, I'm the candidate. I brought my car and driver with me. Not that I need it here. Everything's for the common good, right?"

Cassie was conscious of sitting between two adversaries with the eyes of all others upon them.

"You're the candidate because of our support, Seth," Ann Marie said.

He bristled visibly. "What does that mean?"

"We put you where you are and you need to respect that."

"Ann Marie…Seth, what's happening here?" one of the older men asked.

"Seth thinks he's larger than all of us together. A law unto himself."

Seth pushed his chair back and stretched to his full length. "I think nothing of the kind, but I'm not going to be treated like a misbehaving child. Are you forbidding me transportation?" His brows shot up into a question. "Ann Marie, what is this, a dictatorship?" His voice softened. "What's happened here since I hit the campaign trail?"

With a brief glance, Cassie noticed the woman beside her flush. She wished she were away from here, back in her safe room at the farmhouse.

"Let's not quarrel in front of our guest, Seth."

"Cassie's not a guest, Ann Marie. She's one of us."

"She's new here and doesn't understand that while we disagree, we still possess a united purpose."

Seth hesitated, clearly wishing to answer her, yet holding back.

"We work together for the good of all," Ann Marie said. "Without each other, we are nothing."

"True," Seth agreed, "and none of us rules the other."

"We follow rules, otherwise we would have chaos."

"Our rules include common decency," Seth said. "Respect for others."

"Of course," Ann Marie conceded.

"Which includes hospitality to visitors?"

"Yes."

Even Cassie realized Seth had Ann Marie cornered.

"Even when they're wrong," Seth continued, "especially when they're wrong, as I am now." He finished with a good-natured grin.

Defeated, Ann Marie smiled. "True, especially when they're wrong, and it's a wise man who admits his error."

"Ha!" Seth passed a hand through his wiry hair.

There was a sprinkling of applause around the table. Cassie

sensed that peace had been re-established within the group. Seth emanated good cheer, and Ann Marie seemed content with the outcome of their disagreement.

She had difficulty knowing whether Seth or Ann Marie had won the dispute. Or even what the dispute was.

"If we're through eating, I think I'll be going," Ann Marie said. "I've work to finish tonight."

Cassie looked up. "Should I leave with you?"

Ann Marie's expression was blank. "That's entirely up to you."

"I need to talk to you, Cassie." Seth touched her arm. "I'll see you home."

"Is that what you want, Cassie?" Ann Marie asked.

She hesitated before answering, knowing in her heart she wanted to be with Seth, if for no other reason than to talk once again about Nate. "I'll go with Seth."

"As you wish," Ann Marie said. "I'll tell Lucille and Rupert."

Outside in the last afterglow of the sunset, the air was as still as only a warm summer evening can be. Seth led the way toward a parked golf cart. "Jump in, I'll show you around the place."

Cassie hesitated. "Will Ann Marie mind if you take the golf cart?"

Seth laughed. "Don't worry about her."

"What went on in there between you?"

He turned the key and drove away from the building. "Remember what I said earlier about control?"

"You said it caused problems in the community."

"Right. It's all about control. It's about who gets to call the plays, who pays the bills, and who gets what salary."

"Sounds like money problems to me."

"Money is a big part of it, I'll give you that."

"I wouldn't have thought the Peace Seekers would feel money was high on their list of priorities."

"After all, we're human." Seth smiled. "Mainly it all boils down to control. Think about it, Cassie. These people form an institution, elect an administrator, put on a united front, are determined to improve the environment, the government, whatever…and most of them think they have special orders from on high."

"But I thought if they were called Peace Seekers, they would get along a lot better."

"There's a difference between power and abuse of power— between control and violence. All people want control over their lives. And we would all like the power to make others follow our wishes. But there's a big difference between arguing over small matters and using violence to get our way. We believe in non-violent conflict resolution. You saw a sample of that at dinner. People will always argue. After all, we're not angels, well, anyway most of us are not even close to being angelic. We just want the violence to stop."

"You were angry with Ann Marie."

"I don't dislike her. I merely lose my patience when she forgets the bigger picture. Now, politics are different. At least in politics, a person knows who his enemies are."

"And these other enemies," her voice quieted, "the ones who killed Nate. Do you know who they are?"

"Do you mean specifically, names and the like? No, I couldn't say we actually know who attacked you and Nate."

"But do you have an idea of who is responsible?"

He hesitated. "You were with Nate a lot in the past couple of weeks."

Cassie sighed. Seth once again avoided answering her question. "Yes, I was." They had packed a lot of living, learning, and loving into two short weeks. However, a lot of their time together had been spent arguing, jousting for control, and concealing motivations from each other. It wasn't until their last days together that they finally worked out their differences, and then it was too late.

"What did Nate tell you?"

Clearly, Seth wanted to know what Nate had revealed to her when they were together. He was either cautious or stalling. Either way, she'd had enough of mentally sparring with those closest to her.

"I think we need to level with each other, Seth. Although I'm not happy about it, I'm here at the Peace Lake community. I was a part of your plans from the beginning, and if you think I can be of assistance to you in your career—and I'm considering such a move since there's nothing left of my prior life—then we need honesty between us. Because of the attack on Nate, I can't go back to my life in Northfield or to my job at the library."

Seth slowed the golf cart and turned it down a lane past a building that she thought might be a gymnasium. The sun had set and twilight cast an eerie glow over the red clay tennis courts cut into the gently sloping ground.

He pulled into a shadowy spot under a spreading tree filled with developing fruit. Her heartbeat increased with the hope she and Seth were going to have a meaningful exchange, possibly the first since she'd met the ambitious politician.

He extended his arm along the back of the seat behind her shoulders and idly fingered the edge of her polo shirt's collar. To her surprise, even the lightest and briefest of physical contact with Seth lifted her spirits. She realized how empty her life had been of human contact in the past. It was a self-imposed isolation, certainly, but it had kept her from developing a completely mature personality.

Despite her twenty-nine years, she had been emotionally insecure when she'd met Nate on a lovely June afternoon on Michigan's Mackinac Island. Her long, silvery hair, confined only for her work as a research librarian, had hung in a casual cloud around her shoulders. And she wore childish clothes back then. Was it only a month ago? She smiled thinking of her fringed leather jacket and matching headband that often set her mother's teeth on edge.

Cassie had been thrown into a panic by Eudora's terrible fall down the Mackinac Island bluff—that fall cost Cassie's lone relative her life.

"It's a peaceful night," Seth said, interrupting her mental excursion into the past.

"It is." She looked down at her bandaged hands lying stiffly in her lap. "I was thinking about this past summer. Do you think the people who pushed Eudora off the cliff were the ones who attacked Nate and me in my condo?"

"Possibly...probably."

"It's frightening to think anyone would want to kill me. It's even worse to think there's a conspiracy, an organized effort to eliminate me...us, or people like us." She shook her head. "Can you help me out here, Seth?"

"I can try to explain what's happening. You know change threatens people, Cassie, and the twenty-first century is bringing rapid change." He leaned forward earnestly. "That's why we, you and I, have returned to Earth now, to help with those changes."

"So you say."

"Right. Now let me ask you this: if you were deeply involved in an illegal enterprise, say arms smuggling, drug dealing, or corrupt dictatorships, or anything else you can think of troubling to today's civilization as we know it, wouldn't you want to keep things as they are?"

"What things?"

"Well, war for one thing, or planning for war. Or use of natural resources, distribution of wealth, even land ownership. With the population growth we're experiencing, ownership of the world's land becomes vitally important."

"I thought population growth was slowing."

"It did for a while, but not any more. We have to learn how to preserve and multiply the world's resources."

"But why kill Eudora and Nate? Are all the Peace Seekers targets?"

"We are always at risk from those who want wars to continue. Nate and I are well-known advocates for change, for moving the country and eventually the world toward a more peaceful society."

"But to kill people to keep others from working toward peace, I can't imagine that happening."

He shook his head. "Peace Seekers cannot solve the problem of violence. It is probably in our human genes. Instead, we advocate conflict resolution without going to war. We can show the way."

The glow of the evening sky softened his features and made him appear younger and more idealistic than when she first met him. At this moment and in this light, he had an aura about him that seemed familiar. If she could just remember—

"Cassie—"

"I know." She shrugged. "I know. After all that's happened, it was a dumb question. More than anyone, I should know these people kill their opponents."

He gently stroked a strand of silvery hair that fell across her shoulder. "Your innocence is your charm."

"I'm not innocent, at least not any more." She thought of all she'd gone through recently, remembering Nate, his blood pooling on her kitchen floor.

Seth stared at her, and she realized he'd read her thoughts.

He cupped his hand around her shoulder and hugged her. "You're not innocent, just unspoiled, and more natural than most women."

She covered her face with her bandaged hands. "I don't know what I'll do with the rest of my life."

"You can help with my campaign. We'll put you to work after you've lived with the community long enough to get your emotions untangled and learn the true nature of your being."

"The true nature of my being," she said. "That sounds so theoretical."

"You talked with Nate about who you are and why you're here, didn't you?"

"Yes, after I knew him for a while, and before we left for my condo. We talked and, afterwards, he put me in sort of a trance, a dreamlike state. I saw scenes from what he said were a past life. I've always been able to move in and out of different realities. But I don't know what actually happened that night."

Thinking about Nate and Eudora, revisiting the past, called up a host of feelings, both good and bad. She grimaced with pain.

Seth reached out and lifted her chin so he could see her expression. "It's too soon for us to talk. It was only yesterday. You're still in shock."

Giving in to the loneliness filling her heart, she turned and rested her head against Seth's shoulder. Unexpectedly, her eyes remained dry. Instead, she experienced a deep aching dread that filled her center until she felt as if all life had been squeezed out. The premonition that her future held promise of more unhappiness, that the peace she felt in Seth's embrace was momentary and short-lived, made her shiver.

He gently rubbed the back of her neck, massaging tense muscles in easy circles, increasing the size of the circles until she relaxed under his touch. The ache within her subsided. The anxious feelings eased. She sighed and allowed herself to be consoled.

She closed her eyes and her thoughts drifted along on Seth's scent as a butterfly catches the smallest breeze. Under her closed lids, brilliant colors sprang to life, bringing undulating waves of blues, greens, spots of pinks and purples. Her breathing slowed. She forgot she sat with Seth Hawthorne, the U.S. Senate candidate whom she'd despised so recently.

"This is nice," she said against his shoulder.

"It feels familiar, peaceful."

She did know him from the past. The feeling of his arm around her was as comforting as a father's embrace. "I need to work through this terrible loss."

"You'll get through it, and you'll be stronger when you emerge from the other end."

"I wish I could believe that."

"Let yourself believe."

"How?" The idea seemed impossible.

"Just affirm it. Say aloud the affirmation, 'I will get through this and grow stronger because of it.'"

She pulled away to check Seth's face, to see if he was serious or if his expression contained the slightest hint of a smile. What she saw startled her more than if he had laughed aloud. The rising moon cast a golden glow on Seth's face. His love couldn't be clearer if the words were written on his forehead.

Chapter Five

Raucous blue jays called morning greetings from the lilac bush outside her window. Cassie opened her eyes to the serenity of the whitewashed bedroom with its simple furnishings. Her stomach growled. The bit of food she'd swallowed at the evening meal wasn't enough to sustain her energy.

She was hungry, rested, and extremely curious about the community. She hoped Ann Marie would show her around today. It was quite a change from yesterday's dark mood, she realized as she wrapped plastic around her arms, hoping to keep the bandages dry while she showered. She thought of Seth and their quiet time together in the golf cart and thought her healing had begun. *So soon.* The thought surprised her.

Without warning, despair over Nate's death washed over her. She stood under the shower, where no one could hear, and sobbed. Then she remembered the affirmation Seth had given her. "I will get through this and grow stronger because of it." She said the words aloud while hot water splashed against the back of her neck and her shoulders. She stayed in the shower until her tears ceased and she felt calm enough to face what awaited her.

Last night she had returned to her room to find a white terry robe and a cotton nightgown laid out for her. This morning, she wore the nightgown and robe down to the kitchen, where Lucille had coffee ready. "That smells good." Cassie sniffed the nutty aroma arising from the steaming mug that Lucille handed her. "Thanks for the robe, Lucille."

"Ann Marie brought it over after dinner yesterday with other things she thought you might need. You poor soul, losing everything."

Lucille's expression of compassion tugged at Cassie's heart, but she disliked being an object of pity. "I didn't actually lose my things. They're at my condo. They haven't been released. I'm sure they'll be there when I return to Northfield."

Lucille raised her eyebrows. "Ann Marie said your stay here is permanent."

Not likely, Cassie thought. "What I mean is, someone," her voice faltered, "maybe Willie or even the authorities, will pack up my belongings and ship them to me."

"We'll see," Lucille answered agreeably as if she realized her remark had put a knot in Cassie's thinking. "For now Ann Marie said to give you breakfast. She'll collect you later to show you around."

After eating what Lucille said "wasn't enough to keep a bird alive" and wearing the clean clothes Ann Marie had left—walking shorts, a brightly colored sweater over a T-shirt—Cassie waited for her ride by strolling around the farmhouse yard. She identified many types of wildflowers. Among thistles and wild asters, she spied a lovely white Queen Ann's Lace.

The sun was starting to feel hot on her face when Ann Marie drove up in one of the standard golf carts. She had a briefcase beside her.

"You're up and around I see," Ann Marie said.

"I'm ready to go." Cassie thought that Lucille must have phoned the director with news that she was awake. She realized it would be difficult having any kind of privacy in this community of Peace Seekers. They seemed even closer knit than a small country town. Living communally, they ate together and worked together. Whatever else they did, they probably did it together. She climbed into the cart and settled next to Ann Marie.

"How did you sleep?" Ann Marie asked.

"I was exhausted. I slept straight through and didn't wake until the birds started making noise."

"Did the lack of air conditioning bother you?" It was a clear reference to Seth's attitude toward the room. It wasn't Cassie's intention to renew the disagreement, but since Ann Marie had, there was no harm in soothing her feelings.

"I slept with my windows open. It was pleasant."

"Your wounds didn't bother you too much?"

"No. When I left the hospital, the nurse gave me some pills." Cassie looked at her arms. "My bandages got slightly wet in the shower this morning. I covered them with the plastic Lucille gave me, but water leaked through. I didn't think it would matter because the dressing is being changed today."

"We're heading to the clinic now."

Cassie had been following the progress of the cart as they'd talked. Ann Marie appeared to be guiding it down the same path she'd used last night on the way to the community center.

"The clinic is on the fringe of the campus, away from most of the activity and away from the town itself, but we'll cut through the center of things to shorten the ride."

"Are golf carts the main transportation around here?"

"When distances are too far to walk. Most people enjoy walking, and it's healthier." She gave Cassie an interested look.

"We're dedicated to maintaining our physical health, and we use a lot of natural ways to aid healing. Are you familiar with spiritual healing? Or chakra healing?"

"Yes, I am," Cassie said. "Last summer at a Chippewa village in Michigan where Nate and I stayed—" She paused to deaden the memories flooding her mind. "I saw a child healed through his human energy field. It was impressive."

"The results of auric and chakra treatment are most encouraging."

"Ann Marie?" Despite her resolve, she couldn't keep her mind off Nate and the tragedy of his death. "If spiritual healing is so powerful, why can't it restore life to a fatally wounded person?" She caught her breath at the sharp pain that passed through her at the image of Nate's crumpled body.

"It's not possible, Cassie. When the life force has left the body, it's not possible for it to return, especially if the physical injuries are such that physical life can't be maintained."

"But if healing is possible through the spirit, and there are forces we can't see, such as chakras and angels or whatever, then why would death need to occur?"

"You mean why can't an angel jump in front of a person and take the bullet for him?"

"Something like that. Why can't situations be corrected before they happen?"

"It's hard to understand, Cassie, but at times healthy people have to leave this earthly plane. It's just right for them to go. It's also necessary for them to leave so other changes can happen that couldn't take place if they stayed. You're talking about Nate, of course."

"I suppose it's obvious. What I don't understand is if Nate was important to the community and to earth's evolution, why would he go now? Why when we'd found each other and recognized each other, and loved…" She couldn't go on.

"Exactly. There you have it."

"What?" she whispered the question through her tears.

"It wasn't meant to be, you and Nate."

She gasped. "You can't be serious."

Ann Marie pulled the golf cart to a stop in front of a one-story building similar to the other community buildings. She placed a gentle hand on Cassie's shoulder. "I don't mean to hurt you, dear. I'm just reminding you that you need to move on as soon as you can. Your development as a leader is too important to the movement to let you remain stuck in sorrow."

"But Nate—"

"Nate's left, he's gone."

"But he kept us safe all through the past weeks when we'd been in danger, and then, just like that…" She snapped her fingers. "It's over."

"That's right," Ann Marie said as she climbed out of the cart. "What is supposed to happen, happens. Nate kept you safe all those weeks. It was his duty."

"But we were going to marry, to spend our lives together." She followed Ann Marie out of the cart. "We wanted to work together to help Seth's political career. Now Nate is gone, and it was too fast."

"As I said, it wasn't Nate's destiny to spend this lifetime with you, nor yours to spend it with him. You both have more important work."

She choked back a sob. "How can his leaving improve anything?"

"Don't worry about Nate, Cassie. He's happy wherever he is. He wouldn't want you moping about, mourning him."

She walked toward the clinic with Ann Marie. "You're all so heartless." Her voice became harsh. "You're hard and uncaring."

"Please believe me, I don't mean to hurt you." Ann Marie held the clinic door open. "I know the pain you're experiencing. I feel it the same as you. That's why I'm determined to have you give it up quickly. It hurts to grieve. It hurts so much." Ann Marie held her hand over her heart and averted her face.

Cassie watched the woman's shoulders shake and then reached out and touched her shoulder. "I'm sorry for not understanding how much you care. I know you've also lost a friend."

The clerk at the counter looked up as they approached. "Good morning, Ann Marie, how may I help you?"

The clerk's manner was so welcoming, Cassie couldn't resist answering. "I'm here to have my dressings changed." She showed her bandaged hands and arms by way of explanation.

Beside her, Ann Marie noisily blew her nose. "Excuse me. I'm, uh." She shook her head as if clearing her thoughts. "This is Cassie West, a new arrival. I'd like her to see a practitioner before removing the bandages."

After the receptionist left the room, Ann Marie motioned toward two leather chairs.

Cassie sat, wondering what lay ahead. "Are they going to pray over me like they did in the Michigan village?"

"She'll work with you to assist in your healing," Ann Marie said. "To tell the truth, healing is not my field. A lot of training goes into the making of a healer. I leave their work to them."

"You're an administrator then?"

"Right."

"How did you become head of the community?"

"I'm not the head of anything!"

"I thought—"

"Cassie you can come in now," the receptionist said. "Please follow me."

She took a step then looked back at Ann Marie.

"I'll wait here for you," the woman said. She touched her briefcase. "I've reports I need to read."

Cassie followed the receptionist down an interior corridor then into a darkened room with a padded table in its center. At a corner desk, a woman sat studying papers. A dim desk lamp was the sole illumination. Quiet, peaceful music played. As far as Cassie could make out, the instrument was a wooden flute.

The woman rose. "Come in. I'm Rona. I'm pleased to meet you."

"I'm pleased to meet you also," she said, "except for the circumstances."

"Ah, yes, well, I hope you'll be completely healed soon." She indicated the table in the center of the room. "Just take off your sandals, lie down, and we'll get to work." She pulled a wheeled stool to the end of the table and sat.

"My arms are injured, not my feet." She bent over and kicked off her flip-flops. As she slid onto the table, its paper cover crinkled under her. She squirmed trying to relax.

"I'm going to balance your energy, and I like to touch your feet while I'm working. Do I have your permission?"

"Of course."

"Hmm," Rona murmured, as she lightly rubbed Cassie's feet. "You're tense."

"Imagine that." She didn't hold back the sarcasm, didn't even try. She wanted her dressing changed, not a therapy session.

Rona laughed. "Naturally, you would be tense. We'll try to work with your tension. See if you can relax. Give up your desire for control and quiet your mind."

Control was, Cassie thought, the keyword here according

to Seth. Nevertheless, the dim light, the soft flute music, the padded table and Rona's gentle manipulation of her feet and ankles was producing a state of relaxation. She took a deep breath and let it out slowly.

"Good," Rona encouraged. "Draw in two more deep breaths through your nose and blow them out slowly through your mouth."

Cassie had to admit the foot massage and deep breathing produced a drowsy sense of well-being, but… "What does this have to do with my wounds?"

"Try to relax. We'll get to your hands and arms soon. Another deep breath, please."

Her muscles gave up their tension as the stale air left her lungs. She closed her eyes. Her jaw slackened. She swallowed.

After she was completely relaxed, she sensed Rona leave the stool at the end of the table and stand beside her. Rona's hand passed over Cassie's forehead with a touch so slight she wondered if she'd been touched at all. Only the faint passage of air across bare skin affirmed any movement.

Not knowing what to expect next, she lay tensed. Anxiety increased her pulse. Her heart beat loudly in her ears. What was the woman doing? She slanted a look at Rona and found her slowly moving her hands in the air approximately two inches above Cassie's body.

Rona looked as if she were in a light trance. Her breathing was irregular and raspy, as if she were engaged in exercise. Her eyes moved slightly, yet it seemed as if she saw Cassie in each swift glance.

Beneath her summer clothes, Cassie felt her skin tingle. Excitement? More likely curiosity or anxiety. Yet, she wasn't afraid anymore. In fact, she felt the same resonance she'd felt with Seth last night, as if each cell vibrated to an unseen energy source.

After what seemed an eternity—perhaps because her eagerness to discuss the process with Rona was so intense—she heard the woman return to the stool at the end of the table. The soft music continued with riffs of wood flutes alternating with long mourning tones.

Rona's touch on her feet was warm, drawing heat into the end of her toes. She drifted into sleep.

"That's it for now," Rona said.

Cassie awoke, feeling a little dazed.

The therapist released her feet and stood. "You can rest for a minute if you wish, and then we'll talk."

A tear ran down Cassie's cheek. She wiped it with her bandaged hand and propped herself on an elbow. "That was exceptional." She sat up and let her legs dangle over the edge of the table. "My muscles feel so…relaxed, yet I'm filled with energy. How did you do it?"

With a warm smile, Rona retrieved Cassie's flip-flops from the floor. "It wasn't such a bad idea to remove your sandals after all, was it?"

"Not bad at all." She reached for her footwear.

"Here, let me." Rona placed one of the flip-flops over Cassie's toes. She pushed her foot into it. "Thanks."

Rona put a flip-flop on Cassie's other foot and said, "Now, let's talk." She helped Cassie down from the table and motioned toward two chairs at the desk.

Cassie sat on the edge of one of the chairs. After hesitating she said, "What you did was very nice and relaxing, but about my arms…will you change the dressings yourself?"

"The nurse will do that. I sensed heat in one of your wounds. It might be festering. The rest are healing nicely. The infected wound may give you trouble, but it's not the shotgun injury that concerns me."

Rona's gaze grew soft, caring. "You have other wounds, deeper hurts lying far beneath the surface."

Cassie took a deep breath and willed herself not to react.

Rona continued. "And they're not all recent. True, your mother's passing and Nate's death shocked you, but I have a sense you feel that you belong nowhere. A sense of isolation and loneliness. Naturally, the wounds on your hands and arms trouble you," she paused, "but, if nothing's done, your wounded psyche will eventually cause you more pain."

Cassie swallowed to keep her tears in check. With the intimacy and love she shared with Nate, she thought her loneliness was over, but then he was taken from her. They'd only just given themselves to each other.

"But we won't discuss this now." Rona smiled. "We'll take your healing in small steps." She nodded at Cassie's bandages. "Heal your body first, and then we will tackle your other hurts."

After the clinic nurse had done a careful job of replacing the surgical wrappings with smaller bandages, she sent Cassie back to the reception room, where Ann Marie waited.

"How did things go?" Ann Marie asked.

"One of the wounds is infected. The nurse coated it with antibiotic ointment. She'll check it again tomorrow. She said to remove the bandages when I shower in the morning. The water will do them good."

Ann Marie snapped her briefcase closed. "And Rona? Did you get along with her?" She held the door for Cassie.

She shrugged and headed toward the golf cart. "I guess we did all right. Is she a therapist?"

Ann Marie smiled. "She has a degree in something or other."

"Don't you know?"

"It's not important. She's an intuitive healer. The institute thinks a lot of her." She gave Cassie a questioning look. "Didn't you like her?"

"I liked her, but she wanted to talk about Nate and my mother. I don't want to think about that."

"It's painful. Unfortunately, it's also the path to healing."

"Not now." The lump in her throat threatened to choke her.

"No, not now." Ann Marie laid a gentle hand on Cassie's shoulder. "You can talk with Rona later about your losses."

The next morning Ann Marie again picked up Cassie in the golf cart. She took her to see Rona for another healing session, and the nurse for a change of dressings. At the same hillside overview where Seth had stopped with Cassie the first night, Ann Marie drew the golf cart to a halt.

"Cassie, I'm wondering if you have any questions you want answered, or any concerns about your treatment."

Cassie hesitated, and then decided to trust Ann Marie. She did need answers and now might be a good opportunity to get them.

"Tell me all about the Peace Seekers."

Ann Marie looked surprised. "Didn't Nate explain them to you?"

"Not really. When we were together, we did a lot of arguing."

More raised eyebrows. "That doesn't sound like Nate."

Cassie flushed. "I suppose it was my fault."

"I didn't say that."

"No, but if you had, you would be right. I had trouble believing what Nate was saying, and he stopped trying to explain things. He said I would learn everything about the Peace Seekers when we reached Peace Lake." She paused while she fought back tears. "I always thought we would be here together."

Ann Marie stretched and then relaxed. "It's hard to know where to start. The Peace Seekers are a loose-knit association of different groups all working to heal the planet. Specifically, Peace Seeker individuals are reincarnated souls who delay entry into Nirvana, or Heaven, or whatever you want to call it, to return to Earth. You might say they are advanced souls who choose their parents and their destinies. The Buddhists call them Bodhisattvas. Other religious groups have different names, but essentially they all imply the same: people of higher consciousness with concern for others, and a dedication to improving conditions on our planet. Examples of well-known people we would consider Peace Seekers—although I can't confirm that for you—might be Gandhi, Martin Luther King Jr., Deepak Chopra, or even farther back in history, Francis of Assisi, and Ignatius of Loyola with his Spiritual Exercises."

"Nate did tell me about Bodhisattvas. He called me one. He also called me an Ancient One. Obviously, the idea seems strange. I have a problem accepting it. But what about Peace Lake Village. How did it get started?"

"It was established in the early 1800s by farmers who built a dam on Peace River, forming a lake. After the dam was torn down, the name Peace Lake persisted. When early Peace Seekers were looking for a place for a community, they said the name of the town appealed to them. Over decades we formed several charitable nonprofit institutions that exist side by side with the ordinary people of the town."

"What sort of institutions."

"We have a graduate school offering degrees in philosophy, environmental studies, and conflict resolution; a healing institute—you were in the clinic today—and a political action group."

"But I haven't seen the name Peace Seeker anywhere around here."

"No, we only call ourselves Peace Seekers in our own intimate circle. Otherwise to the world we are known as the institute for the Peaceful Advancement of Co-Creation, or IPAC."

"IPAC?" Cassie hesitated. "Nate never mentioned that name."

"Seth and Nate are loosely connected to our institute. As Peace Seekers, we are all aware of each other, but we mostly act independently. By staying independent, we avoid being labeled a cult. That might turn people away."

"I think you're wise," Cassie said. "The name Peace Seeker and the word Bodhisattva bothered me the first time Nate discussed it."

"We aren't a cult, and it is important to keep our identity as concerned individuals, not a formal organization. We created the institute to serve as an educational area for individuals. People come here for training, and then they leave."

"I'm a research librarian, and I'd never heard of Peace Seekers before I met Nate."

"People have written nonfiction books with that title, but you won't hear the name in general conversation. When we talk about ourselves anywhere except in the most intimate settings, we call ourselves 'Movers.' If questioned, we say 'movers and shakers.' You know the common saying."

Cassie smiled. "Sure, I've heard it a thousand times."

"Okay, that was Indoctrination 101, as Seth would say."

Cassie shook her head. "He certainly is different."

"Headstrong," Ann Marie said. She swung the cart in a wide circle and headed back to the institute.

"I'm not sure I completely trust him," Cassie confided.

"Didn't Nate tell you Peace Seekers are human in every way, including all the normal vices, such as dishonesty and deception?"

"Yes, he did." She recalled their talks together in the forest community. "He used it as an excuse for his behavior whenever I was angry with him."

"Well, Seth is very human, if you know what I mean."

Cassie remembered his hand pressed over her mouth at the hospital. "Can Peace Seekers physically hurt other people?"

Ann Marie stared at Cassie. "They can, but it is rare. When I said normal vices, I meant ordinary. They will never purposely hurt another person unless their life is threatened. Then they are allowed to defend themselves, but usually they use other defensive measures such as auric protection and psychic force fields."

Cassie looked at her feet clad in donated flip-flops.

"Has someone hurt you, Cassie?"

"Not really."

"I suspect Seth has a mean streak in him, something unusual for a Peace Seeker."

It was exactly what he had said about Ann Marie.

CHAPTER SIX

Her first week at Peace Lake passed quietly. Cassie's superficial wounds healed, and removing the bandages and seeing fresh pink skin brought a sense of freedom. Of course, the skin was still tender, and daily healing sessions with Rona continued. Ann Marie had Cassie moved into a one-bedroom apartment in an institute dormitory. The apartment had its own small kitchen where she could have her breakfast and lunch, but she continued to eat dinner in the main dining room to discuss the happenings of the day and—she suspected—so Ann Marie could check up on her.

July led into August, and August into September, and the first leaves fell to the ground, reminding Cassie that nature had its cycles, the same as mankind. With Ann Marie's help, she shopped for a new wardrobe and accessories, welcoming the opportunity for a fresh beginning.

She started soul-healing sessions with counselors and gradually slid into the routine of the Peace Seekers colony. When Cassie felt up to it, Ann Marie assigned her to the institute's library, where Cassie recovered her energy and interest in her profession. The books and audio-visual materials were different from those she'd studied in earlier jobs. During her free hours, she buried herself in learning about soul healing, angels, and other psychic phenomena.

In October, she listed her condo for sale with a Realtor and had a personal representative sell all her furniture and clothes, except for some items she wanted to keep and her jewelry. They were in storage in Northfield. One day she would deal with them, not now. It was too soon.

Although she hadn't seen Seth since the day he left in late July, she followed his campaign on the Internet and, in November, cheered with the rest of the Peace Seekers when he won Michigan's U.S. Senate seat. The institute staff was disappointed when Seth didn't visit in the weeks following his victory, but they understood his life was undergoing a drastic change. He was immersed in the multitude of details related to his swearing-in and his move to Washington, D.C.

The colony keenly felt Seth's absence during the December holidays, but Cassie didn't care. As the months had passed, he had called her nearly every night. They discussed his campaign and his victory, her healing and her growing knowledge of psychic phenomena. She became familiar with his teasing tone and his habit of finding humor in everything, even in himself. And they were becoming friends. Something she would not have expected last summer.

January and February passed with Cassie engrossed in a renovation project for the library. Ann Marie attended Seth's swearing-in as a new senator, but Cassie didn't feel ready for the public occasion.

On a gray March day, Cassie cuddled up on her living room sofa with a book, a couple of pillows, and a rose-colored knit throw. She loved her tiny apartment with its overstuffed sofa and comfy armchair. The dinette set wasn't new, but the chairs swiveled and tilted, and she enjoyed having her morning coffee sitting at the table looking out the sliding glass doors that led to a small balcony.

Two sharp raps on her apartment door drew Cassie's attention away from the book she was reviewing. "Come in," she called. Nine months had passed since she first arrived at the Peace Seeker's colony, and she'd adopted their practice of leaving doors unlocked.

The door swung open, and Ann Marie peeked in. When she saw Cassie on the sofa she asked "Are you resting?"

"That's okay. I'm just reading." She smothered a yawn and put the book down.

"I wanted to tell you that Seth is going to be here for dinner."

"He is? Now?"

Ann Marie smiled. "The new senator will be our dinner guest!"

Cassie thought Ann Marie looked suddenly younger, happier than she had in months, although happiness seemed to be the director's normal state of mind.

Seth's election victory after such a hard-fought battle brought elation to the entire colony. He was their first national office holder. Many served in appointed positions, on presidents' cabinets and the federal courts, but no one from Peace Lake had reached such a high office in a U.S. national election. Seth's victory was considered a sign of more to come.

Cassie stood up and folded the shawl she'd used as a cover. "It's strange," she mused. "He didn't mention he was planning a visit when we talked last night."

Ann Marie frowned. "I didn't know he called."

Taken aback by the woman's negative reaction, Cassie hesitated before answering. In the time she'd been with the Peace

Seekers, she'd learned honesty was best in nearly every relationship. "He calls on his cell phone most nights. I thought you knew."

Ann Marie's lips tightened into a thin line. "How would I know if you kept it to yourself?"

"Of course," Cassie added, "we—you and I, that is—haven't seen each other a lot lately since I've been working in the library, but I thought you knew Seth called me. A lot of people did."

Ann Marie shrugged. "It doesn't matter."

"But it does, Ann Marie, if it makes you angry."

"I'm not angry." She turned to go.

Cassie stopped her with a light touch on her arm. "There's nothing between Seth and me. It's nothing to worry about."

The older woman put her hands on her hips and gave her a hard look. "Really, Cassie, why would you think I cared? And don't try to deceive me."

Cassie recoiled as if she'd been slapped. "What do you mean?"

"You're telling me Seth Hawthorne takes time out of his busy schedule to call every night, and then you expect me to believe it means nothing."

"He knew I was mourning Nate." There, she'd said his name aloud without hesitation and without a tear in her eyes. Rona would be proud.

"Seth has never been a compassionate person."

Cassie felt the flush of annoyance. "That's not kind."

"Kind? Don't speak to me of being kind."

"Ann Marie, what's wrong? I've never seen you this angry."

"You know why he's coming, don't you?" The woman peered at her.

Cassie shook her head mutely. If she had been a third-grader standing at the chalkboard under the eye of her teacher, she couldn't have felt more intimidated.

"He's coming to take you to Washington."

"I…" She had no words, nothing to describe the shock she felt. "I'm sure you're mistaken."

"No, I'm not." Ann Marie stood at the glass doors and looked out upon the Japanese garden separating the two wings of the dormitory. "I don't want you to leave. I've discussed it with him often."

"You discussed me with Seth?" She knew she would feel indignation later. Right now she was numb with surprise and could do little except stare at the director.

Ann Marie turned and paced across the room. "Did he neglect to mention he was setting you up?"

"What?"

Ann Marie sighed. "He wants you with him in Washington."

The truth was beginning to register with Cassie. She sat on the sofa. Seth's interest, his nightly calls. She'd come to expect them, grown to rely on them. They had seen her through more than one rough time.

She said, "You know that's what Nate, Seth and I planned originally."

"You mean you would consider it?" Ann Marie shook her head. "I gave him an outright 'no' for an answer. You're in no condition to enter the political arena."

Despite her gratitude for Seth's nightly calls, Cassie had no desire to be with him. But even more strongly, she resented Ann Marie's voicing the thought that she was inadequate for whatever lay ahead.

"Do you think I can't handle a move to Washington?"

Ann Marie smiled wanly as if she knew she'd made a mistake. "I didn't say you were incapable. I, uh, actually believe the opposite."

Cassie bristled. "*You're in no condition* were the words you used."

Ann Marie spread her arms in supplication. "Cassie, you're taking things out of context. I meant you aren't ready to face the world."

"Nate would want me to go on with our work. He tried without success to convince me to work for Seth." She fought back tears, hoping she had won the battle without Ann Marie's noticing her distress.

Ann Marie put her hand on Cassie's shoulder. "You see," she said softly, "you can't mention Nate without tears. It's too soon, only nine months."

"It will always be too soon for me. I'll never forget him." She took a tissue from her pocket and wiped her eyes and nose. "We were soul mates in a way Seth and I can never be."

She didn't care how foolish she sounded to this pragmatic woman, an administrator who'd probably never had a breath-taking love affair in her entire life. Of course she hadn't, Cassie realized with a rush of insight. Nate had told her from almost the very beginning: Peace Seekers had evolved beyond intimacies of the flesh. They sublimated sexual drives in their work and practiced blending of souls in what he called celestial sex. They had become supra-sexual creatures. She smiled inwardly. Only sometimes...

Cassie lifted her gaze to Ann Marie's. "I was told Peace Seekers don't make earthly attachments as we ordinary people do."

Ann Marie sighed as if taking up an old argument. "I'm forever reminding you, Cassie, you're as much a Peace Seeker as I am."

"So you say." Cassie gestured in frustration. "Well, if I am,

I'm an immature Peace Seeker. When my parents were killed in a cabin fire, I was sidetracked. I grew up like a normal person, Eudora saw to that."

Ann Marie gently took Cassie's hands in hers. "You didn't grow up like a normal person. Eudora kept you hidden and attempted to repress your natural psychic talents. It was a terrible waste of an advanced soul's talents and wisdom."

Cassie pulled away. Everything Ann Marie said was true. She'd known almost forever she was different from most people. And Eudora had known Cassie's background and had kept it secret from her. She needed to recognize that, needed to admit it. Ann Marie was right again. Unfortunately.

"I don't want to quarrel, Ann Marie." She intentionally softened her voice. "You've been like a mother to me."

"In the past nine months, you've become the daughter I never had."

Relieved, Cassie hugged her. "I appreciate that, and I'll talk to Seth tonight. If what you say is true about his wanting me with him, I'll make up my mind after talking to him." She looked at her wristwatch. "Do you suppose I've time to shower before dinner?"

"I'm sure you do." Ann Marie turned to leave. "But don't think badly of me. If I seem interfering, it's because I care so much about you."

✦　✦　✦

This evening with Seth was important and she wanted to look her best.

In the corridor that connected the dormitory to the community building where meals were served, she paused and smoothed her hands over the flowing red silk dress that ended at her knees. Four-inch black stiletto heels bought specially for the dress complemented it perfectly. Although when she bought the shoes, she had no idea when or where she would ever use them. The time had arrived.

Oh, admit it, she thought. What woman wouldn't dress carefully if she was having dinner with a U.S. Senator? Thinking of being with Seth, seeing him after so many months, made her pulse beat faster. He had phoned almost every night. She wondered if Ann Marie was right. Would a man call a woman so often for such a long time if he wasn't interested in her?

She drew a deep breath and opened the door. *One step at a time, Cassie. One step at a time.*

She put on a bright smile and strode into the nearly deserted main lobby. A glance at her watch showed she was ten minutes late for dinner. In honor of the special guest, Seth, it was a table-service meal tonight instead of a buffet. She quickened her step. Now she would have to make an entrance. That wouldn't do. She circled around the outside of the dining room and went in by the rear door.

Inside, she stopped, enthralled by the sight of Seth at a podium in the front of the room. His tanned complexion and perfectly styled hair and his impeccable dark suit and tie made his appearance even more impressive. Although the Peace Seekers in his audience were also dressed nicely, she thought their appearance reflected the more relaxed and casual style of the southern Ohio countryside.

Shivering with excitement, she stood at the rear of the room, listening to Seth speak. Was this her future, her destiny standing before her?

Seth's gaze swept past her and then returned. His face broke into a wide grin and he nodded. Cassie's cheeks warmed under his attention. However, he didn't pause, didn't end his presentation until he came to an appropriate stopping point.

"Once again, thank you all for your loving help," Seth said to the assembled diners. "Without your work, my campaign would have failed." He looked again at Cassie. "Each one of you is important in our plans for the future. Each person must perform his or her job for success to be ours. You all performed perfectly. I do thank you."

He stepped away from the podium to enthusiastic applause. His eyes never left Cassie. Her heart pounded wildly. He was speaking to her, telling her these good people had all performed their jobs in getting him elected. Now she needed to lend her support to the cause.

She hoped she was capable of doing what was necessary. Despite Ann Marie's fears, she knew she was.

Seth walked toward her with Ann Marie and other leaders behind him. "Cassie." He took her arm and guided her toward the private dining room off to the side of the main room. He bent his head toward her. "I thought I was going to have to go to your room to get you."

She whispered, "I couldn't decide what to wear."

"You're lovely."

"I'm not looking for a compliment."

"I didn't think you were." His gaze traveled the length of her. "Have you grown since I saw you last?"

She laughed freely. Seth could be charming when he chose. The little-boy look on his face made her lighthearted. "It's the shoes, silly," she whispered.

His hearty laugh brought everyone's attention to them. She hadn't heard it this strong for months.

"Thank God for you," Seth said. "No one has called me 'silly' since I was ten years old."

"Seth," Ann Marie gestured to him. "You're at the end of the table."

"And Cassie is on my right."

Ann Marie gave him a quick look. "Of course."

But Cassie thought if Ann Marie wasn't careful her icy voice might freeze the blood in her veins.

Seth held her chair for her. "Beautiful," he said in her ear as he assisted her.

She flushed, but took a deep breath to control her reaction. *It is what it is,* she thought, reciting one of the Peace Seekers' favorite mottos. Accept what is and go with it. Her breathing quieted. Seth reached under the table and squeezed her hand.

When the party ended, Cassie stood at Seth's side as the diners exited. She listened to his words of encouragement as he shook each person's hand.

He had the talent, she thought. He made each person feel special. She remembered the first day she met him. It was on Mackinac Island at a garden party her mother gave in his honor. She had thought him too perfect. He charmed the women too easily and struck a sincere note with most of the men within seconds.

Now she stood by his side. As Nate had predicted. And Nate was...

"Ready to leave?" Seth touched her elbow. "We're finished here."

She didn't know what to expect or how to answer. She looked at the people who still milled around in the reception area. "Leave for...?" she asked.

Seth laughed. "Sorry. I want to talk to you privately. We've been getting to know each other for months over the phone. Could we go to your room and talk, or would you prefer a more neutral setting?" He looked in her eyes. "You'd like neutral? Right?"

She opened her mouth, closed it, and then nodded. "Right."

"The SUV is outside. How about taking a ride on a crisp spring evening?"

She hesitated. His car didn't sound like neutral ground, but she'd love a ride outside of the complex. "I'll need to get a coat."

"You can have my jacket." He took her elbow and guided her toward the front door and the traffic circle beyond.

"Seth, I can't wear your jacket."

"Why not?"

She pulled up short. "Because then you won't have one."

"I don't need a jacket."

"Really?" She couldn't help laughing, didn't know what had come over her. "You're that hot then?"

Pleasure showed on his face. "Cassie." He tenderly touched his hand to her cheek. "You're really feeling better."

Her skin felt hot where he touched her, and her throat closed at his show of affection. She forced the words out. "I guess so."

Ann Marie stood guard at the door. "Are you going out wearing that?" She inspected Cassie's thin, elegant dress.

Cassie thought Ann Marie sounded like a disapproving mother, especially after her earlier confession. "Seth says it will be all right." She almost added *Mom*. "He's taking me for a ride and he'll turn on the heat."

Seth laughed. "The heater, Ann Marie. Cassie, don't get me in trouble with the warden here. I always ride with my jacket off. We'll be all right. What time do you want me to get Cassie home tonight?"

Ann Marie gave him a cold stare.

"Just asking," Seth said. "I thought you might care."

Ann Marie smiled without warmth. "I believe she will soon be thirty years old. I'm sure she doesn't need a chaperone. Especially with you. I know you'll be careful of your reputation. Politicians have been removed from office because of scandal."

Outside, Willie stood at the door of the vehicle.

Cassie squealed, "Willie," and ran to him. He had been Nate and Seth's driver for a long time and had seen Cassie through many rough times.

"Hi, sweets." He crushed her to his chest in a bear hug. "It's been too long."

Tears filled her eyes at this bittersweet reunion. "Oh, Willie. Do you remember when we were at Walloon Lake, and..." He had helped Nate rescue her when she'd been in trouble with the law. *Last summer, in June.*

Willie held the rear door open. "Get in. It's cold," he said with a husky voice.

Seth joined her in the backseat and placed his suit coat over her shoulders. He slid close to her and put an arm around her. "You'll have to keep me warm until it heats up." He pounded on the back of the front seat. "Heat, Willie, more heat."

Willie waved a hand as if to say, 'cool it,' but as he pulled away from the curb, warm air poured out of the heating vents.

Cassie looked at Seth and then quickly away. The energy of his gaze was too strong. "Seth, Ann Marie had to tell me that you were coming. You didn't mention it last night."

"I wasn't sure myself. But I'm glad to have a break in my schedule." He put his hand over hers. "Are you glad to see me?"

"You know I am."

"You haven't always been."

"Seth, you've been so good to me, so kind, helping in any way you could, and calling so often while working in Washington. I do appreciate you."

He shifted slightly. "Okay. I accept that for now, your appreciation of my help. It might be a first step leading to a closer relationship later."

She had been afraid this was coming. Now it was here, she didn't know what to say. She sat quietly with her hand in his, feeling the hum of his energy. She wondered what she actually thought of Seth. How did she feel about him?

"I'm wondering the same thing," he said.

He'd read her thoughts. She drew a deep breath. "Okay. I'm all right with that." She glanced at him. "Remember how angry I was because Nate and you always read my mind? Well, he did anyway. And now you're doing the same thing."

"And you're not angry anymore?"

She shook her head. "No, at least not as much. Living with the Peace Seekers makes acceptance of unusual things much easier."

"You're finally accepting that?"

"Yes, they're always saying, 'don't resist things or feelings. Acknowledge what is. It isn't good or bad. It just is. Let it go, then move on.' If you live with that philosophy long enough, it starts to make sense." She smiled with sudden understanding. "Is that what you meant, Seth?"

"Yes, I'm accepting where you are now, but I hope your feelings about me will change one day."

"My feelings about you have changed already."

He laughed. "When we first met, you didn't like me at all."

"You're right about that." She smiled, teasing him. "Was I a real problem?"

"You were never a problem. I liked you from the moment

I saw you."

She hooted. "A lie if I ever heard one."

"No, it's true!"

"Not!"

He moved his finger to her lips and touched them. "You win. But I like you now."

"What a relief. I'd hate to be with you in the backseat if you didn't like me."

"What would you be afraid of?"

"I'm not afraid of you, Seth."

He leaned over and kissed her just above her ear. "Not even a little bit?" He kissed her softly on her lips. A spark of energy moved between them.

Cassie swallowed hard. "No kisses. Can you just sit with me for a minute?"

He pulled her to him and held her against his chest. "You're so thin."

She whispered, "Don't talk, please." She drew a deep breath and pressed her face against his starched shirt. His heat came to her through the cotton. "I wish I could stay here, safe like this."

"You can."

"I mean in the dark, alone, no one else around. Just the two of us, with no responsibilities, no memories." She trembled slightly.

"Can you feel that?" Seth asked. "Our energies are harmonizing. Soon our hearts will beat in the same sequence. Our auras are blending into one. That's why I need you, to calm me, help me clear my head and keep me on track."

Seth continued, "We'll have our moments of peace, Cassie, but we can't run away from the world. I've been sworn in as a U.S. senator. I need you by my side. I need you as my wife helping me through the first year, the beginning of my career in Washington."

She shook her head. "Please, don't talk about it."

"We have to talk about your leaving here." He leaned away and looked at her. "We need to make plans. I need to know your decision. Will you help me as we planned before we were born into this lifetime?"

"I don't know what to say."

"Why don't you ask Nate?"

She stared at him. "What are you talking about?"

"Tonight when you go to bed, meditate, and ask to enter the Inner Kingdom, the time between lives. When you get there, ask Nate what he thinks you should do."

Her eyes widened. "Are you saying I can talk to Nate in this Inner Kingdom?"

"It's possible."

A rush of anger rose within her. "Why didn't you tell me this before now?"

He looked confused. "What do you mean?"

"All these months! I could have been talking with Nate." She hit his chest with her fist. "Why didn't you tell me?"

"Cassie." Seth clamped his hands around her fists and held them against his chest. "Haven't you learned any self control in these past months?"

She sobbed. "But I could have seen Nate."

"You can always see him. You know that."

She quieted, with tears running down her cheeks. "I don't understand."

"You have the talent, the psychic talent, to talk with and see whoever and whatever you want."

She drew a deep breath. Seth took out his handkerchief and wiped her cheeks. She said, "I could have gone back in time."

"Right."

"But I didn't."

"Right."

"Why not?"

"Because it wasn't good for you. Your abilities were blocked for your own good while you were healing—for your safety."

"You blocked my psychic abilities? Ann Marie blocked my abilities?"

"No, we didn't do that. We couldn't. Spirit blocked them. You're constantly guided toward good by Spirit."

She stared at him.

"You know you're not alone. You've learned that much, haven't you?"

"Yes, of course. I'm guided. We're all guided to our highest good."

"Do you believe it?"

She laughed away her tears. "I have no idea."

"Typical." Seth gave her a crooked smile. "Do you want me to stay with you tonight and guide you to the Inner Kingdom?"

She stared at him with a raised eyebrow. "Can you ask that with a straight face?"

Seth spread his arms out innocently. "Have you no faith? I'm completely trustworthy."

She shook her head. "Maybe so but, no, you can't stay with me tonight. For one thing, Ann Marie wouldn't allow it."

"She has nothing to say about what we do."

"Maybe not, but I wouldn't want to be on the wrong side of her for too long. I think she's a little too bossy for a Peace Seeker."

"She wants the best for you, Cassie. Unfortunately, what she thinks is best and what I want from you are two different things."

He slipped his hands under the jacket she wore and wrapped them around her waist. "What do you say? Are you with me? I need you in Washington."

"Can I let you know tomorrow?"

He studied her silently with what looked like respect.

"What are you thinking?" she asked.

"Don't you know?"

She shook her head. "I'm too tired to try to read your thoughts."

"I'm thinking you are quite a woman."

She made a brief gesture with her hand, meaning to brush off his comment.

"No," he said. "I mean it. Don't put yourself down. I admire you and how you've handled everything you've been through. You *are* quite a woman. But know, Cassie West, I intend to have you with me in Washington."

⚓ ⚓ ⚓

Seth and Willie dropped Cassie off in front of the dormitory. Seth would have walked her to her room, but she refused his offer.

Now showered, with her clothes put away and not tired enough to sleep, she thought back to what Seth had said. He intended to have her with him in Washington, and that meant marriage as they originally planned.

She didn't want to marry Seth. If she married him, it would be like an arranged marriage. Not love, but respect and affection. No sexual overtones. Wait a minute, who was she kidding? Seth was a sensual man. He made no secret of finding her attractive.

She lay down on her bed and closed her eyes. After

meditating for several minutes, she asked Spirit how she could delay their marriage. A feeling of peace came over her. She saw a university. What could that mean? She might go to school for an advanced degree. That would give her time to adjust to her future plans.

She continued breathing deeply in slow even breaths. But what would she study? The answer came, law. Okay, a lot of politicians had law degrees. But could she manage it? She'd have to take the LSAT exam. Get together a résumé of her education and work experience. Possibly, she'd need a personal statement or essay, and letters of recommendation. Her career as a research librarian at the Northfield Library should help. And Seth could write a recommendation. If she could be admitted, law school might work. She would like the competition and mental discipline. Then she would be more Seth's equal partner rather than his...his whatever.

But there was more she needed help with. She needed to find a solution with him as to a sexual relationship. She couldn't be with him in that way, just couldn't. Not with Nate's best friend. And certainly not this soon after Nate's death. It was unthinkable.

Although she continued meditating, no further answer came.

She crawled under the covers and rested her head on the pillow. It was time to contact Nate. He had taught her to first meditate, and then ask to be shown the Inner Kingdom, the place where souls rested between lifetimes. Meditation was not as strange to her now as it had been when she first met Nate. She closed her eyes and prayed for protection.

God's light touches all of us.

God's love remains within us....

She yawned and recited the rest of the poem. Her eyelids

felt heavy. It never failed. The repetition of the simple prayer slowed her heartbeat and calmed her. As she continued the prayer, she fought against sleep. One more thing was necessary. She had to ask. She'd learned if she wanted help, she always needed to ask. Show me, she prayed, take me to the Inner Kingdom. Inner Kingdom.

Cassie!

A pink mist surrounded her. Nebulous shapes floated around her. Where was she?

Cassie, it's you.

Nate?

Yes, love, welcome home.

Nate, I miss you.

I know. We miss you, too.

We, not he, she thought. *I miss you terribly. Why did you leave?*

It was time. Some things are meant to happen when they do.

But you left me alone.

Not alone.

Something brushed her arm and she looked down. But where was her arm? Her Light Body glowed, pulsed with a white energy. She could barely make out the form of her fingers. She raised a hand to see it more clearly.

Someone laughed softly. *Child, you don't need a body here. It will materialize if you desire, but it is out of place. Enjoy your freedom from the physical realm. Rest with us before you return.*

Where is Nate?

I'm here, love.

She had come for a reason that was unclear to her now. She struggled with her earthly memory. Then the word *Seth* came into her mind.

Nate, Seth wants me to go to Washington. He's been elected senator from Michigan.

Yes, we know. We're so proud.

There was that "we" again. Was Nate purposely distancing himself? Did one lose one's individuality in the Inner Kingdom? In this restful place between lives, was one's identity lost? If so, how could she know Nate's voice? How did he recognize hers?

We know you, Cassie. We will always know you and love you, but you need to live your earthly life as set out for you before we can have you with us again.

You think I should go with Seth.

You need to fulfill your destiny as you see it. Others cannot make plans for you. What your mind conceives, you shall receive.

Then I should do it.

We cannot say. Do what your heart tells you. It must be your own free will, but do not waste this time on Earth. Do what you will, learn what you may. Then return to us when you are finished.

Peace fell over Cassie. She was released from any obligations except those she chose. She would do it. She would go with Seth, marry him, and assist him in any way she could.

So be it. It will be so.

CHAPTER SEVEN

Cassie fumbled for her cell phone on the nightstand. "Hello."

"I'll meet you downstairs in ten minutes for breakfast."

Seth. Reality returned slowly as she struggled up from a dream. Unlike her visit to the Inner Kingdom, this dream had been vivid and filled with strangers. In it, she had watched painters dressed in coveralls paint the inside of her house with white paint. She knew it must be her house, but she hadn't seen it before.

"Cassie, did you hear me? How about breakfast in ten minutes?"

"Oh, sorry. I heard you. Yes. No. Make it twenty minutes. You woke me." She would ask Ann Marie later about the dream and its significance.

"I'll be there in ten, so step it up." Seth broke the connection.

She shook her head, remembering the decision she'd made last night after visiting the Inner Kingdom. She would go to Washington with Seth. She would carry through with the plans Nate, Seth, and she had made for this lifetime. A search of her soul for signs of dread or anxiety uncovered only peace, confirming her decision.

Twenty minutes later, dressed in a casual sweater and pants outfit, she entered the dining room and saw Seth sitting at a round table with five other people. When he spotted Cassie, he stood and gave her a stunning smile. He pointed toward the private dining room where they'd eaten the previous night.

She started to protest, but gave in. For months now she'd eaten in the main dining room with the other Peace Seekers. If she were to be a senator's wife, she'd have to adapt to the privileges and restrictions that went with the position, as well as not question his decisions in public.

When he joined her at the door of the private room, he wound an arm around her neck and shoulders and pulled her close. "You look good," he murmured, dropping a kiss on her cheek.

She shook him away. "Don't do that." She headed toward the table where a waitress stood waiting for them.

"I kissed you last night."

"In the limo, in private."

Seth helped her with the heavy walnut chair. A small bouquet of fresh flowers sat in the middle of the table. "So whatever I do with you in private is okay?" His hand lingered on her shoulder.

"I didn't say that." Under the warmth of his fingers, her cells vibrated to his touch. He had way too much power over her.

"What do you want to eat?" he asked. He gave the waitress the same dazzling smile he'd given Cassie, and the young woman smiled back.

"Regular coffee, orange juice, a poached egg and English muffin, please." She smiled at the waitress who seemed unable to look anywhere but at Seth, who returned her gaze with unveiled interest.

"Seth?" Cassie asked.

He turned to her. "What?"

"Did you eat already?"

He shook his head. "Could you bring me a fresh cup of coffee and two pieces of raisin toast?" he asked the waitress.

"Is that all you're having?" Cassie asked.

He grinned, leaned toward her, and gave her sweater sleeve an affectionate tug. "We might as well be married already if you're watching my diet."

She drew a deep breath and played with the napkin in front of her. When she looked up he was still watching her. She asked, "Is it obvious I've made up my mind?"

He leaned back in the chair and stretched his arms wide. "Ah, yes," he said with a satisfied grin.

A rush of fear pounded through her. He'd won, his posture told her. She was his now. What had she done? Her heart beat faster, and she licked her lips.

Seth lowered his arms and looked at her closely. "Are you okay?"

"I'm okay. I just need time to accept the idea of going with you."

"How long do you need?"

"How long?" She looked at him blankly. She had no idea.

"Senator Hawthorne?" The waitress placed his plate of toast in front of him on the fresh white tablecloth, and then set Cassie's plate in front of her. "Coffee, sir?" the young woman asked as she turned Seth's cup over and filled it with steaming fragrant brew. "Cream?" She leaned closer to him and placed a silver pitcher on a small plate.

Seth gave the waitress a wink and patted her hip.

Cassie straightened. "May I also have coffee?"

The waitress gaped at her as if coming out of a spell. "Sorry." She poured Cassie's coffee, overflowing it into the saucer as she looked at Seth.

Cassie finally caught his eye and Seth smiled. "Thanks, darling," he said to the waitress, and then reached over to take Cassie's hand. "They love me," he murmured. "What can I do?"

She looked at their hands joined as one, and slipped hers away. "How difficult for you," she said in a lightly sarcastic tone.

He sighed. "It's all part of the job."

She laughed. "And you hate it, don't you?"

"Not at all." He gave another of those *I own you* looks. "You know how I feel about women."

She picked up her cup and slipped a paper napkin under it to soak up what was spilled. "You're right. I do know."

"And I've made it apparent how I feel about you."

"You have." She sipped from her cup.

He took a bite of raisin toast, slowly chewed and swallowed before speaking. "And it's okay with you?"

"We need to talk about our relationship. Settle some issues."

"Okay." He stuffed more toast into his mouth and washed it down with coffee. "What's on your mind?"

"This marriage thing."

Seth cleared his throat. "What about it?"

"I'm been thinking about it, and I'm not ready."

He scowled. "You've had nine months. Did you visit the Inner Kingdom last night?"

"I did."

"And that didn't settle your doubts?"

"It did, and I'm committed to working with you, but marriage—"

"You can't come to Washington as my girlfriend."

"Of course not." She opened her hands expansively as if she were giving a lecture. "I could be your aide, work in your office."

"Not good enough. I told you I need you with me. How will it look if you're by my side, but not my wife? Everyone will think I'm having an affair with you." He finished his toast, folded his napkin and placed it on the table. "We'll get married here at Peace Lake, a small ceremony. Then we'll leave for Washington together. It's all planned."

She hadn't touched her food. Her stomach contracted. "Who planned the wedding?"

"I did."

"Without consulting me?"

He shrugged. "I talked with Willie and others. They're creating a new identity for you. A foolproof identity. You've got a new name, birth certificate, passport, social security number. The whole thing. You've spent recent years working as an assistant to Eudora, helping her manage her horses and her investments."

"Wait!" She held up her hand. "You've done all this without consulting me?"

"I called you every night on the phone. What did you think I was talking about when I said I needed you, and we would take care of everything to remove you from any possible danger?"

She stared at him. "Ohmigod!" It didn't make any sense. She'd still look the same. Was he also thinking of changing her appearance?

Seth asked, "Didn't Nate talk to you about changing your identity before, well, before he left us?"

"We talked, but I didn't think it would ever happen. I had no intention of letting him change my identity. I told him that!"

The waitress reappeared. "Would you like anything more,

Senator Hawthorne?" She included Cassie in her gaze.

"More coffee for both of us, please." He glanced at Cassie's cup sitting on a coffee-soaked napkin. "And bring her a fresh cup." He dismissed the waitress without a look.

He placed a hand over Cassie's. "I thought all this was decided long ago."

She looked at his firm hand pressing down on hers, its pressure transmitting warmth and energy. "I was so stupid."

"Don't say you're stupid because we both know better. You're grieving, and I've pushed you too fast."

She shook her head. "You're only being kind."

Seth gave her a gentle smile. "I know how to be kind." His thumb massaged her palm. "I'm not all talk and protest. Underneath the senator bit, I'm a Peace Seeker the same as you."

"Not like me. You're far, far more developed as a soul and a teacher than I am."

"Stop putting yourself down."

"It's true. What am I? What have I ever done? I'm a research librarian. I buried myself in a library and hid my psychic talents because I was afraid of them."

"Cassie…"

She interrupted him. "Let me finish. While you and Nate were out perfecting your skills, getting higher educations, developing strong personalities, I was sitting with my books, feeling sorry for myself for being an orphan, an adopted orphan with only an elderly woman for family."

"That's over now."

"It's over, but I am still the person I was then. Maybe I'm less than I was before I knew Nate." She paused to get her feelings under control. "Now he's gone, and I feel less capable than ever."

"I wouldn't ask you to marry me if I agreed with that assessment."

"Seth, you haven't asked me." She removed her hand from his and watched the waitress set down the fresh cup, pour refills for them, and walk away.

His eyebrows rose. "Is that right? I didn't ask you to marry me?"

She shook her head forlornly. "No."

"You're joking with me, right?" His eyes became slits. "You want a proposal of marriage? Down on one knee with a big ring?"

She put a hand over her mouth to stop the smile she could feel starting at the corners of her mouth. "When the time comes, I'll expect it."

He leaned his chair back on two legs and hooked his thumbs under his belt. He raised an eyebrow. "You want a little romance?"

She knew she could drag this on. At this moment, seeing how much he needed her and wanted her with him, she knew she could get what she wanted from him. Her inadequacies left her. She had the upper hand. "Every woman wants romance in her life."

He nodded and his eyes narrowed. "You want me to court you like an old-fashioned suitor?"

"That and more."

"More." He smiled. "You want more." He rubbed his chin. "This demand is becoming more interesting. What else do you want from me?"

"I want to go to law school."

The front legs of the walnut chair hit the carpeted floor with a thud. "Why the hell do you need a law degree?"

"I've figured it out. I need to be your equal, or…" She held up a hand as his protest started. "I'll be as near your equal as I can be. Never your equal, Senator, never, since I don't have your background, your celestial memory, or your position in the federal government. But I will feel more worthy of you. And that should eventually help our marriage, and our other plans, succeed."

She sat with a cat's smile on her face and waited for the storm to begin.

Seth made a tent out of his fingers and watched her. "You want to go to law school."

"I do. And I think you can assist me in it the same as you've created a completely new identity."

He rubbed his chin. Cassie took the gesture as a sign he was thinking seriously. "It might work," he said.

Her mouth went dry, and her heart beat faster.

Seth asked, "Where would you want to go to school?"

She drew a breath. "I've just now thought about this but, if I could get admitted, how about Georgetown University? It's in DC. We can see each other often. Perhaps I could volunteer at your office before the next semester." She waited for him to speak, but he merely continued rubbing his chin. "I'd get an apartment, apply for law school. Get used to the area and to being on my own again. Get my confidence back." She threw all her big guns at him, and he didn't flinch.

"And then?" He looked into her eyes. "After you've finished law school, what then?"

"Then..."

"Then you'll want a little romancing and this big down-on-one-knee proposal with a ring?"

He was squeezing it out of her, and she didn't want to agree, but she had to if he accepted her terms. She nodded. "Yes."

"And a big DC wedding. It might be good for publicity…"

"No!" She swallowed. "Not a big wedding. We'll be married here, as you said, at Peace Lake."

"I don't want to waste the opportunity for PR."

She held up a hand. "We can have a big reception in Washington. You can do as much as you like. I'll agree. But I want our wedding, our vows, done here." Her voice wavered. "We'll be married among our Peace Seekers." Nate's face flashed in her vision. She shook her head to clear it. "I think it would be fitting."

Seth placed his large hand around the back of her neck and drew her closer. He kissed her cheek, her chin, her lips. "Okay, sweet babe." He kissed her again, a little more forcefully. "We'll do things your way, but I'm counting on you. We are all counting on you. Don't let us down."

He might have been using the royal "we," but she remembered Nate's words to her during her time in the Inner Kingdom and felt at peace. They were all counting on her: Nate, Seth, and the rest of the Peace Seekers, wherever they were in the world, or suspended in time.

✣　✣　✣

Cassie sat at the maple desk in her apartment living room and planned for her move. She felt unexpectedly dejected by Seth's absence. Even if she didn't love him, he certainly made things interesting when he was around. And his little boy behavior in that brawny body almost made her laugh aloud. She had started a list for packing and her pen was poised to add another item when her cell phone chimed.

"Hi, Cassie, this is Detective Mike Riley from the Northfield Police Department in Michigan. How are things going?"

She took a deep breath. "Detective Riley, I'm doing fine,

I guess."

"Took you by surprise, I bet." His voice had a smile in it.

Flashes of the night she'd spent in the Michigan hospital appeared before her. "I'm surprised to hear from you. Is something wrong?"

"No, just the opposite. We have two suspects in your fiancé's murder."

Her legs turned to ice. "How did that happen?"

"We've had another murder with the same MO as your case. Fortunately, the men left fingerprints at the scene. We were able to identify one of the men, and he ratted on his friend. They fit your description, and they used a sawed-off shotgun the same as in your case. I'd like you to take a look at them, see if you can make an identification."

She didn't want to do this. "I don't know if I can be of any help."

"Cassie, this is important. You need to come back."

She stared out the sliding glass doors at the Japanese garden. "Do I have to return to Michigan? How about online? Could you send me photos?"

"I could but that's not always satisfactory. I'd like you here tomorrow, if possible."

She sagged in her chair. "How is it that you have a suspect now after six months?"

"We had help from the FBI. The man's fingerprint was on file with the Criminal Justice Identification Services. The federal guys are interested because they're charged with halting violence by foreign nationals in the U.S. This is a courtesy call. You're a witness. We let you leave the state with the understanding you would return if needed."

Her heart sank. She'd have to return to the city where Nate was killed. "I suppose I'd better make arrangements then." Her thoughts whirled. With her move to Washington and so many other things to plan, she barely knew which way to turn.

"I'll come down and get you if you'd like." His voice held new warmth she hadn't heard before.

"You would?"

"I wouldn't object to a day away from the office." He laughed softly. "A day on the highway is better than any day at my desk."

She smiled at his offer. "That's okay. I can get there. As you said, it's nice to get away. And I need to tie up loose ends in Northfield."

"I went over to your condo. I saw the 'For Sale' notice in the lobby."

"Yes, it's on the market. I could see the real estate agent while I'm there." She would tell the woman to accept any offer she got for the condo. Her heart clenched. After all, it was the scene of a murder.

"You'll come then? I need you as soon as possible."

"I'll have to make arrangements." She doodled on her list, thinking. "I'll want to stay a day or two. I'll find a hotel."

"Do you want me to help with arrangements?"

"No, I'm familiar with the area. I'm just thinking out loud."

"And, Cassie…"

"Yes?"

"I appreciate your coming and making it easy for us."

"It's my duty, plus I'm feeling much stronger than I did last fall. Shall I come to your office?"

"You know where the Northfield Police Department is?"

"Sure, right in my old neighborhood."

Cassie had so many plans to finalize. Although she'd been

wrapped in a fog of grief, the details of her old life were slowly being finalized with Ann Marie's help. She knew she couldn't live again in her Northfield condo, the scene of such violence. Her Northfield bank would take care of the real estate closing.

That same bank handled her inheritance from Eudora, but Cassie had kept the large Victorian cottage on Mackinac Island. A property management firm was in charge of its maintenance and rental. Eudora's horse farm and estate in Metamora were leased to neighbors who needed more room for their animals.

And now she had to plan a trip to Michigan.

At a knock on her door, she raised her head from her list. Ann Marie peeked into the room. "Are you busy, Cassie?"

"No, come in. I want to talk to you."

"I need to apologize—"

"Not necessary. Here," she gestured toward the sofa, "sit down. Let's talk." She sat beside her.

"I'm sorry about my reaction when you mentioned joining Seth."

She held up a hand. "Please, Ann Marie, I understand your anger, or at least I think I do. I appreciate what you've done for me."

"It was nothing."

"You healed my wounds and strengthened me by your love so I can leave here with confidence." She leaned over and hugged Ann Marie. "You've been like a mother."

Ann Marie patted Cassie's back. "And you've been like a daughter." She smiled and gave a little laugh. "And we both know families have their problems."

Cassie nodded. "I only had my adoptive parents, but I know what you mean."

Anne Marie rested against the cushions. "I understand you had breakfast with Seth this morning. Did you settle anything with him?"

"Didn't you speak to him before he left?"

"No, I think Seth slipped out quietly on purpose."

"He does consider you a rival of sorts," Cassie said.

"For your affection," Ann Marie finished the thought.

"He doesn't have to feel that way. I love you both in different ways."

"But Seth is too much an egotist to be anything but first with you."

Cassie sighed quietly. "That might be true, but I wanted to ask you about something else."

Ann Marie's eyebrows rose. "What's that?"

"The detective from the Northfield Police called today. He wants me to return and take a look at some men who were possibly involved in Nate's murder." Her throat closed.

"And you're going?"

"I have to go. Detective Riley hinted they could make me come back if they wanted."

"I doubt—"

"But that's not the main reason I'm going. I've decided to join Seth in DC, and I need to take care of things regarding my Northfield condo and my trust arrangements."

Ann Marie stiffened. "I accept your decision to join Seth. I hope you are ready."

"I have to be. I need to say goodbye to my old life."

"I'll make arrangements for you to be driven to Michigan tomorrow."

"I'm planning to go on my own. I'd like to rent a car."

Ann Marie stared at the floor. When she raised her head, she had a smile glued to on her mouth like a Band-Aid. "We can arrange it."

"Good. And I'll stay at least one night at a local hotel."

"One thing," Ann Marie said, "I don't want anyone to trace your movements. I'll give you a credit card to use while you're gone."

If she changed her identity, she would have a new name and a new credit history. But she'd talk with Ann Marie about that later, if it ever came to pass.

Ann Marie stood. "I guess that's all for now."

"There's something else, Ann Marie. Please sit down. I'd like your opinion on a dream I had last night." After Ann Marie sat, Cassie continued, "I dreamed I was in my home, but it wasn't a house I remembered from anywhere. It was lovely with carved oak moldings and banisters, original oil paintings on the walls, and handmade carpets."

"And this was your home?"

"Yes, I definitely lived there because I was talking with my husband when the door chimes rang."

"Your husband? Can you describe him?"

"No, he seemed familiar, but in a nondescript sort of way, sandy hair, but nothing like Seth, slender, rather self-effacing." Cassie waved her hands as if waving the image away. "Anyway, when I answered the door, two painters with ladders walked right past me. They said, 'We've come to paint your house.'"

"With a gasp, I remembered hiring them, but I hadn't told my husband. When I turned to tell him, of course, he was annoyed with me for not consulting him. While we discussed the matter, the painters set up their ladders, took out sprayers and started spraying everything white. And I do mean everything! They sprayed the oak moldings, the paintings, even started on the floor before I screamed for them to stop."

Cassie paused and folded into herself, remembering the fear of the dream, the anxiety that her husband would be angry with her. Everyone would be angry, from the painters whose work was halted to the decorator who had helped select the furnishings.

She held her hand over her mouth as she relived the sinking feeling of regret.

"I know what it is," Ann Marie said. "Don't look so lost. It is a wonderful dream, and one that eases my worry."

Cassie straightened her back. "Really?"

"In dreams, your home represents your soul. Painting your home white is the purification of your soul. The fact that your home was already filled with lovely furnishings means you were well on your way to spiritual healing and growth. Having it painted white indicates additional purification has taken place." Ann Marie smiled broadly. "Welcome to your new home. Now I have confidence you will be all right wherever you are."

Cassie knelt and wrapped her arms around the older woman's shoulders. "Thank you, Ann Marie. I didn't want to leave here without your blessing." She kissed the woman's cheek and then returned to her chair.

"Now, a ton of other things need attention." Cassie indicated the papers on her desk. "If I'm leaving here, I have to know that everything is taken care of while I'm gone." She paused and tension rose inside her. "Am I allowed to come back and visit as Seth does?"

Ann Marie laughed. "What a mixture of strength and vulnerability you are. Of course, you may always return."

Cassie wrung her hands. "I've been upset," she paused, "ever since I told Seth I would move to DC." She drew a breath and waited for Ann Marie's reaction.

"I knew you would go. Seth always has his way."

"This was my decision, not his."

"If it helps you to believe that, then I accept it."

"Please, let's not argue," Cassie said.

Ann Marie held up a hand. "I've said I accept it, and I do. It was your decision, and your dream affirmed it was correct."

Cassie nodded. "But…?"

"But nothing."

"Okay then," Cassie drew another deep breath, determined to stay focused. "He's obtained a new identity for me."

Ann Marie waited.

"I'm not happy about it," Cassie said. "I'll need your help in accepting it. I need to tie up all the loose ends concerning Cassie West. I don't know how to do that."

"Our Columbus bank can arrange everything. We've worked with them before on cases like yours. They will contact your Michigan bank to transfer securities, property, and so forth, into a new trust."

"I don't understand, but if you say it will work, then it's okay with me."

"We'll go to Columbus next week and work out the details," Ann Marie said. "We can stay overnight and shop for new clothes and get our hair styled. It will be fun. Ladies' day out." She smiled.

Cassie relaxed in the feeling of goodwill. It would be all right after all. Ann Marie and the rest of the Peace Seekers would help her.

"When are you leaving for DC?"

"It's not decided yet." She paused. "Ann Marie, I would like some advice."

Ann Marie looked up from the notes she had been taking in her ever-present notebook. "What is that?"

"Even though you now feel confident about my abilities, I think I'd like more training." Unsure what Ann Marie's reaction would be, Cassie blurted out, "I might apply to law school."

She hoped this wouldn't spark another disagreement. "What's your opinion?"

"Superb." Ann Marie laughed. "Whatever made you think of that?"

"It came to me while meditating."

"Meditating? Interesting. You have latent psychic abilities emerging through your imagination and meditation."

They weren't so latent, Cassie thought, but she didn't want to talk about that subject at the moment.

"Does Seth know about law school?" Ann Marie asked.

"I mentioned it to him and he reluctantly agreed, because it will set our wedding back. Seth said he had planned to hold it here."

"He didn't mention it to me."

"He said he planned it with Willie, but now our wedding will be delayed."

"Which means you will be living in Washington, going to law school, but won't be married to Seth. That could cause problems."

"Do you think so?"

Ann Marie nodded. "Oh yes, definitely, there will be problems."

CHAPTER EIGHT

In her rental car, Cassie sped northward along I-75 through Ohio's rich, flat farmland and past smokestacked cities. She followed her GPS all the way through the Detroit area until she reached the Northfield Hilton Hotel, north of the industrial city. After registering, she went directly to her room and called Detective Mike Riley.

She sat on one of the room's queen-sized beds and punched in the detective's cell phone number. While the phone rang, she routinely checked her reflection in the mirror hanging on the opposite wall. Despite the uneventful ride, her returning to the city where she'd lived so long, and where Nate was murdered, upset her. She thought she looked tired, with circles under her eyes. She startled when the detective answered.

"Hi, it's Cassie," she said in response to his greeting. "I'm at the hotel."

"Great, I hope the drive went well, but I have bad news. I need to put off our meeting until tomorrow morning. Is that all right?"

She sighed. "In a way it's a relief. I'm still not sure I'll be of any help. This delay will allow me to search my memory for details I might have forgotten."

"I hate to change things after making it sound so urgent yesterday. Um…how about having dinner with me tonight so you won't have to eat alone?"

His invitation surprised her. "I have other plans." Dinner with the detective was the last thing on her list of fun things to do.

"How about breakfast then? I'd like a chance to talk privately."

She smothered another sigh. She didn't want to sound too reluctant. She was hoping to stay on good terms with Detective Riley. "Breakfast might be okay."

"We can go from there to headquarters."

"I suppose that would work."

"I'll pick you up at the hotel lobby. How about 8:30?"

"Okay, breakfast at 8:30. I'll be waiting outside."

On her own for the first time in months, she took a hot shower and changed into fresh clothes. She would order room service for dinner, or perhaps eat at the hotel restaurant. It was still early afternoon and she wanted to talk to her cousin, Liz, whom she had met for the first time last summer at a forest village in Northern Michigan.

At that time, Liz had helped her over a rough spot when a local sheriff harassed her. That was when she learned Liz was her cousin. How long had it been since she'd talked to her soul sister, the woman who shared her psychic talents and even looked like her? Too long. She hadn't had much contact with Liz during the past winter.

"I'm fine, Liz," Cassie said after she'd made the phone connection and her cousin asked how she was doing. "I'm at a hotel in Northfield just for tonight." Holding her cell phone to her ear, she walked to the window and took in the suburban scene. Gray stone office buildings were the hotel's neighbors, with tree-lined streets stretching out beyond them.

"The detective asked me to come back to identify two men who are suspects in Nate's murder, but I've completely blocked memories of that day. I'm wondering if you can help."

"It's possible you don't want to remember."

"Probably not. I'm frustrated because I've come all this way and have nothing to offer the police."

"You're in Northfield for a reason, Cassie. Nothing happens by chance. Use your talent to return to that day and see the events again."

She shuddered at the thought of reliving Nate's murder. "At Peace Lake, they said my psychic abilities have been blocked for my own health. Probably for my sanity."

"Cuz, I know you as well as anyone. You are a strong woman and you can do this. Don't let your fear keep you from remembering."

"Liz, I've tried going back to the past, but nothing happens."

"I'm sure I can help you. Let's try something. Think back, what were you wearing that day?"

A red cloud blossomed in Cassie's mind. "Oh."

"What's happening now?"

"I'm seeing red."

"Don't panic. You're safe. I've surrounded you with an auric field of white light. What clothes were you wearing?"

"I left Mackinac Island with Nate. I wore casual clothes. Teal blue pants with a white cotton T-shirt, a print blouse over it." Red filled her vision. Her clothes were covered with Nate's blood. She shook her head.

"What about jewelry?"

"With the teal, it would be something simple, casual."

"Can you see it?"

"Give me a minute." She exhaled, drew a deep breath, exhaled again. Red filled her eyes. "Liz, all I see is red!"

"You're safe, Cassie. Where is your jewelry now? Do you have it with you?"

"No, it's in storage with my other things. The bank representative hired someone to clear out my condo and put my things in storage."

"Can you go there?"

"I guess. I don't have the key. I think the bank has it."

"Get the key. Go to the storage place and call me back."

⚓ ⚓ ⚓

An hour later Cassie walked into the storage facility's office and asked the manager to show her the interior storage unit where her possessions were stored.

The silver-haired man walked her down a long corridor and stopped in front of a room-sized unit. "This is it. You put the key in here, turn it. That releases the lock." He slid a solid bar free and swung the door open. "There you are."

She stood, mouth open, looking at the leftovers from her prior life.

"Go ahead, walk in," he said. "Plenty of room inside."

She looked at her desk piled high with boxes. One contained her old laptop, the bank representative had told her. Ann Marie had supplied her with everything new at Peace Lake. A new beginning, she'd said.

The manager continued with his list of virtues for the storage space: "Air-conditioned, clean, well-lit, completely private, insured. You'd need a bomb to break in."

"Thank you," she said frowning at the image he'd placed in her mind. "I appreciate your help."

"The bank paid for thirteen months. No need to move your things now."

She nodded. "Okay." She wanted to be alone.

"Extra month for free, you know, when you pay for a year."

"Thank you. I'll be all right now." She put out a hand and guided him into the hallway. "I'll stop by your office when I leave."

She approached the wardrobe boxes where the clothes she'd worn in what seemed like another life hung on hangers, just as they had been lifted from her condo closet. She opened one and touched the white cotton dress she'd worn on the island the day Eudora had been fatally injured. Her skin hummed with a faint charge.

Here were the suits worn at her library job. They would be useful in DC. She shook her head. No. She needed new clothes for a new life. Her hand touched a natural linen jacket. Felt its coarse texture. No energy charge of any kind there.

Jewelry, Liz had said. Cassie had a piece of furniture with drawers. A jewelry table. She shook her head. She had been so organized, this librarian she barely knew anymore. Everything changed when she met Nate and Seth.

There it was. A walnut cabinet with drawers and long carved legs stood in a corner behind a large carton. How could there be so many cartons? One medium-sized package was marked "jewelry."

She took it in her hands and sat down on a box labeled "books." She used a key to break the tape that sealed the box of jewelry. Inside were dozens of smaller packets. Had Peg, the representative, done this? Probably, with help.

Here were her gold hoop earrings. They felt warm to her fingers.

Another box held a necklace of black beads, a favorite.

She held it in her palm, felt a ping of energy. No. With the teal she'd worn…she closed her eyes. *Go back, Cassie. What were you wearing that day?* Natural stones. Her turquoise.

She looked at her wrist and remembered. At the hospital they'd removed her turquoise bracelet, ring, and earrings and put them in a bag for safekeeping with the clothes she had worn. The police had them.

She took out her cell phone and called Liz. "The police have the jewelry I was wearing, Liz. My turquoise jewelry."

"Are you certain?"

"Yes, they took my jewelry and my clothes for evidence."

"Can you get it back?"

"I can ask Detective Riley."

"Then do it."

"What if he won't give it to me?"

"Then ask to see it. You'll know what to do after that."

She knew. "I'll use the jewelry as a channel, a guide back to the past."

At 8:30 the next morning, Cassie stood in the hotel's circular drive and watched a dark sedan drive up. Detective Riley got out of the car, walked around the front, and held the passenger door open for her.

She gave him a bright smile. She thought it was the least she could do. "Thanks."

He drove carefully, what she expected from a law officer with a witness in the car. "Where are we headed?" she asked.

"How about the Coney Island restaurant in Troy for breakfast?"

She laughed. "I'd love it! They don't have Greek restaurants named Coney Island where I live in Ohio."

"I think it serves the best breakfast in the city," the detective said. "Glad you feel the same."

Cassie walked into the gray brick and glass restaurant as though she were in a dream. "Crooks Road," she said quietly. "I always thought it was an odd name for a street, but no one else ever mentioned it."

The friendly hostess standing by the cash register waved them toward a nearby booth.

"Knowing where the crooks are makes it easier for law enforcement." Mike Riley smiled.

She slid into the orange vinyl booth. "If only it were that easy." She handed the detective a menu that was behind condiments lined up against the wall.

When the waitress came with her order pad and pencil, Cassie asked for coffee and a breakfast of pancakes and sausage. Mike ordered the same, and then sat gazing at her.

"What did you want to talk to me about?" she asked.

He stirred the cream in his coffee. "I was curious to see how you were doing, personally. You went through a rough time. I've thought a lot about you."

Her chin rose slightly. This was not what she expected from this man. She'd expected business. Although, he might be playing *nice cop*. "I'm sorry I can't return the compliment. Not that you were anything but kind, but I've tried to forget that night."

"How are you getting along in that Ohio town? Peace Lake?"

Still slightly on edge, she released her tight hold on her muscles. "Oh, Peace Lake. What can you say about a small town in the middle of nowhere? It is a change of pace, and I'm doing well."

When he continued to stare, she went on, "My wounds

have healed. I've recovered mostly from losing my fiancé. Seth Hawthorne has been a big help."

"Oh, yes, our new senator. I followed the election."

She couldn't resist teasing this serious cop. "Did you vote for him?"

He grinned. "By all means. But then I wouldn't tell you if I hadn't."

"I suppose not." She looked into his eyes. They were honest eyes, a hazel green. She liked the twinkle in them and the creases at the corners. "I don't think you're the type of man who would lie. If you say you voted for Seth, I believe you."

He leaned forward and captured her gaze with his. "I'll always tell you the truth, Cassie."

Tears formed at the corners of her eyes. She stuck her fork in a sausage and cut off a piece with her knife, and then pushed the bit of meat around her plate.

"I didn't mean to upset you."

She swallowed over the lump in her throat. "I'm not upset."

"Good. Can I ask what your plans are for the future?"

She chanced a look at him. Her heart rate had slowed, and she could pretend a calm she didn't feel. "I don't know. Is your interest official?"

As he sipped his coffee, he looked at her over his cup. "I'm sorry. I'm messing this up. I should have said this breakfast is strictly personal. I asked because, ah, you fascinate me." He set down his cup and folded his hands. "And it's not fair to say that to you." His words came out in a rush. "I'm sorry if you're angry. I can be totally professional if you want."

She opened her mouth and then closed it. "I'm sorry, too. I…" She gaped at him. "I'm relieved your interest is personal. And I'm glad to hear I'm fascinating."

"You didn't know I cared about you?"

She met his gaze again and she shivered. "Had no idea." His eyes were mesmerizing. She had difficulty looking away.

"What do you think you'll do next?" he asked.

Should she tell him? Why not? Even if he were lying to her and his interest was entirely as a law enforcement officer, her life would soon be an open book to the public. "I'm moving to Washington DC to work in Seth Hawthorne's office and then attend law school if I'm admitted."

"No kidding! You are better then, aren't you?"

"I'm on my way. I'm much stronger than I was a few months ago."

"And your, uh, relationship with Hawthorne. Is that settled?"

"We've talked about marriage, if that's what you mean. But I haven't committed myself." Actually, she had, but this man didn't need to know everything. "It won't be soon because I'm excited about law school and terrified they won't accept me."

"And these men who murdered Nate Chambray. Are you worried they will come after you next?"

She studied him. There was something about his eyes. The look he gave her was filled with concern, much like Nate's look and the other Peace Seekers at Peace Lake. Her scalp tingled.

"I am worried," she confided. "We all are, Seth as well." She drew a breath and realized she trusted him. "He wants me to change my identity so that I can't be traced."

Tension drained from her. She took another deep breath. "Mike, you're one of us, aren't you?"

He grinned.

She leaned forward and put her hands on the table. "Mike Riley, I'm so glad to meet you."

He placed his hands over hers so that they were joined. "The same to you, Cassie West."

The waitress brought their food, and Cassie sat smiling at Detective Riley while he poured syrup on his pancakes and dug into them with a man's appetite. She picked at her meal, too excited to eat after learning he was a Peace Seeker.

Mike finished eating and accepted a coffee refill for both of them from the waitress. He pushed his plate away. "Are you surprised to learn we're on the same side?"

"It's amazing." She lowered her voice. "What's a Peace Seeker doing as a police officer?"

"Detective."

"Ah yes, detective. How did you choose your profession?"

"I always wanted to help people. To help society. I wasn't smart enough or rich enough for medical school. And I enjoyed working with people, helping out any way I could. It seemed a natural place for me."

"And your family?"

He smiled. "It helped that Dad was a police officer." His attitude changed. He looked at her solemnly. "We need to talk about changing your identity. I don't think you should."

"Why not?"

"You can do a lot of good as Cassie West that you can't do if you're hiding your true identity."

"That's what I thought exactly." Excitement ran through her veins. "I'd always be hiding a secret. I'd feel as if I was lying constantly. And if people found out, it would be terrible for Seth and his career."

"Precisely."

A burden lifted from her shoulders, and then she remembered the jewelry. "Mike, if possible, when I view the suspects, I need to hold my turquoise jewelry."

"You can have it and," he stared into her eyes, "I need something from you."

In a darkened room at police headquarters, Cassie stood with Detective Mike Riley and stared intently through a one-way mirror at the five men standing against the far wall. All were swarthy, as she remembered Nate's killers had been. All were slender men of medium height. Some had distinguishing marks, beards, unruly hair, a tooth missing, or a crooked nose.

"Do you recognize any of them?" Mike asked.

"Not yet." She felt as though she was standing in a tomb. The room even seemed sound-proofed, with no outside noises to give a sense of orientation. There was only the completely dark room and the view of the lineup through a window. She felt she needed to whisper. "That's why I need the jewelry, to see if I can sense any clues while I wear it."

She slipped on the ring and wrapped her fingers around the turquoise bracelet on her wrist, the one Mike had checked out from the evidence room. Her fingertips trembled as she touched the natural stone. She closed her eyes. *Go back. Go back to that night when Nate and I arrived at my condo.* They'd been so happy. A small sound escaped from her throat.

"Cassie, are you all right?"

She nodded without opening her eyes. Nate and she had been in the kitchen, talking about having a glass of wine, when the door to the hallway had opened, and…her ears filled with the sound of a shotgun blast. In her mind, she peered intently at the men who had entered her condo, doing her best to memorize their faces, but it had happened in an instant.

Her eyes flew open and she was back at police headquarters. "It happened so quickly. I'm not sure. My senses tell me that some of these men are evil, but I can't identify any one person for certain. It wouldn't be right to guess."

"No, we don't want you to do that." The detective studied her. "When your eyes were closed, did you return to the murder scene?"

"Yes, how did you know?"

"I felt vibrations coming from you."

Her eyebrow rose. "Are you sensitive, too?"

"No, but I felt you tremble. It was as if a slight charge was going through you." He reached out and ran his hand from her elbow down to her wrist.

Her skin responded eerily and she pulled away from his touch. It was too intimate. But how could that be? He'd barely touched her. She looked into his eyes and a sense of peace fell over her.

Mike's smile went right to her heart. She stared at him.

He clasped her elbow gently. "It's a nice feeling, isn't it?"

Warmed through to her center, she stepped closer, put a hand on his arm. "What if all of life could be this way?"

"Like this moment?" he asked. "In a dark room alone together, knowing what we know about each other?"

Tears dampened her eyes. "What's going on out there?" She gestured toward the world beyond the door. "Why are people killing each other? They're not using violence for survival. They're killing out of hate."

"And we're working to bring peace, Cassie." He touched her cheek. "You and I have a divine appointment. I want you to work with me to find the men who killed Nate Chambray. Even though the case is cold, we need to find these hired killers, discover who their bosses are and bring them to justice, one at a time."

She put her hand in his. "I'll do what I can."

"Even if it puts you in danger?"

She pulled away. "Whatever is necessary, I'll do it."

"What if you had a chance to assist in catching these guys who are messing with your life?"

"I'd like nothing better."

"Not afraid?"

She smiled. "Of course, I'm always afraid. I think I was born afraid. That doesn't mean I lack courage."

"Where did you get this courage?"

"I didn't always have it, but a lot of fear left me when I was shown the Inner Kingdom. Do you know what I mean?"

"I understand."

She folded her arms across her body. "It's hard to explain. I know the life I'm living is real, but it's an outer reality. I'm a spiritual being living in a mortal body. I understand now there is more going on than what we can see. We have a lot of knowledge inside us that we don't access."

A muffled knock on the door drew her attention.

Mike opened the door where another detective stood waiting in the hall. "Did we have any results?" the other detective asked.

"No positive ID," Mike said, "but I think good things will come of this meeting."

He led her out of the room and down a hallway into a dark gray, carpeted office that was divided into lighter gray cubicles. "Here's my domain," he said.

He motioned for her to sit down. He sat at a swivel chair at his desk. "Here's my idea. I think these guys are going to keep after you until they find you." He paused and looked closely at her as if trying to guess her thoughts.

She purposely kept her expression neutral. Reading of the other's thoughts usually happened between people who were in harmony with each other. She felt harmony in Mike's presence, but it was possible to block thoughts if she was aware of the intrusion.

"You can hide from those men," Mike said, "but you can't escape them. They know Hawthorne's record and the work he's doing to foster peace between countries and here at home. And they know he's interested in you. They can't touch Hawthorne, he's too powerful, but they can discourage him by harassing you."

"Why would they do that?"

"Hawthorne campaigned on ending war and violence and setting up an international commission to search and destroy weapons of mass destruction. Nearly everyone who champions peace comes under harassment."

"Are they terrorists?"

"No, they're hired thugs. It's an international group of anarchists. We think we know who the leader is, but there's one problem."

"What's that?"

"This guy lives in Canada, and the Canadian government doesn't take kindly to U.S. operations on their soil. We want to extradite him for questioning, but we can't do that until we have probable cause."

"Won't Canada cooperate?"

"They'll help us, yes, but they want evidence. We can't go in and arrest someone on suspicion. We can't even question him."

"And you think I can help?"

"We don't know for certain, but if you change your identity, it will make apprehending them more difficult."

She brushed her hair back from her forehead. "What you're saying is, if they're after me, that I might be used as bait?"

Mike grinned sheepishly. "You could say that, but I would

rather think you're the vessel through which we can capture them."

"Are you sure I can do this?"

"Are you?"

She shrugged. "I don't know. My self-confidence took a dive when Nate was…" She looked at the floor.

"Are you willing to at least give it a try?"

She took a deep breath and nodded. "What do we do first?"

Mike stood. "Follow me. I'm going to show you the gym and introduce you to the guy who handles self-defense training."

Karate? She rose, but pulled back from him.

"Don't worry. He's going to show you some moves and then he will give you printed instructions. You'll do the real training at a gym in DC after you move there."

She loosened her hold on her muscles. "Okay. What else?"

"I'm going to set up an appointment for you with a special agent at the FBI office in DC. He's the one I've been working with on this case. Their mission is to cooperate with local and state police as partners in threats to the U.S."

The enormity of what she was undertaking started sinking in. "You're serious about this, aren't you? You think this is a national threat?"

"Anytime you threaten a U.S. senator, or one of his team, it's a national concern. I am serious and I hope you are."

"And you think I can handle this?" she asked again, looking for reassurance.

"The question is, do you believe you can?"

She hesitated, thought about her decision.

"Cassie, you can achieve whatever you believe you can. Your mind controls your thoughts and actions." He curled his hand around her shoulder. "Listen, I don't want you to start if you have any doubts."

"Of course, I want to do it. These men have killed people I love." She choked up. "I don't know if you understand, but I can't live with the guilt that I was responsible for Nate's being in my condo that night." She covered her face with her hands.

Mike wrapped an arm around her shoulders. "I didn't know Nate Chambray, but from what I heard about him, he wasn't the kind of guy to be led around by a woman. If he was with you in your condo, it was because he wanted to be."

She lifted her head and straightened her shoulders. "Let's get started."

CHAPTER NINE

The next afternoon after an appointment at the bank, Cassie listened to music from *Mamma Mia! The Musical* while driving south on I-75 through Detroit toward Toledo. This stretch of road was the difficult part of the drive. Trucks would control the highway until she was past Toledo, but then everything would be smooth going. She was glad to say goodbye to the city that had been her home.

Goodbye to the Detroit area, hello to Washington DC. But first she had to tie up loose ends at Peace Lake.

What would Seth say when he heard she wouldn't change her identity? It didn't matter. She finally felt in control of her life. Instead of grieving and whining about the past, she was taking action to help solve Nate's murder.

And no one was telling her what to do. Not Seth, not Ann Marie. No one.

She laughed at the irony in the thought. No one controlled her, except the FBI and the Northfield Police Department. In reality, she was a partner with them. What had Riley called her? A "civilian asset" with instructions to contact the FBI field office as soon as she was settled in DC.

It was all coming together. Fate was bringing good people into her life. She had opened her heart, given up feeling isolated, and the universe responded.

Seth might be unhappy about this turn of events. She had to admit he wanted to control her. It was only natural. He was a newly elected U.S. senator, full of himself.

She slowed to allow a truck in front of her to merge onto the freeway. Imagine Cassie the librarian, and maybe a lawyer, married to a U.S. senator. She needed a new haircut. A new style. New clothes.

Ann Marie had said they would take care of that in Columbus. She'd wait for DC and do it on her own, or with Seth. She smiled. Had she actually promised to marry him?

Nate. Are you there? Is it okay if I marry Seth?

She waited. Listened to another song and waited for his answer that she was certain would bring his approval.

A burst of sunlight fell across the windshield.

The following day dawned bright at Peace Lake. Feeling buoyed by the sunny day and the decisions she had made, Cassie completed arrangements online to take the LSAT after her arrival in DC. And she ordered catalogues from two law schools in the DC area. Later, when she applied, she would e-mail her alma mater, Michigan State University, and request they forward her graduate and undergraduate transcripts to the law schools.

In the afternoon she drove with Ann Marie to Columbus, where she had her long hair cut to shoulder length. It was now a contemporary style, straight and sculptured, but one that she could pull back in a ponytail for working out. They stayed the night in suburban Dublin at a local hotel.

After a casual dinner, they strolled through a shopping

center, where they stopped for frozen yogurt cones. Cassie said, "I don't want to buy my entire wardrobe here, Ann Marie. I'll wait until I reach DC and see what everyone is wearing there."

Ann Marie looked disappointed. "We have the same clothes in Ohio."

Cassie believed otherwise, but didn't want to argue. "Shopping will help fill the time while I'm applying to law school."

"I thought you would be busy working in Seth's office."

Cassie licked the delicious frozen treat. "That's what I thought, but Seth said that could wait until I had my apartment furnished and learned my way around the city."

"When did he say that?"

"Last night when he called my cell."

"I didn't hear you talking."

She had shared a hotel room with Ann Marie. "I didn't want to disturb you. I had the phone on vibrate and I took it into the bathroom."

"Oh." Ann Marie bit into her cone. Her shoulders sagged a little as if she were sad.

Cassie brushed her hair back with one hand. "Anyway, I love my new hair cut."

Ann Marie frowned and ate the last of her cone. "If you're not buying clothes here, we might as well go back to Peace Lake in the morning."

Cassie finished her cone, wiped her hands on the soggy napkin and threw it into the nearby trash barrel. "For the most part, I want to window shop. I'll make some purchases, but I won't buy everything here."

Ann Marie stood, her mouth a firm line. "Then I'll cancel the boutique appointment."

"Don't. It will be fun and maybe I'll find that special

something. You never know."

The next day Cassie shopped in the local mall with Ann Marie. She bought casual outfits that would see her through the first semester of law school—she crossed her fingers, if she were lucky enough to be admitted. The jeans she tried on fit perfectly, so she bought one blue pair and another in black. She found a great pair of low boots made of soft leather that would go with everything. And she bought new walking shoes. Seth had told her that the place he'd rented for her was close to transportation. It was close to everything, he said. She would not need a car.

When she thought of moving to DC, her stomach quivered with tiny needles of excitement. This move was out of character for her. She'd lived her entire life in Michigan and when she traveled, she always went with a tour. Now that she understood her psychic talents, she was more at ease in her own skin. The chronic fear she'd experienced after Nate's death was almost gone.

In the window of an outdoor clothing store, she saw a leather jacket with fringe, just like the one she wore to Mackinac Island when she first met Nate. She'd left it behind with the rest of her clothes when she moved to Ohio.

"Ann Marie! I have to have this jacket."

Ann Marie put her nose in the air. "It's hardly appropriate for DC. I thought you wanted more sophisticated things."

"I do, but…you wouldn't understand. I'm going to buy it." She entered the store with Ann Marie following behind.

Cassie found the jackets in the back of the store. She ran her hands over the soft deerskin. Memories of Nate flooded her mind. She chose a jacket, medium size, and slipped it on. She closed her eyes. *Are you here, Nate? Do you remember my jacket? I was wearing it when we first met.* She swayed.

"Cassie, are you all right?"

She opened her eyes and turned around. "I'm great, Ann Marie." She handed her selection to a salesperson that approached. "I'll take this jacket."

"It's beautiful, isn't it?" the woman asked. "And it will last forever."

Cassie smiled. "Forever should be about right."

That afternoon Cassie drove the SUV back to Peace Village with Ann Marie as her passenger. "I won't be driving much after today," Cassie said. "Seth said I wouldn't need a car in DC."

"You're going to miss having your own car."

"I suppose. Especially for shopping." She thought of all the department store bags in the trunk. And then she remembered the red convertible she had owned in Michigan. The bank had sold it for her. "After a while, maybe I'll buy a convertible."

Ann Marie laughed scornfully. "You wouldn't want a convertible in that city."

"Don't bet on it." She focused her attention on driving. Everything was a battle with Ann Marie. Whether it was jealousy or control issues, Cassie mused, it simply confirmed she was doing the right thing by leaving.

Ann Marie touched Cassie's shoulder. "I don't mean to be negative."

Would Ann Marie read her thoughts? She never had before.

"We'll plan a going-away party for you, Cassie."

The last thing she wanted!

"It will give the friends you've made a chance to say good-bye. Lucille and Rupert will want to be there."

"I see them at dinner all the time. We'll spend a quiet moment together when I can thank them. Besides, I thought no one was supposed to know where I'm going. I haven't told anyone."

"That's right."

"Then why a party? Why don't I just say goodbye to those I know well?"

"We usually have a farewell party when a person leaves. It gives closure."

Cassie shook her head. "I'm not going to lie to everyone. It's bad enough telling the people I know that I'm moving to my aunt's horse farm in Michigan for a while. I hate lies, I won't do it." Her voice shook. "I'm going to call those I've been close to and that's it."

"But people will ask."

"Then you tell them what you want. I won't be a part of this."

Ann Marie leaned over and touched her arm. "Cassie, we don't want you traced from here to DC. Only Seth, Willie and I will know where you are. In this case, deception is necessary."

They were playing the fugitive game. Personally, she thought it was a lot of fuss over nothing. People would see her with Seth in DC and recognize her. She shook her head and wondered what the Peace Seekers would think when they learned, if they ever did, that she was going to be a "civilian asset" of the FBI.

Two days later, Cassie climbed into the SUV with Willie for her trip to DC. He would drive it back to the Peace Seeker's village so it couldn't be traced to her. Her income from Eudora's estate was wire-deposited to a numbered account in the Cayman

Islands, then wired to a trust account at the Peace Seeker's village, then wired to her new bank in DC. She'd also have a new cell phone number.

No matter how much Seth argued with her, Cassie refused to accept a new identity as "Emily Proctor," the name he'd chosen for her. He was such a control freak, he wouldn't let go of his idea of a name change. For his sake, she compromised. Cassandra was now her middle name. He worked with the authorities to set up a different social security account with a new birth date and no work history, and a passport with a new first name—Emily.

Detective Mike Riley approved the name change. He agreed with Cassie that Nate's murderers already knew of her connection to Seth Hawthorne. They knew what she looked like, and she was keeping the same last name. They'd find her if they tried hard enough. But Seth was happy. For now, that was all that counted.

The authorities did as much as they could to erase her personal history, health insurance, e-mail addresses, credit cards, and charge accounts. She was as safe as they could make any person in hiding, except she was hiding in full view of the public as Emily Cassandra West.

CHAPTER TEN

Sweating from his two-mile jog, Grady Hagen stood on the sidewalk across the street from his Georgetown townhouse. He studied the woman who was knocking on his front door. It was her all right. Tall and slender, shiny blond hair, with a real sense of purpose in her posture. She was Emily West from Ohio.

Senator Hawthorne's aide had said to expect her today. The senator's aide hadn't even looked at the place, just asked for the favor. Any self-respecting newspaper reporter did as many favors as possible for a senator. He had to be crazy otherwise.

The sweat dried on his body as he watched the woman peer into an oval window set into the front door. Okay, he'd kept her waiting long enough.

"I think you're looking for me," he called as he crossed the quiet residential street. "I'm Grady Hagen. Senator Hawthorne's office told me you would be here today." He wiped his sweaty hand on his shirt before he extended it.

Her smile showed more relief than pleasure. She shook his hand. "I'm Emily West, as you probably know. My friends call me Cassie."

"Yeah." He continued to study her as he fished the door key from his zipped gym shorts pocket. "I suppose you want to take a look at the apartment."

"Yes, that's the reason I'm here, to see where I'll be living."

"Law student at Georgetown?"

"I'm seeking admittance, but I haven't been accepted yet."

"You will be, knowing Hawthorne and all. You're traveling in big company."

She backed away from him, and he wondered if he reeked of sweat after his two-mile run. Too bad if he did. At least he didn't smell of whiskey anymore. He'd quit drinking three years ago, when he was thirty-one. That was the year of his divorce. He shook the thought off.

He opened the door into a cramped foyer. There was a door off to the right, and straight ahead were stairs that led up into his second-floor apartment. "You'll be on the ground floor." He took a key off a hall table that wobbled, unlocked the door, and pushed it open for her.

Her eyebrows rose, but she went in before him as he held the door open. "Oh," she made a small sound, "this is nice." She walked to the front bay window. "It's charming."

He grunted. "I don't know about charming, but the rent helps pay my mortgage on the place. I'll show you the rest."

He sensed her following close behind as he led the way out of the living room and into the dining room. There was a tiny kitchen on the left, bedroom and bathroom in the back. In the bedroom he said, "You've a nice courtyard back here." He unlocked the French doors and opened them. "Goes with the ground floor apartment."

"It's lovely."

Grady shrugged. "Does it suit you? Do you want the key?"

"Oh, yes, I'll take it."

"Thought you would." The senator had paid six month's rent for the favor Grady was doing him by renting the apartment on a month-to-month basis. It wasn't any of his business why Hawthorne was installing this beauty in Georgetown. All politicians had their secrets.

"When do you plan to move in?"

"Is today all right?" she asked in an uncertain voice.

Behind the woman's smile, he picked up a mixture of sadness and anxiety in her attitude. He shrugged. "Sure. Whenever." He looked at the sparse furnishings. "You'll need to bring some of your things." The room held a worn sofa and lounge chair with a couple of tables and lamps. It must look shabby to a senator's girlfriend.

"My things are in the SUV." She nodded toward the curb where Willie, who had driven her from Ohio, sat in the driver's seat. "I didn't bring much, but I can buy what I need. Do you have an inventory so I'll know what to get?"

"Yeah." He thought the woman looked lost. "I'll help you out. I'll have a cleaning service come in. Don't worry. It will clean up good."

She sighed deeply. "It's not the apartment. I like it fine." She glanced around, looking almost distraught. "It's just… ah…it's different, that's all."

"Yeah, well, I will help you."

"Thanks."

Damn, her eyes were moist. Grady drew a deep breath. "I've got to go now." He saw her eyes widen. "You've got the key, right?" He backed away. "The electricity is on, furnace and A/C work." He was in a rush to leave before she broke down, but he should offer some assistance. "Do you need help carrying in your stuff?"

She shook her head.

"If you do, just call up the stairs. I'm going to shower now." He pulled at his jersey. "Jogging, you know." He smiled what he hoped was a genuine smile, but he wanted to get away from this compelling woman with the sad eyes. "Glad you're here. I'll check back later." Then he left, closing the door quietly behind him as he retreated to his upstairs apartment.

Cassie hesitated before she went outside where Willie waited in the SUV. She'd told Grady things were different here, and they were. Since Nate's death nine months ago, she'd lived communally, taken nearly every meal with other Peace Seekers, was hardly ever alone except to sleep. Now she was in a new city with no friends except for Seth, on her own again as she had been in Michigan. It would be an adjustment. She drew a deep breath and went outside.

"Is everything satisfactory?" Willie asked.

"It's a nice place. I think I'll like it."

"I'll help with your suitcases."

"Thanks. I'd appreciate that. I'll show you around the apartment."

Willie set the suitcases in the living room and looked around. "This place has a lot of possibilities."

"I know. I love the bay window, and there's a garden in the back."

He gave her a hard look. "You going to be all right here?" he asked.

She hugged him. "I am. Thanks, Willie, for stopping at the grocery store. I've everything I need for now. I plan to explore the neighborhood tomorrow. My landlord can give me hints on where to shop for things I need." She smiled. "Are you hungry? Would you like soup and a sandwich before you leave?"

Willie laughed and shook his head. "I know how it is with

you women. You want to get settled, and I need to start back to Ohio."

"Thanks for everything."

"You're not alone, Cassie," Willie said. "Give me a call if you need anything."

⚓ ⚓ ⚓

One day the next week, Seth walked into the apartment as if he owned it. That bothered Cassie. She didn't want to be indebted to him. She had to laugh at her logic. She'd practically promised to marry the man, but didn't want to be obligated. She probably owed him her life. Without Seth, she'd be back in Michigan grieving, stuck away in the library staring at the books and assisting students.

"How do you like it?" Seth asked.

"I love it!"

"It's a sweet apartment. Right?" He grinned.

"Yes, I owe you." She grimaced. Just what she didn't want to say, or feel.

Seth laughed and put an arm around her shoulders, squashing her against his large chest. "I'll expect payment in return."

She wiggled out of his embrace. "I'll never be able to pay you back for your kindness, so don't get too optimistic."

"It's enough payment to know that you're happy again."

"As happy as possible."

The smile left his face. "Naturally, that's all anyone can ask." He walked through the small dining room into the smaller kitchen. "Nice kitchen. Going to fix me something to eat?"

"Sure." Cassie couldn't help smiling at his good-natured teasing. Nothing seemed to bother the big guy. However, she didn't want to relax too much. She remembered his hand across her mouth in the hospital room. Like a flash, she wondered if he'd done it with the purpose of showing her what to expect if she didn't stay in line.

"What do you want for dinner?" she asked, knowing she was safe because he wouldn't be interested in the things she'd bought at the grocery. "I've a frozen pizza, and a bag of peas. How about cereal?"

Seth turned around and put his hands on her shoulders. "I'll have to pass on tonight." He ran his hands down her arms to her elbows and up again. "But I wouldn't mind an appetizer."

Cassie studied his expression and thought she saw a sensuous glint in his eyes. "No appetizers unless you want corn chips and salsa."

With his hands on her shoulders, he drew her to him. "I was thinking of something sweeter."

He was making a pass at her, and she wanted to handle it without offending him. She pressed her face to his shoulder and breathed in his familiar scent. She needed to be strong.

"How about some sugar?" he asked.

At his choice of words, she drew back, but he pulled her against him.

"No sugar tonight, Seth." She put an elbow against his stomach and pushed away. She walked into the dining room. "You have no idea how difficult this move to DC is for me."

He followed and grabbed her hand, stopping her forward motion. "I understand, but this isn't all about you, Cassie. Other people have feelings and needs. The world doesn't revolve around you."

She tried to remove her hand from his grasp, but failed.

"Come here." He pulled her to the worn sofa and sat, pulling her down with him. "Let me tell you about life in the nation's capital. Let me educate you."

At the rough tone in Seth's voice, Cassie's throat tightened.

"This is a city with a lot going on," he said. "Do you understand?"

"Not yet. Remember, I've only been here a short time."

His arm fell away from her shoulder, and he exhaled heavily. "That's right, only a week or so."

Cassie nodded.

"I've been busy," Seth said. "Sorry I haven't been around to help."

"Willie carried my things in. The guy upstairs gave me a hand. I'm getting used to being alone."

He lowered his head and rubbed an eyebrow. "I think we all need to get used to this city."

"Is everything going okay with you?" Cassie asked.

He came alive. "It never ends, the social life, the meetings, and the bull." He reached for her hand and gripped it. "I need you to remind me who I am, of my purpose, our purpose for being here. I need to relax with you and recharge my energy."

"I'm here now."

"And I'm glad. It's too easy to get caught up in my power. Do you understand what it means to be a U.S. senator? Once a person reaches that level, anything is possible. I could be elected vice president, or even president. When my term is over, I could be a cabinet member or ambassador."

He leaned back and rested his head against the cushions. "That's why I need you, Cassie, to keep reminding me that I'm here to serve others in the name of peace. This isn't about me and I know it, but sometimes I forget."

He stood wearily. "Can I have a hug before I go?"

"Yes, of course."

He opened his arms and Cassie leaned against him. Winding her arms around his neck and clinging to him, she buried herself in his strength.

"Let's give ourselves a while, okay?" She pressed her cheek against his shoulder. "I need to get settled, fix up this apartment, and learn my way around the city. I'd be out of my depth if I tried to keep up with you."

"I'm not asking you to go around with me, Cassie. But... men have needs. And powerful men have powerful needs, if you know what I mean. I've wanted you since that time at Walloon Lake when I walked in and saw you in bed with Nate."

She pulled away. "We weren't in bed. We were lying on it."

"Don't fool with me, Cassie. I'm not dumb. I know what you were doing."

"It wasn't what you think."

He laughed. "I know, you were messing around with that stuff called celestial sex, weren't you?"

She felt her face flush. "Don't talk that way. It was beautiful."

"But it didn't stop there, did it?"

She turned away. "I don't know what you mean."

"Nate agreed to marry you because he slept with you."

"You don't know that."

"Believe me, I know. You're not a virgin, and neither am I."

Well, that was true. She waited silently for whatever else was to come.

"Do you realize what's going on out there?" He gestured toward the door. "If you buy a girl a drink, she'll take you home with her for a little fun. No problem. There are a lot of women in this city who would give me anything I wanted if I showed interest. A new U.S. senator...a bachelor. Think about it." He placed his hand beneath her chin and made her look at him.

She pulled away.

He walked toward the door and then turned back. "Think about it, Cassie. You're the one preventing our having a closer relationship."

She stared at him and felt familiar moisture gathering under her lids.

Seth shook his head. "Don't do that. Don't cry. It's okay. What you need to remember is I am the one in control here. I found this apartment. I'm getting you into law school. We have our future together. I'm not the kind of man who needs to force anyone to do anything. There are plenty of willing women. If you won't take care of my needs, someone else will."

"Seth, I'm sorry. I didn't think things through when I said I'd come to DC. I thought you would give me more time." And she'd thought she could follow through with the plans she'd made with Nate and Seth in another lifetime. Now, she has having strong doubts.

As if he realized what he'd done, Seth's expression turned sad and all the energy left his stance. "It's hard for me, too. I know you want time, and courting, if I remember correctly."

He smiled and the whole room brightened. "Remember that night in the golf cart at Peace Lake? I want that feeling back."

"So do I."

"Then what the hell is wrong with a kiss between the two of us?"

CHAPTER ELEVEN

Faint gray light leaked through her bedroom shutters. In the seconds before being fully awake, Cassie vowed to contact the FBI today. Mike Riley had given her the phone number, but she'd put off calling. She told herself she was too busy getting settled, too busy finding her way around the city, and just too busy to think about getting involved in this scheme to trap Nate's killers. The truth was she was scared. Whenever she thought about the FBI, her throat tightened. What she was about to do was completely out of character. She thought perhaps she'd been mesmerized by Detective Mike Riley when she met him over breakfast in Michigan. She had let herself be talked into something she didn't want to do.

She picked up a translucent crystal she kept on her nightstand and palmed it. The gemstone felt warm in her hand. She drew a deep breath in through her nose, held it, and gently blew the breath out through her lips. *For Nate.* She would take this step for Nate.

Do it for yourself, Cassie.

She looked around as if expecting to see him behind her. But the thought inspired her. Yes, she would do it for herself.

She would help put these killers behind bars for a long time.

She picked up the phone and punched in the number before she could change her mind.

"Special Agent Rosetti," a man's voice sounded in her ear.

"Emily West. I'm checking in, for the first time."

"Ah, Ms. West. Detective Riley said you'd be calling. Can you come into the office tomorrow?"

✣ ✣ ✣

Cassie stood outside the Capitol Martial Arts Academy and shivered with excitement. *Nate, how you've changed my life.*

You're in charge now, Cassie, and I'm proud of you.

She entered the building and a man in black pajamas looked up from the desk. "How may I help you?"

Cassie introduced herself. "I've an appointment with Mai Li." Yesterday, Special Agent Rosetti had suggested she take martial arts training. He'd recommended Mai Li.

When the man left to find the instructor, Cassie looked around. It was a small reception area, but beyond she could see a larger open room with wood floors, mirrored walls, and something that looked like ballet bars. Down a hallway were a series of rooms with closed doors. She wondered what went on in those rooms.

A young Asian woman approached, bowed and introduced herself as Mai Li.

Cassie bowed awkwardly. "I'm Emily West. I called yesterday for an appointment."

The woman bowed again. "Come with me, please." She led the way through the main area into a private room that was filled with fitness equipment.

For the next hour, Mai Li ran her through a series of activities that were designed to establish her fitness level.

Cassie was perspiring heavily when they were through. "I'm not in good shape, am I?"

"To the contrary, your scores show that you have been diligent with your physical fitness."

Cassie nodded. "That's true. At the institute where I stayed, I exercised several days a week. I'll admit I'm tired now." She bent over and rested her hands on her knees.

"You should be tired. I've worked you close to your limit."

Cassie straightened and brushed away some sweat that was running down her neck. "Will we be doing this every time?"

Mai Li smiled. "Today was to take a baseline. It will not be so bad in the future. But we want to keep your conditioning at least where it registers now."

She led the way toward the front of the building. "You rest tomorrow. Do the stretches shown on this paper." She held it out. "Then I will see you the day after tomorrow to start your self-defense training. Same time?" She opened an appointment book.

Cassie nodded. "Okay with me."

Outside on the street, she drew a deep breath and decided to walk home to keep her muscles warm until she could get into a hot shower. It was a thirty-minute walk and it was probably easier than taking a bus or finding a cab.

⟡　⟡　⟡

She returned to the martial arts center two days later.

Mai Li led her to one of the small private rooms and handed her white pajamas. "Please remove your outer clothes and put these on. I'll return shortly."

She followed Mai Li's instructions and, striking one pose after another, Cassie stared at her startling reflection in the floor to ceiling mirror.

When Mai Li returned, she said, "We will start with Kung Fu today. I have carefully considered your fitness level, body type, and personality. Although we will acquaint you with all five animals of Kung Fu—the Tiger, Love Bird, Dragon, Snake, and Crane—I believe you might be best off if we concentrate on the defensive movements of the Crane."

Cassie tightened the belt around her pajamas. "The Crane?"

"Yes, the Crane moves silently, spearing fish with its beak. Its nervousness is an illusion." The woman extended her arms and moved them over her head and then down to shoulder height. "The Crane's shield of feathers will distract any attacker. The Crane softly uses mobility and speed."

As Cassie imitated Mai Li's movements, she felt powerful and couldn't hold back a grin.

The instructor smiled. "I see it appeals to you. As the Crane, you will redirect the opponent's force before unleashing your strength. It takes patience, grace, and balance." She patted Cassie's shoulder. "Something magical happens in Kung Fu. The secret is in the breath. Come, we will start your first instruction now."

She followed Mai Li to a private training room with mirrored walls and mats on the floor. "How long will I be training with you?"

Mai Li shrugged. "Until you no longer need me."

Special Agent Rosetti had said that Mai Li was an excellent trainer. Cassie had no idea what else he told the woman. "And how will I know that?"

"When your mission, whatever it is, is finished."

Through her front window, Cassie saw her landlord park his

car and run up the townhouse's steps. She quickly opened the door into the hall and stopped him.

"Can I speak to you?" she asked.

"Sure, is something wrong?"

"Not really, but I do have a question. Maybe you can help me." She opened her door fully and walked into her living room.

He followed her inside. "What is it?"

"I thought I'd like to get some new furniture, maybe a table and chairs. I was wondering—"

"I told Hawthorne's aide that the apartment wasn't completely furnished. I suppose you want me to pay for it."

"No—"

"Why don't you ask the senator about it?" He walked into the dining room and looked around. "It is bare in here."

"I'm wondering if you could recommend a nearby furniture store where I could shop."

His manner softened. "I suppose I could pitch in and help with the cost."

She shook her head. "It's not that. I have plenty of money."

"That makes one of us."

She sighed. "I need advice."

"Advice?" He stretched. "That's all?" For the first time he gave her his full attention. "I'm good at advice, go ahead and ask."

She brushed a strand of hair off her face. "Look..." She paused, staring at him, and then gestured to the sagging sofa. "Why don't you sit down? I'll get us some iced tea."

When Cassie returned with the cold drinks, Grady was lounging on the sofa. He rubbed a hand on the upholstered cushion. "This thing could use some work, too. I didn't realize how bad it was. It's okay for a guy, but you must be used to better."

She sat at the other end of the sofa. "I plan to get a new sofa and a rocking chair, too."

"I could help out, I guess. How much would it come to?"

"Look, Grady, all I need is advice. I've got the money."

"You and my ex-wife." He took a pull at his iced tea.

"Let's agree not to talk about that."

"What? The money or the wife?" His eyes crinkled.

She realized he was putting her on. "Both. No money talk, no wife talk."

"Sounds good to me. What do you want to talk about?"

"A furniture store!" She laughed. "Men! Can't you stay on the subject?"

He smiled. "Can't you take a joke?"

She stared at him and then sheepishly returned his smile. "I guess not."

He sucked down a long drink of tea. "Sure, I know a store. I'll take you there."

"That's not necessary. I'll call a taxi."

"Naw." He stood and placed the glass on the end table. "You've got the money. I've got the car. We're a team. We might not be in the same league, but I wasn't always broke. My ex-wife's father is a U.S. representative. I had—"

"No wife talk." She held up a hand. "We agreed."

He grinned. "This afternoon okay?"

"You name the time. It's all I have," she said, smiling at him.

"And money."

"Hey!" She shook her head and held the door open.

"One o'clock okay?" he asked.

She was ready with her purse over her shoulder when she heard him stomping down the stairs. She pulled the door open as he was about to knock.

He nodded. "I like a woman who's on time."

"First time ever for me." She preceded him down the cement steps.

"The store I'm thinking of has a decorator and everything," he said.

"Grady, why do I think you're putting on an act?"

"What act?"

"I know you're educated and a reporter for one of the biggest newspapers in the city. And you were married to a congressman's daughter."

"No wife talk," he reminded her. He held his car door open for her.

"And," she continued, "you didn't buy this Georgetown house for nothing."

He sat in the driver's seat and shut the door. "You should see my mortgage."

"So, why the act?"

He laughed softly. "It's not an act. I became disgusted with everything I'd ever said or done. Now with the help of a twelve-step program, I'm living a more simple life." He pulled at a piece of fringe on the sleeve of her suede jacket. "You're not Miss Sophisticated yourself to look down at me."

"I'm not looking down at you," she said.

"You are."

She sighed. "Let's forget it."

They stopped at a red traffic light, and their gazes met. Grady smiled. "You mean forget the wife and the money? We'll run out of topics. What can we talk about?"

"Furniture! We're on a furniture hunt."

"I forgot my gun."

The store was in a renovated part of the city and modest in size. Cassie selected a cream-colored microfiber sofa and a white wicker rocking chair with a colorful teal cushion.

After a brief argument, Grady bought a tall lamp with a table base to put beside the rocking chair. "Just to keep you happy," he said.

But Cassie realized he had a kind heart once she got past his defenses.

Then he insisted on her selecting a tall, dark walnut, tavern table and matching chairs for the dining room.

She wavered. "I'm thinking now that I can get along without a table and chairs. I don't know how long I'll be here."

"Why not? Don't you like the place? And you're going to law school. You need a table and chairs," he told her. "You can put your laptop on it and use it as a desk."

"You're right, of course. It's just that I feel this is temporary."

"Why? Where would you go? It's perfect here, and you're connected with Hawthorne. Besides, with a table you can put your elbows on it when you eat. That's what I do," Grady said.

She laughed. "You would. Okay, I'll buy it."

Grady reached for his wallet.

"Don't even think about it. It's my table and I'm buying it." She realized she had taken the first tentative step toward friendship.

CHAPTER TWELVE

Two weeks later, Grady was returning from an afternoon jog when he saw Cassie on her way over to their neighbor's townhouse. He slowed his steps so he wouldn't have to speak. After he had helped her get settled, he'd avoided her as much as possible.

Women like Cassie, single and new on the Washington scene, were best left alone. Sure, he'd keep an eye on her, but he didn't want to get too close. Didn't want to give the wrong impression. The job at the newspaper was going well, and the mystery novel was taking shape. If he added those achievements to finally having a decent relationship with his ex-wife, life was picking up. Of course, since Cassie was here, he'd do what was necessary to make certain nothing bad happened to her.

She was a threat to his upward progress. It had been a long fall from being a top reporter and husband of "the congressman's" daughter. The climb back had taken longer than he expected, but once again his life and drinking were under control. And the Big Boss in the sky was pleased. He might even get his halo back.

After their trip to purchase furniture, Cassie had come and gone daily from the apartment. When the sound of music or hair dryer intruded on his space, Grady tried not to think of the long blond hair spilling over her shoulders or how good her slender legs would look moving gracefully on a dance floor. Those thoughts could get even an angel into trouble.

Several days after they shopped for furniture, she brought him a serving of lasagna. He refused the meal, but did so with a smile. She caught on and didn't bother again. Once a man started eating a woman's cooking, no telling where things would end up. More than once he'd been criticized for lack of self-control.

Grady waited until Cassie entered their elderly neighbor's home then quickened the pace toward their own gray brick townhouse with the crooked black shutters that needed repainting. One of these days, he would fix them and put on a fresh coat of paint. The house was one of those remaining that were still divided into individual apartments. All of the other houses on this street had been renovated and sold for big bucks.

He had bought the house as an investment with his father-in-law's help, never thinking he would end up living in it. Now it was all he had left of his marriage.

❖ ❖ ❖

Inside her townhouse, Mrs. Williams greeted Cassie and urged her to sit on a carved chair upholstered in faded olive velvet. She hesitated only because she recognized it as a Louis XIV chair. They chatted for a while, and then Mrs. Williams asked if she would like a piece of homemade cake.

Cassie smiled. "I'd love it."

"Thought you might," the woman said. "I used to be a good

baker, but I don't have many excuses to make a cake now."

Mrs. Williams disappeared into the kitchen and reappeared carrying a tray with two plates of cake, forks, and two cups of tea. Several magazines cluttered the coffee table, and Cassie hastily pushed them aside to make space for the tray.

The first bite of cake revealed its moist texture and rich chocolate flavor. "This cake is the best I've tasted in years," Cassie said.

The elderly woman's eyes shone with the compliment. "I cut the recipe from the newspaper nearly thirty years ago. Later I heard a fancy restaurant down in New Orleans sued the paper for publishing it." Her laugh ended with a hacking cough.

Cassie looked affectionately at her first Washington friend. She couldn't count Grady Hagen. He'd turned down her lasagna with such distaste that she'd stayed clear of him ever since.

"I'm glad you asked me over," Cassie said.

"It's the least I can do for a neighbor. I was happy when I saw you come home early, and I had this cake baked. I confess I baked it because I've got an investment fellow coming over later to talk about my account."

Cassie raised her eyebrows. "Not many brokers make house calls."

"This one does. And he should with the size of my investments. Besides, with my swollen legs, I can't get around much." She stretched out her legs and displayed the orthopedic shoes on her feet.

"If I had a car, I could drive you to your broker's office."

Mrs. Williams looked pensive, and then brightened. "If you need money, I can loan you enough for a car."

Cassie shook her head. "It's not money, I'm all right that way. I just don't want to be bothered with a car. But thank you for the offer."

The doorbell rang. "Now who is that?" Mrs. Williams muttered as she limped to the front door.

While her neighbor answered the door, Cassie looked around the room and admired the Victorian furniture.

"I told you before," Mrs. Williams's voice carried from the front hall. "I'm not paying you for last week because you didn't sweep out the basement like I asked."

Surprised by her neighbor's angry tone, Cassie listened for the reply, but couldn't make out the words.

"I don't care if you need the money. Finish the job and you'll get paid."

The door slammed, making a loud noise. Cassie's heart pounded and the room started rocking. A sea of red swam before her eyes. She gasped and shut her eyes tightly. When she opened them, the red was gone. The world had settled down from the flashback.

Mrs. Williams shuffled back to her chair. "I don't know about that kid, Ramon, who helps around the house. He seems nice enough, but once in a while I have to get tough."

"Anyway, where was I?" she continued. She looked at Cassie. "Oh, that fellow down at the brokerage. He's coming over, and later my son's stopping in. He wants to manage my money, says I should fire the broker if he can't explain the shortage in my account."

Although she'd shaken off the sickening flashback of Nate's death, Cassie wanted to leave. She put the plate with the unfinished cake on the coffee table. "I need to be going." She trembled when she stood.

"Is something wrong, dear?"

"No, it's just...I'll tell you about it some day. A memory. Don't worry, I'm all right. Everything will be all right." She drew a deep breath. "Thanks for the cake. I made a casserole for dinner. Later, I'll bring some over for you."

"Thanks, dear. I'll leave the door unlocked."

On her own porch, Cassie took three envelopes from the metal mailbox. *Occupant, Occupant, Occupant.* Oddly the bulk mail eased her sense of loneliness. She unlocked the outside door that led into the hallway.

Before she could unlock the inside door, she heard her landlord's door open and Grady's feet thundering down the stairs.

He drew up short and held up a black bag. "Hi. I'm putting out my trash."

Her gaze slid to his wide shoulders and the crisp cotton shirt pulled tautly across them. She backed away, trying to keep some distance between them in the hallway that suddenly seemed too small.

"Sorry if I startled you. Uh…how have you been?" His unsmiling face and emotionless dark brown eyes made the question seem insincere.

"I'm fine." She wondered if he regretted helping her. They hadn't actually spoken since that day at the furniture store. She fumbled with her keys and then dropped them in the process of unlocking the apartment door.

He picked them up. "Need any help?"

She shook her head and accepted the keys. "It's just that I can't talk and use my hands at the same time."

The hard creases of his face softened and his eyes brightened. "Happens to me all the time."

The key slid home at last, and she opened the door. She couldn't help notice Grady's quick inspection of the newly furnished living room. "Do you want to take a look at the furniture?" she asked.

He shook his head. "Not now. I'll see it later."

She stifled a rush of irritability. He hadn't shown any interest in the furniture since its delivery. She waited until he left before slamming her apartment door as hard as she could. The tension she'd felt since she'd moved to the nation's capital seemed sharper after the flashback she'd had earlier.

She told herself that Grady's attitude was natural, nothing to be upset about. He had looked into her apartment without wanting to come in. She often spied on him when he returned from an afternoon run. She had in fact, ogled his red running shorts that clung to his firm backside. That didn't mean she wanted to be involved with him.

She kicked off her shoes then tossed her deerskin jacket on her new sofa. Everything in the room was fresh. A cream-colored sleeping sofa—maybe her cousin Liz would visit—the white wicker rocking chair, a new beige area rug and tables and lamps.

She spent an hour reading the evening paper, acquainting herself with her adopted city. When she finished reading, she opened a diet cola, washed some dishes in the sink and then discovered it was five thirty and she hadn't taken the casserole over to Mrs. Williams.

She heated the pasta and sauce, went next door and waited on the cement stoop for her neighbor to answer the bell. Cassie juggled the hot dish and resisted the urge to pick at a bit of peeling paint on the doorframe.

Mrs. Williams didn't answer the first ring, or the second. Cassie put an ear against the door and heard the bell ringing inside the house. Worried, she rapped on the door over and over.

Her neighbor knew she was bringing dinner. What could be wrong? She closed her eyes and saw a sea of red. No! It couldn't be true. *Get a hold on your wild imagination.* She took a deep breath, held it and slowly exhaled. New air in, old air out. She resolutely tried the knob. This fear would not defeat her.

As Mrs. Williams had said, she'd left the door unlocked.

Did she dare enter? She pushed the door open. "Mrs. Williams?" She hoped her neighbor had gone out, but knew that was improbable. Her broker was coming over. Or maybe he'd left already.

In the shadowy hall, she left the front door ajar and scanned the parlor. Nothing seemed different. She could find no reason for her increasing sense of danger.

She shook off the anxiety and started through the dining room toward the kitchen.

Hissss!

She gasped and nearly flung the dish toward the ceiling. Mrs. Williams's tiger cat that had been hiding earlier was perched on top of a tall Sheraton breakfront. Cassie backed away from the spooked animal.

Adrenaline pumped through her veins. She rushed through the swinging door into the kitchen where she stopped short.

Blood spattered the kitchen floor, the white enameled walls, and even the ruffled curtains at the windows. A red sea spun before her.

She closed her eyes and fought down nausea. When she could manage, she looked around and saw the courtyard door standing open. A smashed phone, ripped from the wall, lay on the cluttered counter. Two chairs were overturned. Shards from a broken blue and white teapot littered the floor. And underneath the kitchen table sprawled Mrs. Williams's twisted form, legs turned awkwardly, dress stained with blood.

Cassie stared at the crumpled form and remembered how Nate had looked in her condo the night he was murdered. She struggled with the impulse to flee. The thought there might be a spark of life in the woman kept her in the kitchen. She set the casserole on the stove and forced herself to kneel beside her friend.

Grimacing against the blood, and with shaking fingers, she searched for a pulse in the wrist, then in the neck. Finding none, she placed a finger under the woman's nose and then, impatient with her reluctance, she pressed her ear directly on Mrs. Williams's bloody chest.

Finally accepting the woman's death, Cassie stood in a daze, looked around the room and saw her casserole dish. As if in a dream, she picked it up from the stove and fled the house.

Chapter Thirteen

She needed a phone, any phone, her cell phone. Where was it? Why was this dish in her hands? Weakness kept her from thinking straight. She stood on the outside steps and couldn't find her key. She pounded on the door, rang Grady's doorbell incessantly.

Grady flung the door open. "What is it?"

She started to move past him. "I need to call for help."

He caught her by the shoulders. "What's happened?"

"Mrs. Williams." She pointed north to their neighbor's house. "She's been murdered." Cassie put a fist to her mouth and bit down on a knuckle.

"My God, your hands and face are bloody. Are you hurt?"

She shook her head. "No, but we need to call the police."

"Come on up. We'll use my cell."

In his apartment, he took the casserole from her and set it on his desk in the dining room and then helped her onto the desk chair. "Who's dead?" he asked. "Is it Mrs. Williams next door, the lady who sweeps her porch every afternoon?"

She nodded bleakly and studied her bloodied hands.

He called 911 and gave dispatch the information. Then he

hung up and turned back to Cassie. "Are you all right?"

"Yes."

"Can you stay here alone if I go next door and take a look?"

She nodded.

"Where is she?" he asked quietly.

"In the kitchen."

"Okay, you wait here." He moved away, grabbed his camera and a tape recorder from a table next to the door, threw her one last glance, and then left.

She heard him run down the steps, heard the outside door shut. She closed her mind to the gore their neighbor's kitchen held.

Slumped on the desk chair in front of his desk, she sat unmoving and waited. Only the computer's screen saver kept her company. Now that the original shock was passing, she trembled uncontrollably. That wouldn't do. She needed a sense of icy detachment for what was to come.

Seth. She had to call Seth, but she was in Grady's apartment without her phone. She wasn't sure she could make it down the stairs on shaking legs.

Time seemed to stop. She didn't know how long it was that she sat frozen at Grady's desk until she heard his footsteps pounding up the stairs.

He entered the room in a rush. "You're right. She's dead. What a mess." He stopped in front of Cassie. "My God, you're pale."

"I'm okay."

In the distance a siren wailed. "Come over here." He motioned to the dark leather sofa in the living room, where she sank into its deep cushions.

He sat beside her and held her hand. "As a crime reporter I've been through this before. You'll feel better as soon as the shock passes."

The sirens grew louder, and then stopped outside the townhouse.

He stood. "I'm going to meet the police." He looked as if wondering what to do with her. "You can stay here if you like." He shifted his weight from one foot to the other. His eagerness to leave was clear.

"Go ahead." She stood. "I'll wait in my apartment." She grabbed her casserole and stumbled ahead of him into the hall. As she reached the top of the stairs, her eyesight blurred. She was weaker than she'd thought.

Grady helped her down the stairs, and she managed a shaky smile.

When Grady ran outside, Cassie noticed the sun was setting. Police cars, their blue and red lights flashing, were parked at crazy angles to the curb. Gawkers were gathering in the violet twilight.

She shut herself in her apartment and set the casserole on the kitchen counter. If she hurried she could shower and clean the blood off before the police wanted her. She couldn't believe this was happening again. What was the significance of her being involved in two murders? Three, if she counted her mother, Eudora, last summer.

In the bathroom she started the water for a shower and then one by one stripped off her clothes and dropped them into a heap on the tiled floor. Mrs. Williams's crumpled form appeared in her mind. She shuddered. She was one house away. Perhaps the killer had gone to her neighbor's house by mistake instead of Cassie's.

After the shower she dressed quickly in jeans and a cotton shirt, and then ran a brush through her hair. Gingerly, she picked up her soiled clothes and carried them to the kitchen.

She stuffed them into a grocery bag and then put them at the back of her bedroom closet. They would be available if the police asked to see them. Guilt was growing inside of her. Mrs. Williams had left the front door unlocked because of her.

She saw the casserole on the kitchen counter, dumped it into the sink and ran the garbage disposal. Never again would she eat spaghetti casserole.

In the living room, she sank into the wicker rocking chair and huddled in the darkness. Red and blue police lights danced through the windows and across the walls. She had to call the FBI.

When Cassie had met him in his office, Special Agent Rosetti had given her a specially programmed cell phone. If she pressed 911, the call went to the local police. Simultaneously, a message would be relayed to Rosetti. He'd said it was an example of the new federal/local law enforcement cooperation to fight terrorism and violence after 9/11.

Since Grady had already called 911, she called Rosetti directly.

"There's been a murder next door," she blurted out after he answered.

"Slow down, Cassie. Who's been murdered?"

"The woman next door, my friend." She had difficulty keeping her voice steady.

"Did you call 911?"

"My landlord called them."

"Are the police there?"

"Their cars are everywhere."

"Okay. Let me think."

She waited.

"If the police are there," Rosetti said, "then they'll handle the investigation. I'd rather not interfere unless they request our assistance."

She felt let down. "Okay. I just thought I'd alert you."

"I'm glad you did. You could be involved, or it could be a random crime. One thing for certain, I'll want to see you again and go over what's happened. For now, I'm going to let the investigation play out with the Washington police."

"All right." She hadn't known what to expect, but she'd thought Rosetti would be more supportive.

"Are you okay?" he asked. "Do you have friends you can call?"

"Yes, I'm okay. Don't worry about me." She had to contact Seth.

"I'll want to see you within the next day or so," Rosetti said. "I'll call you. Meanwhile, remember, I've got your back."

After hanging up, she went into the kitchen and found her purse and personal cell phone. When she opened the file of numbers, the one for her Michigan cousin, Liz, leapt out at her. She pushed *Send.*

"Liz," Cassie said, when her call was answered. "I'm in trouble."

"Wait. Before you say more, find a quiet place to sit down." The calm voice soothed her.

"I can't go into the living room. There are too many police lights in there."

"Where can you find a quiet spot?"

"My bedroom."

"I'll wait until you're there."

In the bedroom, Cassie shut the door and climbed onto her bed. "I'm on my bed now."

"What's happened?"

She briefly told the story of Mrs. Williams's death. "I think I'm responsible."

"Because she left her door unlocked?"

"No, because they're following me. They wanted me, not Mrs. Williams."

"You don't know that."

"I feel it. I sense it."

"Everything we sense isn't correct. I think you're scared now and not sure of anything. Are you alone? Someone should be with you."

"I could call Seth, but then he would get involved and the papers would place him with me, and it would get all mixed up. My landlord, Grady Hagen, helped me. He's outside with the police now."

"Then Grady will be back. He won't forget about you. Follow your intuition about calling Seth. If you think it's the wrong thing to do, leave it until later. He may be more helpful afterward. For now, stay quiet in your bedroom. Lean back against a pillow and imagine wrapping a golden robe of protection around you."

Cassie relaxed against a rose-colored pillow and imagined a glowing golden robe lying on the bed. She visualized putting one arm in it and then the other. Her muscles gave up their tight hold. When she pulled the imaginary robe up around her neck, its warmth calmed her.

"I'm wearing the robe now," she told Liz.

"You're safe. There is nothing else you need do until Grady or someone else asks for you."

"Liz, I need to know. Do you think I caused this tragedy? Did I draw this to me?"

"No, Cassie. You can't draw evil to yourself. There isn't an evil cell in your body. Sometimes things just happen and there isn't any way we can control them. We can only control our reaction to the events. You can do that by staying calm and centered in your golden robe."

The doorbell rang. "I have to go now. Someone is here. Thank you, my wise cousin, for your help."

"Stay in touch and take your golden robe with you tonight wherever you go."

A tall uniformed police officer stood at her door next to Grady. "Are you okay?" Grady asked.

"Are you Emily West?" the officer said before Cassie could answer Grady's question.

"Yes," and then, looking at Grady, "yes, I'm okay."

"I need to ask you some questions," the officer said. "Can I come inside?"

"Sure." She opened the door wide. Grady and the officer entered.

She indicated they should sit on the sofa, and then she sat on the rocking chair at the bay window. "How can I help?"

"I'm just getting some preliminary information. The detectives will question you later. What is your full name?"

"Emily Cassandra West."

The officer made a note. "How long have you lived at this address?"

"About three weeks."

He looked more interested in that answer. "Where did you live before this?"

She gave the Peace Lake address.

"How long at that address?" he asked.

"Um." She tried to remember her new history. "About six years." She looked at Grady and was suddenly frightened that the police would ask about Nate's death.

"You're doing fine," Grady said gently.

She nodded and blinked away tears. "It's not fair. She was a nice lady."

The officer glanced up from his notebook. "We'll be finished soon. What's your occupation?"

"I'm a research librarian, but I'm not employed at the present. I'm hoping to enroll in law school."

"Okay. Phone number?"

She gave both landline and personal cell phone numbers to him.

"Anything else?" Grady asked the officer. "It's been a tough night for us."

"Almost done." He focused on Cassie. "I need to know if you saw or heard anything unusual earlier this evening." He waited with a patient expression on his face.

She shook her head. "No, nothing."

"Any suspicious sounds?"

"No, I had music playing."

The officer snapped the notebook shut. "Detectives will talk to both of you when they're through next door. It's my duty to ask you not to leave the city without notifying the police department."

"When will they get around to us?" she asked.

He glanced at his watch. "They have a lot to do next door. If it gets too late, it might be tomorrow morning. The suits like to work nine to five like normal people." He chuckled as if enjoying a private joke.

She followed the police officer to the door and waited while he left. Grady paused before following him out. "I'm going to hang around the scene for a while and see if I can learn anything more. The TV guys are here. I'll probably submit a story for tomorrow's paper." He hesitated. "Do you think you'll call the senator about this?"

Cassie pressed her hands against her cheeks. "I thought I'd wait until the news people leave." She peered at Grady, remembering he was a reporter. "You won't write about his connection to me, will you?"

He looked down at his shoes. "I won't if you ask me not to."

"I'm asking you not to."

He nodded. "I won't write it unless the other reporters pick it up. I'll tell you first if I do."

Her lips trembled. The horror of the murder scene rose fresh in her eyes. She felt her center weaken. "Grady...I don't know what...without you..." She pressed her lids tightly against her eyes, and then straightened. "You've been so kind." She sobbed quietly, a cry from her soul.

He put a warm, steadying hand on her shoulder. "You'll be okay, Cassie. I've had problems of my own, and I know the publicity is no fun. Your private life is safe with me, for now."

He started out then turned back. "Come and get me when the detectives show up. I want to be with you while they're here."

Chapter Fourteen

The doorbell jolted Cassie from a restless sleep. She stirred, half-asleep, but aware of lying in a painful position. When the doorbell rang again, she opened her eyes and realized she had slept on the sofa.

Moaning softly, she stumbled to the door. "Who is it?"

"Police, homicide." The man's rough voice sounded bored, as though he had shouted that phrase a thousand times.

Mrs. Williams. The memory of her neighbor's death hit like a fist in the stomach. "Just a minute." She put a hand against the solid door and waited for the nausea to subside.

"Ms. West?" the rough voice called again.

She arranged her face into what, hopefully, was a mask of composure before pulling the door open.

The man in the hallway was bulky, too big for the jacket that pulled in tight folds across his shoulders and around his biceps.

"Are you Ms. West?"

She nodded.

"I'm Detective Sergeant Ed Souchuk, DC Police. I have some questions about last night." He flashed identification. A shield glinted from a leather wallet. "May I come in?"

"Of course." She stepped aside to let him pass.

Light brown hair framed a wide face dominated by a nose that looked as if it had been broken more than once. His eyes, lively under heavy brows, scanned the room. "You live here alone?"

She nodded.

"Mind if I take a look around?"

Surprised, she said, "Okay, but give me a minute, I just woke up." She motioned toward the sofa. "Please sit down."

When she returned from the bathroom, she found the detective hadn't waited. He was searching through the kitchen cabinets. He shut one and then opened the refrigerator.

She clenched her fists. His size alone was intimidating. At five foot six, she wasn't a small woman, but he was huge. And it wasn't just his height. He was a wide man with Slavic features. Perhaps he was only excessively nosy. She took a deep breath. "Why are you searching my kitchen?"

"I'm not searching it." His cold smile reminded her that this was not a social call. "Just routine. I'm taking a look around. You gave me permission."

She didn't know much about these things, but thought police needed a search warrant to go through cabinets. Intuition warned not to make an enemy of this man. "I'm going to brew some coffee. Would you like a cup?"

"Yeah, sure, that would be fine." He headed into the living room.

As she performed the automatic task, she glanced around the kitchen with a stranger's eyes. Its pristine condition was surprising. Usually a dirty dish or two stood in the sink.

Then it all came back—the moments of pure terror after finding the body. She had emptied the spaghetti down the garbage disposal in a fury of cleaning while she tried to exorcise the memory of her neighbor's crumpled form.

Sickened, she closed her eyes. When the nausea had passed, she started the coffee maker.

Returning to the living room, she found the detective sitting in her wicker rocker, squashing its blue and white striped cushion. "I like rocking chairs," he said, testing its motion. The rocker creaked.

She sat on the couch and folded her hands. Her dislike for the man grew. "The coffee will be ready in a minute." She spoke to fill the silence. "Let's get started while it's brewing. What did you want to ask?"

He drew a notebook from a pocket. "The officer gave me his report." He read aloud the statistics of her physical description, her address, and all the recorded information.

He looked at his notes. "The officer also mentioned someone named Grady Hagen."

"He lives upstairs." She took a deep breath and willed her muscles to relax.

"You're new to the area, Ms. West."

"Right."

"You discovered the body?"

The image of the bloody kitchen hit her hard. *Mrs. Williams.* Her heart fluttered. As she opened her mouth to answer, the doorbell rang.

A dark-skinned woman wearing a tight-fitting electric blue suit and stylish black leather shoes stood in the hall. She extended her hand to Cassie who nearly shook it before noticing the shield in the woman's hand.

"I'm Detective Petter." The woman's expression held a hint of a smile. "I recognized my partner's car. I assume he's here."

"Hell, yes, I'm here." Souchuk's voice bellowed. "I don't

drive my kid to private school every morning."

"You might be eating your words soon." Petter's voice had a bantering tone.

Cassie smiled politely. "Please sit down." The woman detective sat at one end of the sofa. Cassie sat at the other.

"I'm sorry I'm late," Detective Petter said. "I told Ed I would meet him here." She smiled graciously and smoothed stray hairs into her neat bun. She removed a notebook from a handbag large enough to hold a gun. "Have I missed much?"

"You know as much as I do, Petter." Souchuk cleared his throat loudly. "I looked the place over before you came. Miss West is a good housekeeper, if you know what I mean."

Cassie was surprised Souchuk revealed his search to his partner. Perhaps looking in cabinets was standard procedure. She thought it wasn't. She leaned back and watched the detectives.

Petter took a tape recorder from her leather purse. "Miss West, may I call you Emily?"

The name was still strange to Cassie. "Certainly."

"Emily, I understand you discovered the victim next door." She consulted her notes. "Mrs. Williams."

Cassie nodded.

"Can you tell us in your own words exactly what led you to the Williams home last evening?" She pressed a button on the recorder and set it on the table next to Cassie. "Do I have your permission to tape?"

She worried she might be doing the wrong thing by talking to the detectives alone. Grady wanted to be notified when they were here—for a story, she reminded herself.

"I don't like tape recorders," she said.

"Neither do I," Petter agreed. "They make me self-conscious, but the need for accuracy is more important. You want to be quoted correctly, don't you?"

This woman's warm brown eyes had a trustworthy look, setting Cassie at ease. "I guess it's okay."

When the doorbell rang, she leapt to answer it.

Grady, his hair damp, his white shirt unbuttoned at the collar and stuffed into twill pants, stood at the door.

"Come in, come in," Cassie welcomed him.

Souchuk stood and quickly blocked Grady's way into the room. "Who're you?"

Grady's gaze narrowed. "I'm Hagen from *The Inquirer.* I live upstairs."

Souchuk eyed the reporter. "Yeah, I've seen you around. We're conducting an investigation into the Williams death." He held his hand one inch from Grady's chest. "When we're finished, we'll get to you. Keep yourself available, elsewhere."

Grady's expression hardened. "I'd like to stay when you question her." He started around Souchuk, but the detective's broad hand halted him.

"There's no need for that. She's doing fine." Souchuk smiled at Cassie.

She shuddered.

Petter joined them at the door. "Mr. Hagen, I'm Detective Petter, Homicide." She offered her hand. "And this is my partner, Detective Souchuk."

Grady stepped around Souchuk and shook the woman's hand. "I don't think we've met."

"I'm fairly new," she said.

Souchuk growled under his breath. "They stick me with all the rookies, and the women."

Petter's mouth tightened before spreading into a polite smile. "I'm a new detective, but I know my job."

"I'm sure you do," Grady said.

"She should," Souchuk said. "I've taught her everything she knows."

Smiling, the female detective shook her head and continued, "Mr. Hagen, in crimes of this nature, we find it's best if we interview witnesses separately so their observations aren't contaminated by hearing each other's story."

"That won't work in this situation," Grady said. "We spent half the night talking about what happened."

Petter grimaced. "In that case and since neither of you are suspects, I see no objection to your being present. I guess we can waive that requirement." She looked at her partner, her eyes wide and questioning.

Souchuk sighed audibly and, with an expression that said he would win the next one, plopped down in the rocker.

Grady gave Cassie an encouraging smile, raising her spirits. He seemed bright and full of energy this morning, although probably hadn't slept any more than she had. She made room for him on the end of the sofa and was calmed by the feel of his shoulder against hers.

Her stomach growled, a reminder of what she'd started earlier.

"I think the coffee is ready." She stood. "Would anyone like a cup?"

Thirty minutes later they were still at it. Cassie had told the story over and over. She mentioned Mrs. Williams's argument with the yard boy and the appointment with the broker, and that her son was coming over. She told how the front door was unlocked and where she discovered the body.

She cried and then controlled herself and finished the story. Now Souchuk was going over the story once again. She squared her shoulders and faced his cold stare.

"It seems unusual that you would stop to pick up your

casserole dish before going for help."

She met his gaze as calmly as possible. "Everyone reacts differently under stress."

"Yet, I looked in your kitchen this morning and found no evidence of this…" he consulted his notes, "spaghetti dinner."

"I put the food down the garbage disposal. I wasn't thinking."

"When exactly was this?"

"What do you mean by exactly?"

"I mean what hour was it?"

She shook her head. She hadn't consulted a clock or watch after finding the body. She couldn't recall ever losing her memory like this. "I didn't wear a watch."

"If you didn't wear a watch, why were you worried when your friend didn't answer her door?"

"I don't know. I don't understand the question."

Grady shifted uneasily. "You're out of line, Souchuk. I think you've learned all you can."

"I'll be the judge of that."

"No more intimidation." Grady glared at him.

"Ed," Detective Petter said.

At the edge of her vision, Cassie saw Souchuk point a restraining finger at the female detective.

Grady cleared his throat. "Are we suspects?"

His question steadied Cassie. She followed the course Grady had started. "Am I under investigation?"

"Not at present."

"Emily," Petter interrupted, "at this stage we question everything and everyone." She smiled. "Only when we've gathered all the facts can we determine what actually happened."

"I see." With sudden insight, she realized the detectives might suspect she was involved in the murder. "You can't believe I killed my neighbor!"

Detective Petter shook her head. "Not at all. It's just that there are holes in what you've told us. We're only trying to fill those gaps." Petter paused. "May we see the clothes you wore last night?"

"Clothes?" What had she done with her clothes? "I suppose so." Her mind was a blank. "I was upset after discovering…" She felt Grady stir, felt his encouraging hand on her knee.

Then as quickly as it vanished, her memory returned. "My clothes are in a grocery bag in the bedroom closet. You can get them if you want."

Detective Petter disappeared down the hall.

Souchuk leaned forward. "Why did you change clothes last night?"

Her stomach churned. The terror of that moment returned. "They were bloody. I couldn't stand them."

"After you found the victim, you returned to your apartment, disposed of the food, changed your clothes, and then reported the crime to the authorities?"

She raised her head. "No."

He snapped his notebook shut. "What part is wrong?"

"That's enough." Grady started to stand, but Cassie tugged at his hand.

"It's all right," she said. "I want to answer."

Grady sat down and his shoulder brushed hers, giving her strength.

"As I've said before, we called 911 from Grady's apartment. You must have a record of that call."

Detective Petter returned from the bedroom carrying the grocery bag with Cassie's clothes. "Is it okay if we take these with us?"

Cassie nodded.

Petter said, "I think we've all we need for now." She picked up her tape recorder and put it in her purse.

The burly detective sighed, but he pocketed his notebook and stood. "We'll take your official statement this afternoon at headquarters, Ms. West." His face held a trace of a mocking smile. "If you like, we can send a car for you."

She nearly laughed in his face. This man had to be putting her on. After his total rudeness, he wanted to send a police car to pick her up. "No." She shook her head emphatically. "I'll get there on my own."

Souchuk paused in the open doorway. "Don't give any interviews to the media while the homicide is under investigation. That includes the boyfriend here. Understand?"

CHAPTER FIFTEEN

As soon as Cassie closed the door behind the detectives, Grady gently pulled her into his arms. Her mind reeled with questions, but the feel of his arms holding her solidly against him calmed the panic. She was conscious of warm breath on her ear, heart beating against hers, and the comfort of his embrace.

"They don't believe me," she whispered against his shoulder.

"You're okay. Relax."

She indulged herself in the feel of the long length of his body against hers. "That man treated me as if I murdered Mrs. Williams." She sniffed and then swiped at a tear before meeting Grady's eyes.

He touched her hair. "Forget Souchuk. He wants to impress his rookie partner with how tough he is. He has no reason to suspect you." His arms tightened around her. One hand rested at the curve of her hip.

Grady smelled of soap and aftershave. To rest against his male strength, if only for a moment, reawakened the truth of how alone she was. Her arms circled his neck, and she hid her face in his shoulder.

She felt his lips against her cheek. If she turned her face only a little...she felt the stirrings of desire. She shouldn't respond sexually, shouldn't lean on him, a man she barely knew.

Aware of her wrinkled, slept-in clothing, she pulled away and tucked in her blouse. "Thanks for helping, Grady." She hardly knew what to say to him—her landlord—especially since she had just embraced him with the warmth of a woman who wanted a man. She ran her fingers through her hair just to have something to do.

He put a hand on her arm. "That's what friends are for."

The thought pleased her. Now that she and Grady were on better terms, she had another friend in Washington, other than Seth. Although, it was one less than she had yesterday. The remembrance brought another rush of sadness. "If only Mrs. Williams were still alive."

"Yeah." He looked at her with a question in his eyes. "How well did you know her?"

"We only met three weeks ago, but we were close. She filled a void in my life."

"Were you in her house often? Did you see any money lying around?"

She nodded. "She kept cash in an envelope in a secretary desk in her living room. When I first took meals over, she wanted to pay me. I know she had money because just yesterday she offered to give me some so I could buy a car." She sank onto the sofa. "I'm afraid the police think I killed her."

Grady sat in the rocker. "After you've had a chance to think things over, you'll see how silly that sounds."

"Don't you understand? Souchuk thinks I killed her."

He shook his head. "Be reasonable. You wouldn't kill anyone. What would be your motive?"

"I don't know." Her stomach clenched. "But I believe Souchuk thinks I did it. Maybe they think I killed her and then robbed her."

"You're not making sense. Was she robbed?"

"I have no idea."

"Was the house a mess when you found her?"

"No. You were there afterwards!" Her voice rose. "You saw it."

"Cassie," Grady said softly, "don't let the questioning get to you. The police will do their best to find the murderer."

She sighed. "You're right. I know they will. After all, finding the killer is their job. But why did they push me so hard?"

"They'll go after the real killer with as much energy, you can be sure of that."

She took a deep breath. "You're right. I'm not thinking straight. I need fresh air and exercise." But not alone. And she should call Seth, or Mike Riley, maybe the FBI, but the thought sent shivers through her. What would Seth say about this new problem in her life? What would Mike think? As for the FBI? Rosetti hadn't seemed interested.

Her mind spun with all that had happened. Exercise and fresh air would help untangle her thoughts. She eyed Grady, tested her feelings for him. She felt safe enough to risk a rejection. "Would you go for a walk with me?"

He hesitated. Then he stood, stretching to his full height. "Sure. My deadline's later this afternoon. I'll meet you out front in five minutes." He put a gentle hand on her arm. "Don't fret about this. It'll work out."

She closed the door, still feeling the warmth of his touch. If she accepted his offer of friendship, he would be a support for her. Despite his churlish behavior earlier, his tenderness proved he was capable of caring about people.

She continued to be troubled by the feeling that she was reaching out in the wrong direction. Despite the gentleness he had shown, Grady was an investigative reporter. He was probably very much in the middle of the Washington scene.

She should call Seth before she went for a walk.

Seth didn't answer his cell, but that wasn't unusual. He usually put it on vibrate when he was in a meeting. When his voice mail came on, she said, "Seth, call me. I'm okay, but I need to talk to you."

She stared at her phone before placing it on the table beside the rocker. She didn't want it with her on her walk. Her heart raced when she thought of telling Seth about Mrs. Williams. Didn't she trust him? What would he think about yet another murder? She heard Grady's step overhead and headed for her bedroom to change.

She threw on sweat pants and a T-shirt, socks, and shoes. She probably needed to call Mike Riley. She looked at her watch. Probably had a minute or two before Grady reappeared.

"Mike Riley," he answered the first ring.

"It's Cassie. I need to give you a report." She heard Grady's knock on her door. "But I'm going for a walk now. I'll call you later."

"Can't you talk while you walk?"

"No, I'm going with a friend. I don't want him to hear me talking to you."

A pause. "Did you say 'him'?"

She waited. "Jealous?" She was still smiling when she opened the door to Grady.

Neither speaking nor touching, Cassie and Grady walked to the C & O Canal. The city was starting to fill up with visitors. It wasn't as crowded as it was in summer after the schools closed, but there were enough visitors to create crowded sidewalks and lines at restaurants.

They sat on a bench overlooking the canal. The walk along the canal had a cozy feeling. The sun was partially blocked by blooming tulip trees, and the air had a damp smell of spring rain. Exhausted, her muscles gave up their tight grip. She looked down at her running shoes, their pink and white a contrast to the gray cement walk. She couldn't speak, not even to tell Grady how much she appreciated his being with her. She smiled, hoping the smile would say how thankful she was for his presence.

He asked, "What did you do before you became a senator's girlfriend?"

Amused, she shook her head. "After all that's happened last night and this morning, is that all you can think to ask?"

He laughed softly. "I want to know more about you. You didn't just drop out of the sky fully grown did you?"

"I wish." She poked him gently with her elbow. "If you're going to interview me, I'm leaving you here and heading home."

"Are you certain you can make it that far?"

"No, I'm not, but please let me just lean back and take it easy for a minute."

"Sorry. I was only trying to have a little fun."

"Did anyone ever tell you that your timing is rotten?"

"That's what my ex-wife said."

She laughed. "Now I'm sorry for mentioning it. Didn't mean to call up bad memories."

"Don't be sorry. I know I'm a jerk. I'm working on being a better guy. That's one of the twelve steps, 'Make amends for anyone you've harmed.'"

"You haven't harmed me."

"I know. I'm making amends before I do. It's inevitable. I told you, I'm a jerk."

She patted his knee, then quickly drew her hand away.

"Seriously, Cassie. What did you do before you came to DC?" He gave her a look. "Off the record. I promise."

"You won't believe it, but I was a librarian."

He sputtered. "You're kidding me. A babe like you?"

"Librarians aren't nerds!"

"I didn't mean that." He took her hand, squeezed it, and let it go. "I've upset you again. I'm sorry."

She laughed.

He looked hurt. "What's funny?"

"I'm not upset, and you look like a whipped puppy."

"Being a nice guy is hard for a reformed alcoholic newshound."

"I'll make it easy for you then. Here's the scoop, Mr. Newshound. I was adopted."

"No kidding?"

"No." Although she'd accepted it by now, she wished her mother had told her the truth about her birth parents earlier. "And when I was a kid, I was kind of different. So my adoptive mother kept me at home a lot, kept me close to her."

"Is that right? How were you different?"

She looked at him. "Off the record?"

"Yeah."

"I think I had psychic abilities."

"Jeez, no kidding."

"Grady, I thought you were a reporter for a national paper. What's with this 'Jeez, no kidding' stuff?"

He laughed and scuffed his running shoes on the brick walk in front of them. "I don't know. I'm surprised, I guess.

Besides, my mind's not working too well this morning. And you make me feel a lot happier than I am."

Cassie sat in the soft rays of the partially hidden sun and watched the local scene swirl around her. Two joggers passed by at a leisurely pace, water bottles bouncing on their belts. In the canal, kayakers lazily paddled down the protected waterway.

Grady casually placed an arm on the bench behind her shoulders. "What do you mean by 'psychic abilities'?"

"Oh, little things." She wouldn't tell him the whole truth. "I thought I saw things or heard things."

He lifted his eyebrows.

"I was considered weird. Kids teased me. So I learned to hide things from others."

"Can you still do that?"

"You mean hear things and see them?"

He nodded. "Yeah."

"Not really. I've repressed most of it."

Grady drew away and gave her a look. "I think you're holding out on me."

She laughed. "You don't give up, do you?"

"Not very often. That's okay." He took a deep breath. "You've a right to your privacy."

"I only told you about my past because I want you to know I'm not as special as you think I am. I've been a loner."

"Then how did you meet Hawthorne?"

She thought for a moment, and then decided to trust him. "On a ferry."

He laughed. "You picked him up?"

"No, not that way. Actually my mother, Eudora, gave a campaign party for him at her home on Mackinac Island. That's in the Michigan Great Lakes. Have you heard of it?"

"Sure, I've never been there, but I hear it's a neat place."

His eyes narrowed. "So you met Hawthorne and fell in love with him?"

"Not exactly."

"No, but you're together now."

"Together? I'm not sure what you mean. We're friends. Good friends. Actually, I haven't known him long. Well, I have, but that's another story."

"How'd you get together? Tell me. I'm interested."

Her comfort level increased with Grady. Talking with him about the past felt almost normal. "Actually, I fell in love with his friend."

"You didn't!"

"I did."

"What's his name?"

His persistence triggered a protective reaction. She felt the golden cloak fall over her. "Stop it, Grady. This is not a news story. No names. You said it would be off the record."

He slapped his hand against his forehead. "Damn! Okay, are you ready for the 'I'm sorry'?" He hung his head and mumbled. "Please forgive me."

Instantly contrite for causing him more pain in his already messed-up life, she leaned over and put a hand on the back of his neck. "I forgive you." She moved her hand away. His gaze rested on his knees for so long, she wondered if he were truly that upset. "Grady, are you all right?"

He rubbed his fist over his mouth. "I'm okay."

A woman pushing a baby carriage strolled by, bringing Nate to mind. She'd hoped…

"Passing on your left," a bicyclist called out to the mother, chasing the memory.

She turned to Grady. "Anyway, since you asked, I fell in love with Seth's campaign manager. The three of us were going to work together to elect Seth, but then…" She waited, not sure how to continue.

He peered into her face. "He's not here now, so my guess is you broke up."

She shook her head. "Not exactly. He died."

"Ah, shit!" He put his arm around her. "What else can happen to you? First your boyfriend—"

"Fiancé."

"Fiancé? Ouch!" He shook his head. "First your fiancé, now Mrs. Williams."

She nodded, overcome with the enormity of her losses. "And before that Eudora, the woman who adopted me."

"Jeez, your mother too? When was that?"

"She was first. On Mackinac Island, last summer."

He looked at her as if he were trying to figure her out.

"So don't get too close to me," she said. "I'm trouble."

"If you're psychic, couldn't you sense any of this coming?"

"It's hard to see things for yourself," she said, her voice a whisper.

"Did you sense anything about your mother?"

"I had a premonition, repeatedly, that something was going to happen. I warned her."

"You warned her of what?"

"Not to go near the bluff. I tried to tell her. I went back in time."

He pulled away slightly. "You did what?"

Cassie realized what she had said. "I warned her."

"You said you went back in time."

"It didn't work."

"You couldn't go back, or she didn't believe you?"

"She didn't believe me. Grady, you've sworn this is off the record. You can't tell anyone, ever."

"You're safe with me." He patted her hand. "How did you manage this time travel thing?"

"It doesn't matter. Forget it."

He studied her and then went on with his questioning. "What about Mrs. Williams or your fiancé? Did you sense either of their deaths?"

"I had a premonition about Nate, my fiancé, but he didn't sense anything. I guess that goes along with not being able to see your own future." She paused, her head down. She said quietly, "We were happy that day."

"How did he die?"

She closed her eyes. "He was murdered in front of me." She held her hands over her face.

"Cassie." He leaned over and drew her close in a tight hug. "How did you deal with that?"

"I had help. Seth helped me. His friends helped me." She took a deep breath and moved out of his arms. "I was doing well until…Mrs. Williams." She swallowed hard. "Do you think I'm bad luck?"

"Don't talk that way. It's a coincidence. Life is stranger than fiction. If you read your story in a book, you wouldn't believe it."

"I don't know. A lot of people believe there are no coincidences. Everything happens for a purpose. Anyway, here I am involved in another murder, enrolling in law school, wishing I could find the answers to why this is happening." She tugged on a lock of her hair. "And you're my upstairs neighbor."

He smiled. "You could have at least warned me."

"I have now."

"Too late. I'm already hooked." He pulled her hand down into his and rubbed her fingers.

She drew it away. "Don't even think that way. I'm involved."

"With the senator." A statement, not a question.

"In a way."

"Yes or no."

"Yes." She studied him. "Now that you know my past, are you afraid to be around me?"

He shook his head. "The way I look at it, all those people you loved—those who died—they were pretty good people, weren't they?"

She choked up. "Yes, they were."

"That proves the Irish adage that only the good die young. I'm a messed-up depressed alcoholic. No one cares if I live or die. That means I'm safe." He gave her a grin. "Even with you."

She groaned.

"That bad, was it?"

"No, I'm getting tired and I'm thinking about the walk home."

"Stay here. I'll get my car and come back for you."

She stood and stretched and then looked down at the C & O Canal below them. "No, that's okay." Despite her fatigue, she didn't want to appear weak.

"Okay." He stood beside her. "Then let's go." He took her hand and tugged her after him.

She followed him, liked the feel of her hand in his rough one. She couldn't tell Grady everything, but it was good having one friend she could talk to in DC.

On the street, he slowed to let her walk beside him. "So do I know everything about you now?"

"No, there's a lot more."

"No kidding?" They waited on the curb for the light to change.

When it turned green, she started out beside Grady. "I've a cousin who is helping me learn about my psychic abilities."

"Can you tell me about that?"

"Essentially the story is that women from ancient Egyptian days possessed certain secret knowledge that they passed down through their daughters for generation after generation. My birth mother died when I was an infant, and she couldn't pass it down to me, so my cousin is helping."

They'd turned off M Street, leaving its quaint stores and restaurants behind, and were passing down a residential avenue. Bright bursts of yellow forsythia bushes dotted the elegant row of townhouses, and birds searching for nesting materials flew crazy circles through the flowering trees.

"So, you see, Grady, you can't know everything about me, because I don't know everything. And, anyway, I like feeling mysterious."

Chapter Sixteen

"Hi, Cassie. What's happening?"

When she arrived home after the walk with Grady, she had punched in the number of Seth's personal cell phone. She took a deep breath. "You won't believe this."

He chuckled. "I'm used to your drama by now. Tell me."

"There's been a murder, and I'm involved." She closed her eyes and willed the red-splattered wall to disappear.

The silence was palpable. "Are you hurt?"

"No. The victim was my next-door neighbor, an older woman." Her voice broke and she breathed deeply again to calm herself. "I discovered her body in her kitchen."

"What were you doing in her kitchen?" A touch of anger tainted his voice.

"It doesn't matter. The detectives were here this morning, and I need to go to the police station to give a statement."

"That's ridiculous. Did you tell them who you are?"

The question puzzled her. "Of course, I gave them my name."

"No, I mean, did you mention your connection to me?"

"I didn't. I thought I'd talk to you first, just in case you didn't want the press to find out."

He hesitated.

"Grady volunteered to drive me to the police station and go in with me. I thought you might like that better than my going alone...or with you."

"You're right. Not that I'm trying to hide anything. I'll be with you all the way, you know that." He paused. "You're not a suspect are you?"

"No, I doubt it. The detective was a little rough, but I think he was just fishing for information, to see if he could upset me."

"What do you mean a little rough? Did he touch you? What's his name?"

She smiled. "No, Seth, he didn't touch me. I mean he tried to trip me up. I guess he thought I might confess to knowing more, and he was right. I had talked to her and I knew who was going to see her that evening."

"Damn. This is one thing after another."

"Don't you mean that I'm one problem after another?" Her voice rose. "I told you I would be trouble. I told you this wouldn't work!"

"Stop it, Cassie." His voice was deep and forceful. "You know I care about you. I want to be with you, take care of you. Unfortunately, I think Grady might be better right now. I just stepped out of a committee meeting. " He sighed. "Cassie, can you do this without me?"

She drew a deep breath and felt her muscles relax as she exhaled. "I'll be all right, especially if Grady goes with me."

"I'll see you tonight then."

"I don't know. It's going to be a difficult day. It's already been tiring."

"No, sweetheart, I'll see you this evening even if it's just for a few minutes. I miss you."

"I miss you too." Did she? She wasn't certain. It was mere politeness that made her mouth the words. "Then I'll see you later, Seth. Thanks for understanding."

"We'll talk about what happened. Should I bring a pizza?"

She smiled at the thought of Seth in his limo arriving with a pizza. "Sounds good."

She called Grady and told him what Seth had said. He agreed to drive her to police headquarters if she called and confirmed the time with Petter and Souchuk.

Detective Petter sounded pleased to hear from Cassie and suggested she stop by at three o'clock that afternoon. Cassie thought that would work out. She could grab a quick lunch, shower, and even have a little nap before leaving with Grady.

When she called him with the news, he said, "Okay, I'll be down at two-thirty."

Before she took a shower, she called Mike Riley. He was properly sympathetic, not at all like the FBI, and soothed Cassie's misgivings. "If you need anything, anything at all, call me," he said at the end.

The hot water of the shower felt good on her skin. She thought she heard Grady's shower running also, and she smiled. Sharing the old house with him gave her a sense of intimacy. It wasn't living with someone, but she didn't feel as alone in the world as she would have without having him upstairs.

Although Seth called often, he was always busy with one thing or another. Or another woman. She couldn't help thinking about that night shortly after she arrived when he said there were plenty of women who would satisfy his needs if she didn't.

She constantly wondered if she was making a mistake in pledging herself to him. Then she remembered Nate and her acceptance of her role as a Peace Seeker in this lifetime. Seth was on a peace mission despite his blatant sensuality, which she accepted as part of the sensuous energy that made him politically successful. The larger purpose took priority in their lives.

She washed her hair and blew it dry, then put on lounging clothes and curled up on her bed. The floor creaked overhead with Grady's footsteps.

At two-thirty, she heard Grady coming down the stairs and was ready for him. She'd changed to dressy casual separates. Even though she was apprehensive about the upcoming interview with the detectives, she hoped the outfit would convey confidence.

She shouldn't have worried. In the gray stone building downtown, Petter welcomed her into the cubicle she shared with Souchuk. He had called in to say he couldn't make it. He was tied up with a new murder.

Petter shook her head. "Things get worse nearly every day around here. There's hardly time to interview witnesses anymore."

"That doesn't sound too good for solving Mrs. Williams' murder," Cassie said.

"We'll do that. I'm certain. We have three good suspects, and we know one of them did it. It's just a matter of checking their alibis and motives."

Grady looked skeptical. "Cassie...I mean, Emily, isn't one of those suspects, is she?"

"Not at all." Petter shook her head. "We checked out her background and received a good report." She eyed Cassie. "You have friends in high places."

Seth or the FBI, she wondered. "What do you mean?"

Petter shrugged off the question. "Someone I talked to

spoke highly of you. Let's get this formality over with. I'll turn on the tape recorder and let you tell everything that happened. Try to include the hour of the day, any other impressions you had, and so forth."

"I'll do my best," Cassie said in a weak voice.

"Don't be nervous. Just start with your entering Mrs. Williams's home when she didn't answer the door. I'll ask you about anything I think you might be forgetting."

Thirty minutes later, Cassie climbed into the front seat of Grady's car. "That didn't take long," she said. "I'm sure glad it's over."

"Yeah, she's pretty decent for a detective."

"Don't you like detectives?"

He turned the key in the ignition. "Most are good guys, but I'm sick of working the crime beat. It's like purgatory for reporters. Once I've proved I can stay clean, I might get better assignments."

"I hope so. Meanwhile, look at it as an obstacle you have to go through for success."

He smiled. "Yeah, it's necessary, all right." He pulled the car out of the public parking garage. "How about getting something to eat tonight?"

"Are you asking me to dinner?"

"Yeah, informal, you know. As friends."

She liked Grady and she didn't want to be alone tonight. Mrs. Williams's death was too overwhelming. "That sounds good." She grimaced. "Oh, I'm sorry, I forgot. Seth is bringing pizza over tonight." She paused. "In his limo."

He shook his head. "I don't want to like that guy, but I have to admit he has his own style."

"He's really okay, Grady."

"I don't know. You act like you're scared of him."

"Of Seth? That's crazy." But was she? When she was with him, she felt as if she were walking on eggshells. He definitely liked having his own way, and the longer he was Senator Hawthorne, the more demanding he became.

Grady turned the corner onto their street. "You're playing in the big leagues with him. Politicians have huge egos. You'll get trampled if you're not careful."

"I'm aware and I'm pretty tough."

He snorted. "You, my dear Miss Cassie, are a marshmallow."

"I am not."

"Yes, you are."

"I'm not." She looked out the window and spied a parking place. "Grady, look, there's an opening right in front of the house."

He looked heavenward. "It's divine order." He pulled the car parallel to the curb.

Cassie and Grady climbed out of the car. "Thanks for going with me," she said. "I wouldn't have wanted to face the police alone."

"I thought you were tough."

She narrowed her eyes at him. "I can be hard when I need to be."

He looked her up and down. "That's a possibility." He followed her up the sidewalk and opened the front door to their house. "Make sure Hawthorne knows that."

At seven o'clock that evening, Cassie closed her cell phone. Seth had called to say he couldn't make it. She looked out the bay window at the darkened street. She'd eat alone again. Unless…

She punched in Grady's number. She'd heard his printer

working until just a while ago. Maybe he hadn't eaten.

"Hi Grady," she said when he answered. "Seth had to cancel tonight. Are you still interested in eating together?"

"I don't know. I hate being second choice." His voice sounded warm and amused.

"Well, Plan A didn't work, and you're Plan B. That's not too bad if you consider how many letters there are in the alphabet."

He laughed. "You might be right."

"Come on down and I'll order pizza delivered. The treat is on me."

"Nothing I like better than having a sexy woman buy my dinner."

"I don't know about the sexy part, but you're in luck about my paying."

"Maybe I'll be lucky in a different way, too."

"Don't count on that. Be glad for the food."

After hanging up, she thought for a minute about Grady. Before tonight, he'd never called her sexy. She liked him. He was low-key and laid back. But then he could be so intense that she wondered what drove him. He was a recovering alcoholic. Each one had his own story. That didn't stop him from being attractive and fun to be with as she got to know him better.

She was glad to have company tonight. The brutal killing of Mrs. Williams left her feeling vulnerable. It was unbelievable that her new friend had been murdered in the house next door. So much sadness. Being with Grady would help thaw the numb feeling in her legs.

When she heard his footsteps on the stairs, she opened the door. "Come in and sit down."

"How do I know you're not going to poison me?" he asked.

"Is that why you wouldn't eat my lasagna?" His earlier

rebuff still troubled her.

He sprawled on the sofa. "I'd forgotten I did that. I was scared of you."

She picked up her cell phone. "Scared? I thought you said I was a marshmallow."

"That was before I knew you were such a witch." He made a silly face.

She smiled and shook her head. "What do you want on your pizza?"

"Everything."

She gave him a look. "My kind of man."

After she'd ordered the pizza, she asked, "What's your drink?"

"Tonic, if you have it, with lemon or lime. Otherwise cola is fine."

"I've tonic. Seth likes it." Oops. She'd made a mistake.

"Do we have to talk about him?"

"Absolutely not."

"No, that's okay, and I am curious about your boyfriend."

"Don't call him my boyfriend!"

"Well then, what is he? If he's not your boyfriend, how come you're here in Washington with him? He rented this apartment for you, and then he never comes around."

"He comes around."

"What I mean is one of the reasons I was leery of you is that I thought you were his...uh..."

"Lover?"

"Something like that."

"As I said yesterday, he's the best friend of Nate, the guy I was going to marry. After Nate was killed, Seth helped bring me out of the depths. I promised I would help him here in Washington with his career."

"Help him in what way?"

"Just help him."

Grady grunted. "Are you going to get me that tonic?"

"Sorry. I forgot."

She returned to the living room with two glasses of tonic with lime slices and sat down in her wicker rocker. "Anyway, Seth needed help. I'm not entirely sure how far we will go with that, but I'll do what he wants. I owe it to Nate, who was his campaign manager. And before I came here, I promised a detective in Michigan I would help with the investigation of Nate's murder." She didn't want to reveal that she was cooperating with the FBI.

"So you do whatever Hawthorne tells you?"

She rocked a little in the chair. "No, I don't do everything he tells me to do."

"It sounds that way."

"You might be surprised at how I am with him." She sipped the tonic.

"For instance?"

She couldn't tell him about Seth's wanting sex, and her refusing. That was way too personal. But she wanted him to know she wasn't completely under Seth's control. "For one thing, he wanted me to change my name when I moved to Washington. He said I might be in danger from the people who killed Nate."

"That's stupid!" He took a long pull from his glass.

"I didn't think it was stupid, but I saw problems with it, so I refused."

He gave her a look and then smiled. "What name did he pick out for you?"

Her heart warmed toward him. She was actually relaxing despite Mrs. Williams's death. "You won't believe this, but he even had a passport set up for me as Emily Proctor."

"Emily? But that's your first name."

"It was a compromise. Cassandra is my middle name now. I'm Emily Cassandra West. I refused to be Proctor."

The doorbell rang. "That's the pizza." Just in time.

They ate the large supreme pizza in the dining room at the high tavern table, the one Grady had helped select. They didn't finish the pizza, and he agreed to take the leftovers.

She covered the slices in plastic wrap, put them in her refrigerator and threw the paper plates away. "Do you want coffee?" she asked Grady, who had followed her into the kitchen.

"No, but I'll take a cola if you have it."

She poured two colas into insulated glasses and carried them to the living room.

"The pizza was good," Grady said, sitting again on the sofa. "Thanks for asking me down."

She sat at the other end of the sofa and set her glass on the table beside her. "I knew you were home because I heard your printer."

"Oh, yeah, the book." He shrugged. "It's a long process."

"Do you want to talk about it?"

"Not really. What about you, Emily, do you want to tell me how your senator selected your new name?"

She shook her head, bothered by the thought of Seth's plotting.

"Why not...Emily?"

"Don't call me that. I don't like the name."

"What should I call you?" He reached over and took her hand. "You're special and you need a special name. If you could have any name in the world what would it be?"

His grasp was warm and supportive. She clung to his hand, struck by how much she missed touching a male, touching anyone. She'd been isolated for the last month. The only one who wanted to touch her was Seth, and he didn't respect her feelings.

"Never mind," she said, "my name's not important."

Grady gave her a stern look. "No, you're not going there."

"What?"

"If you say your name isn't important, you're actually saying you're not important. And you are important." He peered at her. "What would I name you if you weren't Cassie? Angelina? Carmela?" He leaned closer to her and held her elbows. "Who would you be? Carmela. *Cara mia.*"

He stood and pulled her to her feet. In one gentle movement, he moved her into his arms. "*Cara mia*, Carmela?"

Startled, she tried pulling away, but he wouldn't let go. He held her tenderly, as if she might break. How long had it been since a man had held her with so much care?

"Is that who you are? Are you Carmela? Should I call you that?"

His voice soothed her. It took her out of the harsh reality of this world where kind elderly women were living one moment and dead the next.

"You feel good," he whispered.

And so did he. Wrapped in his arms, she felt safe. All the scared feelings she'd been fighting softened. The tension left her, and she trembled slightly.

She wrapped her arms around his waist and pressed her palms against his back. He felt so solid under her hands, so safe.

"Carmela." The word was a caress.

"Forget the name, Grady. Just hold me. Please." She pressed her face, her lips, against the soft flesh of his neck just under his ear.

His arms tightened around her, and he rocked her a little.

She drew in a deep breath and let it out in a quiet moan. In these arms she was safe again. Mrs. Williams hadn't died. Cassie's mother was alive. In Grady's arms time stopped and she was absolutely safe. *Nate.*

She buried her face in his shoulder and sniffed. He smelled like a man—like Nate had smelled.

"What are you doing?"

"Smelling you," she murmured.

He laughed. "I'm not sure that's a good idea."

Memories flooded through her. She cuddled against him. "I love you."

He tensed and withdrew slightly. "Wait a minute, what did you say?"

"What?"

He held her away from him and his gaze searched her face. "You're thinking of another man, aren't you?" His eyes narrowed.

She awoke from her brief daydream. "Why do you say that?"

"You said you loved me. That's not like you."

She felt like a trapped animal, caught by her carelessness. "But I do like you. I like you a lot."

"You said you 'loved' me, and we both know that isn't true."

She stared at him.

"Who were you with in my arms right now?"

"Grady, please. Please don't do this. Can't you be my friend? Just be my friend. I need you. Can't you see I need you?" Hot tears formed under her lids. She opened her arms to him. "Will you hold me? Please, just hold me."

He drew her against him again. "Okay, then smell me if you want, but I'm not sure this is a good idea."

She tucked her head back into that familiar place between his shoulder and neck and breathed deeply.

"I mean, my God, who knows when I showered or washed my hair."

She laughed softly against his warm skin. "You're always in that shower of yours."

He rubbed her back. "How do you know? I suppose you're down here tracking how much water I'm using. Or…thinking of my being naked."

She moaned. "Just be quiet and hold me."

"I'm not sure if I can. If you know what I mean." He put his hand on her bottom and drew her closer.

"Oh my." She wrapped an arm around Grady's neck. Her body, as if it had a mind of its own, leapt to life at the feel of him against her.

"I know." He breathed deeply. "I think something's coming between us."

Every cell vibrated. She snuggled closer. "Oh my."

"Is that all you can say?" he muttered in her ear.

"Oh, Grady."

"Yeah."

"Oh, my God."

"Yeah."

She couldn't get close enough, and she started trembling. "Please hold me."

"I am."

He drew her against him until they seemed to blend into one. She thought their auras must have blended. Fused like hers had with Nate, and Seth.

"Oh, Grady."

"Are you with me now?" he asked. "Or are you with another guy?"

"I'm with you," she whispered.

"Is that your final answer?"

She laughed softly. Sensations streaked the length of her, up her legs and through her abdomen, and if Grady let go of her she thought she might fall. "Grady, I think we're going to do it," she whispered breathlessly.

She sensed a pause, a slight hesitation in him.

"Are you sure you want to?" he said.

She grabbed his hand. "Come on." She tugged him through the dining room toward her bedroom.

"I shouldn't...I really shouldn't, but," he rolled his eyes heavenward, "I could get in trouble for this but, for better or worse, I'm with you."

In the darkened bedroom, she slipped out of her jeans.

"No, wait," Grady said, "let me undress you."

She shook her head. "I don't like being watched." She fumbled with her shirt buttons. "It makes me nervous."

He eyed her. "Nervous? But I like it. Let me do that." He reached to slip her shirt from her shoulders.

She pushed him away and then turned her back and removed her bra and panties. She looked over her shoulder and watched as Grady quickly removed his clothes.

She lay down on the bed and held out her arms.

He was next to her before she had time to think. "Cassie, you are a surprise."

"I don't understand myself," she said into his ear. "I've never acted this way before. I have to do this. I hope you understand. Oh..." She stiffened under his caress. "Hold me tight. Hold me tight."

She was safe again. *Home.* Nothing could harm her. Grady was strong, masculine. She delighted in the feel of his bare skin against hers. She opened her eyes to look into his. Instead the brilliance of a golden aura around his head blinded her.

"Grady," she whispered in awe.

"Shh." He silenced her.

"But there's—"

"Don't think, just enjoy."

What did it mean? She tried to remember what she had learned at Peace Lake. *Angels.* Had they said angels had a golden aura? She opened her eyes again, but the aura shown so brightly she closed them against it.

A lively tune filled the room. She moaned and stretched an arm toward her night table. "That's my cell."

"Let it go. I'll tell you what. I'll go upstairs and be right back. Then I plan to make slow leisurely love to you."

The phone stopped ringing. She reached for it, but Grady stopped her hand. "No," he said. "This is our time together."

"I'll just see who it was."

He shook his head. "No way."

A loud rapping at her front door startled her. "What's that?"

"Someone's at the door." He rolled off the bed, quickly found his jeans and slipped into them.

"Don't open the door!" She checked her phone. "I've a text message."

"I'm just putting on my jeans."

"It's Seth."

"At the door? Mr. Limo?"

She read the message. "He says he's in front of the house—"

"Damn."

"My lights are on. He knows I'm home."

"Bet he doesn't know I'm here."

A burst of terror streaked through her. The rapping at the door started again.

Grady sat down on the bed and leaned back against the pillows. "Come here and forget him. You don't need to answer the door."

"You don't understand. He has a key."

The look in Grady's eyes saddened her. "He has your key?"

She nodded.

He levered himself off the bed.

"No," she said. "You stay here. I'll put on pajamas and a robe and tell him I fell asleep watching TV."

"I'm not..."

"Please, Grady." She grabbed a pair of pajamas printed with Scotty dogs out of a drawer, put them on and shrugged into a terry robe. "Please do this for me. Stay here and don't come out." She left the room.

At the front door she took off the deadbolt and opened it to Seth. She rubbed her eyes. "Sorry, I was sleeping." She was conscious of her swollen lips and her face flushed from the rub of Grady's stubble.

Seth paid little attention to her appearance. "I thought as much." He pushed past her and stepped into the living room.

"You can't stay. I was asleep, and I'm not in the mood to see anyone."

"I want to talk to you. I was on my way home and thought you might be upset by your interview with the police."

"You should have called."

"I did."

"Yes, but from the street in front of the house. You were already here. I'd like more notice."

He looked at her carefully. "What's going on? Since when do I need an appointment to see you?"

She raised her shoulders. "You don't. I just..."

His gaze became penetrating. "You're not alone, are you?"

She looked him in the eye. *Her Peace Seeker partner.* She couldn't lie any more. "No, I'm not." She was ten years old and she had dropped Eudora's Spode cream pitcher on the hardwood floor. It had shattered into pieces around her toes.

Seth looked at the closed bedroom door. "Do I know him?"

"Don't do this."

"I haven't done anything, Cassie. I think I deserve to know."

She pointed to the ceiling, unable to speak Grady's name.

Seth let out a sharp laugh. "The drunken landlord?"

"Don't." She held her hand up. "Stop now. This is my home and my life."

"Your home? I found it for you and arranged for everything."

"You didn't have to do that, and I've paid for it all. But I'm not going into that now. I want you to leave."

"I'm leaving, but I hope you realize you're risking our plans for the future. All for one good—"

"Stop! We'll talk later. Nothing happened. Go, please."

He grabbed her by the arms. "Cassie, make up your mind. Either you are with me, or you're not."

"I'm with you."

"Then get with the program. I'm not going to put up with this nonsense much longer."

"I understand." She was almost desperate for him to go before Grady decided to leave the bedroom. She shrugged out of his grasp and firmly led him out. "I'll call you tomorrow." After he left, she shut the door and locked it behind him. She stood with her forehead pressed against the solid wood.

She heard the bedroom door open. Grady walked across the living room. "Cassie." He took her by the shoulders and turned her around.

She sighed heavily. "That was ugly."

"I'm sorry."

"Don't be." She drew a deep breath. "I feel alive for the first time since last summer. I was numb, Grady. I felt as if I was living in a dead body. I can't tell you how wonderful it is to know I can feel again. I can respond to a man. Do you know how important that is?" She leaned against him, and he pulled her into his arms.

"Even if Seth arrived," she said, "what happened between us was wonderful."

He grunted.

"Don't you think so?"

"That's what I said," he muttered.

"No, you didn't. You grunted."

"That's man talk for 'you're okay, baby.'"

She laughed and cuddled closer. "I can't believe we almost lost our minds."

"I can't either."

"Sex was the last thing I had in mind."

"Me, too," he said. "Well, not the last thing."

She smiled. "Grady, I really like you."

"I believe you."

"What did you mean when you said you were going upstairs and you'd be right back?"

"What do you think? That I carry protection when I visit neighbors? We're in your apartment. If you wanted to have sex, you should have been prepared. I had no idea you were going to jump me."

"Jump you!" She backed away.

"Yeah." His look said she was on shaky ground.

"I didn't know it was going to happen either," she said in a weak voice. "I was carried away with your voice, your smell…"

"Yeah, my smell."

She shook her head. "And the way I felt when you touched me."

"Oh, ye-ah." His voice was low, grainy, and he drew the word out.

Despite herself, she laughed. "You have no idea how complicated this is—"

"No, you're the one who doesn't understand how complicated it is. But let it go. We'll forget it happened. I had no right to act that way with you. It was wrong. I took advantage of you, and I'm sorry."

"Don't say that. For the first time since Nate…you made me feel alive again." She wrapped her arms around him.

He kissed her forehead, and whispered, "We can finish this later."

She shook her head. "No, we can't. I think I made a big mistake tonight."

After Grady left, Cassie turned off the lamp in the living room and looked out the bay window that faced the street. A shadow in her neighbor's yard moved and caught her attention. Then it slid silently out of sight. A man had been standing behind the magnolia tree. The streetlight cast unusual shadows on the sidewalk and across the paved street. When she looked again at the tree, she didn't see the man. She shivered. She must be imagining things.

Chapter Seventeen

The next morning Cassie considered the art easel she'd set up in front of the bay window in her living room. To fill the months waiting to hear if she was accepted into law school, she'd asked the undergraduate department to let her register for drawing and art history classes. They met on Tuesdays and Thursdays. But she had resisted picking up a drawing pencil. She was always leery about what her unconscious mind would create.

She walked over to the easel. Thoughts of Grady and Seth and the awkward scene that happened the night before ran through her mind like a TV drama. But, oh, she couldn't regret what had happened with Grady. She closed her eyes and drew in a deep breath, could almost feel his arms around her. To think she had undressed in front of him. She smiled a secret smile. What had happened to her inhibitions?

She stood before the bay window, moved the lace curtain aside, and looked across the street. There was the magnolia tree where last night she had thought someone was watching her. A man was there now, or her eyes were playing tricks on her. This might be the break she needed. He could be watching her. She let the curtain fall over the window. If she walked to Wisconsin Avenue, she could stop occasionally and check if anyone followed her. Maybe she could take a picture with her cell. And it was safer to mail the payment for her credit card account from a postal drop box. Mike Riley had warned her against leaving envelopes with enclosed checks in her mailbox for the carrier to pick up.

Acting on impulse, she picked up the envelope from the dining room table, placed house keys in the pocket of the fringed deerskin jacket she'd put on, and then grabbed her FBI cell phone. She was out the door in less than three minutes.

On the cement porch, she paused and looked around before starting out. She didn't see anyone, but that didn't mean no one was there. For an instant she thought she was being paranoid, but then she dismissed the idea and walked swiftly, but casually, down the sidewalk toward the main street.

Once on Wisconsin Avenue, she stopped at a restaurant window to study the menu. She glanced behind her and thought she caught a glimpse of a man who stopped at the same time and looked in the window where he stood. But she couldn't be sure. There were too many people on the sidewalk.

When she reached the postal drop box, she walked past it for ten paces, and then did a quick turn around as if she'd walked too far by mistake. Was that the man who had been behind her earlier? If so, he did a good job of ignoring her.

She mailed her check and paused a moment at the box, but didn't see anyone who looked familiar. Her edginess was disrupting her life. She drew a deep breath and started home. Even if she wanted to, she couldn't stop anywhere to buy a coffee. She hadn't thought to bring any money.

Despair washed over her. Was she becoming delusional? After her foolish behavior with Grady last night, and then the feeling of being followed this morning, she wondered if she should give up the idea of working with law enforcement to trap Nate's killers. This was the stuff of movies, not real life.

She couldn't lose her courage now. These dark forces counted on individual citizens feeling inadequate to do anything to halt acts of violence. She passed a man who looked familiar, and she shivered again. Looking back, she thought she caught him watching her. *Don't panic.* She took her cell from her pocket and held it to her ear as though receiving a call. Then she turned again and followed him. When she drew even with him, she raised the phone and took a picture.

In the process she bumped his arm. "Sorry," she murmured, and then dropped a pace or two behind.

She pressed #2, put the phone to her ear and walked on. "I'm sending a pic to you soon," she left a message for Agent Rosetti.

⚓   ⚓   ⚓

Back at her townhouse, she sat in the white wicker rocking chair and forwarded the cell picture to Agent Rosetti and Detective Riley. When she finished, she leaned her head against the high back of the rocker and closed her eyes. The playback of last night's scene with Grady, and then Seth's arrival, began immediately.

To quiet her mind, she silently recited verses of the Tao that she had studied at Peace Lake. "What is happening is what is supposed to happen. There is no power but good omnipresent."

Her personal cell phone rang.

"How are things going today?" Seth asked after she'd answered it.

With the memory of last night's quarrel fresh in her mind,

she straightened her spine. "Not too good. How about you?"

"I think we should talk. There's a reception tonight at the British Embassy and the new senators have been invited. I know it's the last minute, but I'd like you with me."

"It is last minute." What was he up to? He acted as though they hadn't argued last night. As though he hadn't caught her in bed with Grady.

"Can you make the effort?" he asked. "We need to talk."

She hesitated. "Is this a test?"

"What do you mean?"

"Last night you told me to get with the program."

"Cassie, let's not argue."

She hesitated. "All right, what's the dress code?"

"Formal."

"Like long dress, or what?"

"I don't know. You're the woman."

She sighed. "I bought a nice dress in Columbus with Ann Marie. It will have to do."

"The limo will pick you up at seven o'clock."

The limo would pick her up? "Where will you be?"

A long pause. "I'm going over from the Hill with the new senator from Ohio."

"I don't get this." Blood rushed to her face. "You're asking me to accompany you to a reception for the first time, but you can't be bothered to pick me up."

"I will if it's important to you."

"Yes, it's important! You said you wanted to talk. How are we going to talk if we're never together?"

He sighed. "Okay, forget the senator. I'll pick you up in the limo."

She wished she had an old-fashioned phone so she could slam down the receiver. "Right. Seven o'clock." She snapped her cell shut.

A look in the mirror told her she had to visit a beauty shop. She'd like to have a manicure and pedicure also, but it was probably too late. But then she thought she'd seen a salon on her way home from Kung Fu. What was the name of it? Hair Designs?

Her cell rang again. She set her jaw. This had better not be Seth calling back.

Looking at the name on the screen, she smiled. "Hi, Grady."

He said, "This is last night's big mistake."

She had to laugh. "You are sooo right."

"Do you want to go for another walk?"

She needed to get her hair and nails done. "Another time, okay? I've got girlie things scheduled for this afternoon."

"Such as?"

"I said 'girlie' so you wouldn't ask."

"I can take a hint. Are you busy tonight? Dinner?"

She might as well tell him. The habitual newshound wouldn't stop until he knew the entire story. "I'm going with Seth to a party."

"I'm sorry I asked."

"I'm sorry, too, Grady, but you know how things are. Seth told me last night I had to get with the program. I think he was talking about himself."

"You scared him with me, didn't you?"

"I hope you don't mean I used you."

Silence.

"Grady, I don't regret last night."

"I do. But not in the way you might think. I regret I ever let you answer the door."

Seth was thirty minutes late. She supposed it was his way of reminding her that he called the shots. She sat in the back of the limo with him and felt excited about the glamour the evening promised.

"You look nice," he said.

She smiled. "Only nice?"

He took her hand. "I'd like to kiss you, but I don't want to spoil your makeup."

"You do, and you're off my list."

"Where's your buckskin jacket?"

She gave him a warning look. "That's dangerous territory, partner."

"Whatever you're wearing, it looks good. What are these glittery things?" He touched the front of her crepe jacket.

He was so transparent. "Those are hundreds of tiny black beads sewn on black crepe."

"And this?" He touched the trim.

"Royal blue satin. Do you like it?"

"You should dress up more often."

She turned away and spoke to the window. "If you took me out more, then I'd have a reason to think about what I was wearing."

He slipped an arm around her shoulders and drew her close. "Even though I've been busy, I shouldn't have neglected you."

She had felt neglected. All these long days, she'd thought Seth cared nothing for her, and theirs would be a marriage of convenience only. His kindness in apologizing brought tears to her eyes. She blinked them away. "It has been difficult getting settled here in DC, but it's forced me to become independent once again."

"How have you filled your days?"

"I've been busy. I've started art classes while I'm waiting to hear if I start law school in the fall. And I bought new accessories and furniture for the apartment."

"And…" He kept stroking her upper arm. She moved away, and then he slipped his arm around her waist and brought her back.

She swallowed. This was the man she was going to marry. His touch was not unwelcome. It just seemed inappropriate. If he saved his caresses for after the party, she might be more relaxed. "Seth."

"Mmm?" His hand moved up from her waist.

"Don't wrinkle my dress or mess up my hair."

He stiffened and moved away. "What am I doing wrong?"

"You're touching me."

He drew back as if he'd been slapped. "You're joking, right? I touched you? Who the hell cares if I touch you?"

She wanted to keep her emotions under control. "We're on our way to a party."

"What do you think parties are for? What century are you living in?"

Her energy drained from her. "Let's not fight."

"I suppose if we were in the townhouse in your bedroom, then it would be all right." He mocked her. "What about the drunk? Are you telling me that he didn't touch you?"

"Seth—"

"No, that's right. You were having a pajama party, weren't you? You were there in your cute little pajamas in your bedroom, but he didn't touch you." His eyes challenged her.

She lifted her chin toward him. "You have other women."

The harshness left his features. "What do you mean?"

"That day in my apartment. You said you had other women who would take care of your needs."

"I wanted to make you jealous, that's all."

She tried to get beyond the hostility of his stare. "Seth, what has happened to us? At Peace Lake we were friends, warm friends. I thought enough of you to come to Washington and plan our marriage. Where did things go wrong?"

He ran a hand over his cheek and across the back of his neck. "It's the office. I thought I was prepared, but it's a lot of talking, negotiating and backhanded politics. Always compromising my principles." Seth looked at the floor. "There are times when I'm overwhelmed. Nate handled a lot of things for me."

"I remember." She lowered her gaze.

"I didn't know how much I missed him until I moved here," he said.

"In a way, I'm still grieving," Cassie told him. She sat quietly thinking of all that had happened in the past year. Well, that was over, and what happened had happened. It was over now. Her life was with Seth in DC. "What about your new manager?"

"She's okay, but she's not a guy." His voice sounded regretful, almost lost.

"You probably knew that when you hired her."

"She came well recommended and worked a lot on the campaign. Nate liked her and trusted her."

She swallowed quietly. "Then what's the problem?"

"Like I said, she's not a guy. That can get in the way of things."

"What things?"

He cleared his throat. "Let's not get into details. Vicki and I work together, and I try to keep everything on a professional level. She's not your rival."

Cassie looked at him.

"If you hear things, they're not true."

"What am I going to hear?" she asked.

"Who knows? Vicki will be at the reception tonight. I want you to meet her."

She put a bright smile on her face. "I look forward to meeting her. If she knew Nate and worked on your campaign with him, we should have a lot in common."

He nodded. "You'll have a lot of things to talk about, but don't be catty."

She stared at him.

"Like now, Cassie. Close your mouth. I know that smile is false. You're thinking my manager is a woman, an attractive woman who knew Nate as well, and you're jealous."

"I—"

"And don't deny it. I know women, and I know you."

She blinked fiercely. "You don't know me at all, or you wouldn't feel you have to trot out your office manager and threaten me with her."

"I'm not threatening you." He looked out the window.

Their limo waited in a line at the curb to move ahead to the embassy's front door where other guests were entering.

He continued, "I thought we should become closer since you seem to have other interests. It's important that people think of us as a couple."

Other interests—he must mean Grady. She opened her mouth, and then closed it when their limo drew up to the door. A valet opened the car door for her and extended his hand. She gracefully stepped out of the limo and Seth followed her.

On the sidewalk, he ran a finger across the front of her dress. "I like these beads."

She lifted her chin and stepped toward the door held open by an embassy employee. An inner part of her was amused by Seth's crudeness. Was it possible she was an exhibitionist underneath her prim librarian façade? Flashes of memory flitted across her mind—memories from another lifetime when she and Seth had...

"Good evening, madam," the impeccably dressed man greeted her.

"Good evening." She was caught up in memories from a past life.

Seth reached out and waved the engraved invitation toward the man holding the door. "Senator Hawthorne and guest."

"Good evening, Senator Hawthorne. Enjoy yourselves." The man motioned toward the foyer where security had set up a scanning device and a walk-through metal detector.

Seth handed his invitation to the security guard.

"Your purse, ma'am." The guard reached for Cassie's bag.

She smiled at the clean-shaven young man and handed it over. He motioned for her to step forward and walk through the metal detector. The device pinged as she stepped through it. She put fingertips to her chin and looked at Seth, who waited his turn behind her. He shook his head as if he had expected her to mess up.

"Your watch, ma'am," a uniformed guard said.

"Of course." She undid the catch and handed him the watch. Again, the device pinged when she stepped through it.

He motioned toward the beads on her dress. "Metal?"

"No, they're crystal."

"Then, if I may ask you to remove your shoes."

Cassie stole a look back at Seth who waited to pass through the scanner. The line of dignitaries behind him had lengthened, and she heard the murmur of conversation concerning who was holding up the line.

A woman's voice called out, "Seth, what are you doing up there? Do you have an arsenal with you?"

"Not at all, Vicki. I'll see you inside."

The guard returned her black stilettos. The metal buckles apparently had caused the problem. She slipped them on and felt her elbow touched by Seth as he hastened her away from the entrance.

"Sorry," she said quietly, hoping her embarrassment wasn't apparent. She was surprised when a smile lit up his face and eyes.

"No problem. I've had the same thing happen."

As they walked toward the reception line, she slipped her hand through his elbow. "Thank you. That's kind of you to say."

"No more than you deserve." He patted her hand.

What was going on? Where was the annoyance he'd showed in the limo? And what, if anything, had soothed his feelings?

They went through the reception line where the British ambassador and his wife officially welcomed them to the embassy. Cassie was properly impressed by the pomp and circumstance. She kept staring at Seth as he smoothly worked his way through the greetings. He introduced her to each person as his fiancée, an unexpected turn of events.

White-gloved waiters stood at the end of the line with trays holding glasses of champagne. Satin bag tucked under her arm, she strolled with Seth into the embassy ballroom where the ceremonies would take place.

"I'm your fiancée?" she asked.

"You are."

She sipped the champagne, which was the best she had ever tasted. Then she showed him the third finger of her left hand. "Where's the ring?" she whispered. Seth smiled at her, and she couldn't help enjoy their secret.

"It's at the jeweler's for sizing."

"Is it?" She looked at him over the rim of her glass.

"That's my story and I'll defend it to the end."

"It works for me." She sipped again. "This is wonderful champagne."

He twirled his glass. "Do you think you'll like being a senator's wife?"

"I'm not certain yet. I'm waiting for the courting and bended knee."

Seth laughed loudly. "That's what this is."

"The courting?" She hugged his arm, enchanted with champagne and the elegantly dressed people who swirled around them.

He inclined his head toward hers. "The bended knee comes later."

"Seth! Here you are." An elegantly coiffed and dressed, tall slender woman interrupted and put her arm around his waist. She looked at Cassie. "You must be Emily! How lovely to meet you."

Cassie released Seth's arm. "You must be Vicki," she said as if she'd known about the woman for months.

The evening progressed from informal conversation to formal introduction of the new senators and representatives, and a welcome to their wives and other members of their entourage. They circumspectly sipped champagne, ate caviar and an assortment of other delicious appetizers. They finished off with miniature beef tenderloin sandwiches.

Vicki hovered around the edges of Cassie's sight, never interfering with the introductions and socializing, but always nearby as if waiting to pounce. Cassie did her best to avoid the woman, but as the reception drew to a close, the amount of champagne consumed obviously had affected Vicki's behavior.

As Seth and Cassie waited in line to say goodnight to their hosts, Vicki approached. "Seth, I've heard you're introducing

Emily as your fiancée."

"We're engaged, as you well know, Vicki."

"But I thought you were keeping it a secret." Her voice was low and angry.

Cassie turned away from them and inched forward as the line moved toward the door. She'd had too much champagne and she didn't feel completely in control of herself. Better to let Seth deal with his employee, if that was all she was, than to pretend she liked the woman.

"I've decided now is the right time for announcing it," Seth said.

"You could have told me." Vicki's voice had started out as a whisper and was rising by the second.

"You know now, don't you?" Seth asked Vicki.

"I don't like having someone else tell me!"

Cassie turned toward them. "Seth, we're almost to the ambassador and his wife." She nodded at Vicki. "Maybe this conversation could be continued at the office."

The woman gave Cassie a look that chilled her. It seemed to say, *You might be his fiancée, but I'm his woman.*

Cassie shivered and crossed her arms over her chest. With the motion, her cell phone chimed. She dug in her purse for it.

Seth gave her a surprised look. "You brought your phone? Why didn't you turn it off?" Then he nudged her ahead as the ambassador awaited them.

She finally found the phone and turned it off. She felt her cheeks flame. "I'm so sorry, sir. I don't know how that happened."

Very stiff, very British, the ambassador said, "Not at all to be concerned. Delighted to have met you."

His wife extended her hand. "We hope to see you, Ms. West, more often in the future."

"My pleasure," she murmured and practically fled through the doorway.

Seth was close behind her. "At least they'll never forget us."

She gave him a startled look. "What?"

He smothered a laugh, and then nodded to the doorman who motioned Seth's limo forward. "I said you made an impression tonight."

His fingers rested gently on the back of her neck, and then gently traced a path down her spine. Cassie looked over her shoulder and saw the doorman smiling in amusement as his eyes followed the path of Seth's hand far below her waist. She ducked into the back seat, while Seth went to the other door.

Seth settled himself beside her as the limo drove off. He held her upper arm and pulled her close. "Do you like being courted?"

Her mind swirled with the effect of the champagne and the excitement of the evening. "I love it."

Seth leaned over and put his lips under her ear. "That's what I hoped to hear."

She stretched her neck allowing his mouth easier access to the sensitive flesh. "I think I've had too much champagne."

"So have I." He reached around her waist and drew her against him. "You look hot tonight. I like that dress and the way you're wearing your hair. We need to do more of this." His lips brushed strands away from her temple.

"And weekly manicures and pedicures." She was lost in the dance of emotions that his attention and the champagne evoked.

"And diamonds and limos." He laughed.

She pulled away. "What's happening here? We need to focus on why we're in DC. I thought we were in politics to change the world, not enjoy its riches."

"We are, but everything has its place, and tonight is meant for dreaming." His hands roamed over her.

She groaned. This was too much. Way too soon after last night with Grady. She whispered, "You're not coming in with me."

"Relax, Cassie. I'm not forcing you to do anything you don't want to do."

She tugged her dress tightly around her knees. "Then what is this called?" Her voice was a murmur, and she knew she'd have to overcome the effects of the bubbly drink and take a stand.

"Don't you know," Seth said against her ear, "limos are for making love."

She moved away and smoothed her hair. "Actually, I didn't know. Is this what goes on in DC?" But she gave him an amused smile. Seth was attractive and could be compelling when he wanted. He had a magnetic quality that made him popular with the voters and irresistible to women. It was a part of their relationship that continued to trouble her. His charm disarmed her.

The limo drew to a halt in front of her building. "That didn't take long," she said.

"Not long enough. I could use more sugar." He reached for her.

But she slipped out of his grasp. "You can walk me to the door and kiss me goodnight."

He put his hand on his forehead. "I'm back in school. Fifth grade, I think." But he tapped on the window dividing the limo into two compartments. "Okay, Juan. You can get the door."

She doubted the man could hear Seth through the glass, but he apparently got the idea of what was said because he ran in front of the limo and opened her door.

She slipped out of the limo with Seth following.

"Should I wait, Senator Hawthorne?" the driver asked.

"Definitely wait." With a hand at the back of her waist, he nudged Cassie forward. "This won't take long at all."

On the cement porch, he paused. He gently took her face in his hands and kissed her. She wound her arms around his neck and pressed against him. "Nice," he said, and then released her.

Cassie slipped her key out of her purse and opened the door. "Thanks. It was wonderful."

"It was."

She closed the outer door behind her and let herself into her apartment. She couldn't help but wonder how the evening would have ended for Seth if he hadn't asked her to go with him at the last minute. Would Vicki be in his arms now?

Chapter Eighteen

Cassie was in the kitchen pouring a second cup of breakfast coffee, when a cell phone on the counter chirped. The two phones, her personal and the FBI, were lined up side-by-side in their chargers. After they were fully charged, she would move the FBI phone to the bedside table where, in the lonely hours after midnight, it would be within reach.

She set down her mug and flipped open the FBI phone. "Hello?"

"Emily, we've identified the guy," Agent Rosetti said.

Cassie hesitated.

"You know, the one in the picture you sent yesterday. Information Services has him on file."

Her heart beat faster. If the FBI knew him, that could mean he was dangerous. "What's his name?"

"He operates under an alias. And knowing his name wouldn't help you. Besides, he uses a lot of aliases."

"I thought maybe he was one of yours."

A pause.

She continued, "You know, I thought you might have me under surveillance. For protection." She twirled a lock of her long hair around her finger.

Rosetti laughed. "No, Emily, we don't have that kind of manpower. You're on your own, except for the phone."

"That's not reassuring. Do you mean you're going to wait until you receive a report I've been attacked and then go after the man?"

"Let's hope it doesn't come to that. Until now this guy was involved in low-risk activities. Mostly he's gathering information on sensitive sites. He's part of a group funded by an eccentric billionaire who lives in British Colombia, but who has a Michigan connection. The man spends his winters at Lake Charlevoix in Michigan. You don't need to know his name either, but he's been on our radar for a while. He's an anarchist. Borderline schizoid. We've a tracer on his cell phone, and e-mail surveillance.

He continued, "Nate Chambray's murder, if our information is correct, is the first time we've heard of this kook being responsible for any real violence. We can't touch him as long as he lives in Canada. If he runs true to form, he'll return to Michigan next October. We'll question him then."

As she tried to process the information, she leaned against the counter. "Then, what you're saying is, you know who's in charge of these men, and my work isn't needed."

"Not true. If this guy's branching out into violence, we need to know."

She closed her eyes. "The guy following me looked violent." She would never forget his face.

Rosetti chuckled. "So do a lot of people."

His laugh sent a chill through her. Weren't the FBI taking this seriously? "What I mean is, I *looked into his eyes*." She swallowed. "I didn't like what I saw there. I sensed evil."

"Detective Riley said you were a sensitive. I'm sure you're

right about the impression of evil. We're keeping an eye on this group, but we'd like some solid evidence so we can put his boss away after we've learned what we can from him."

"I hope that's soon." She scuffed her foot against the worn vinyl floor. "I feel anxious, as if I'm being watched."

"Listen, you'll be all right. Keep this phone with you at all times."

"I do."

"Don't hesitate to call if the slightest thing bothers you."

"Okay." She tried to imagine walking through DC with her cell phone open waiting for an attack. Her legs trembled. What had she been thinking when she'd agreed to work with them? She had felt so strong, so confident. With the knowledge that she was being followed, those feelings had vanished.

"How's the martial arts training coming?" Rosetti asked.

"It's a lot of fun, and I like Mai Li, the instructor."

"She's good isn't she?"

"As far as I can tell. I like her personally, that's enough for now." Her voice sounded strange in her ears, as if she were speaking from another part of her personality.

"Emily," his voice lowered, "are you all right?"

He must have picked up on her insecurity. "In what way?"

"With all of this…I know it's a lot for you."

It felt as though someone were strangling her, choking off the ability to speak. "I think people everywhere are following me. I'm afraid of losing it, you know? Perhaps I'm making all this up. Maybe it's a dream."

"It's no dream," he reassured her.

"Is it usual to feel this way?" A whisper, a plea.

"Not for everyone, but some people get alarmed. Especially the first time you realize you're being followed. We call it the mirror syndrome. You think they're watching you, and then you start watching them while they're watching you. It plays havoc with the mind. It usually clears up after a while."

"What if it doesn't?"

"Then it's a form of paranoia that's not useful in the field."

"Do you think this whole thing will work out?"

"You mean finding your boyfriend's murderer?"

Her heart lay heavy in her chest. "Yes, that's what I mean."

"Maybe it won't solve the murder, but it will help in some way. We need to know about subversive groups that are planted on our soil. Some of the members are U.S. citizens disillusioned with life. It's a land of opportunity, but to succeed each person has to work. They're disappointed when they find out they can't sit around all day doing nothing."

"But would they *kill* people because they don't have a job?"

"No, they probably don't care much about working. They're into feeling good about themselves by causing trouble. They enjoy harassing people."

"Agent Rosetti, I was wondering…" She grabbed a swatch of hair and twisted it. "What if something happens when I'm being followed and I drop the phone? Or what if they knock it out of my hands?"

"That's where Kung Fu comes in."

Incredulous, she released her hair. "You expect me to use martial arts for defense?"

"That's the idea. Did you think you were doing it for fun?"

She sputtered. "Well…well!"

He laughed. "Emily, it's okay. I understand how you feel. We don't want anything to happen to you. Now that we've verified you're being followed, we'll keep in close touch."

"You mean the FBI will follow me, too?" She hoped the relief she felt wasn't too obvious.

"No, we have other means. Let me look at my calendar for

a minute."

She took a sip of her coffee and wondered what, exactly, Mr. FBI had in mind.

"How does tomorrow look for meeting with me?"

The thought intrigued her. Perhaps they *were* taking this seriously. "I don't need to look at my calendar. I'm free all day."

"I'll be at the Justice Department in the morning, but we could meet after lunch. I'll bring something with me that will make you feel more secure."

"One other thing," Rosetti continued. "You haven't revealed to anyone that you're working for us, have you?"

"I was instructed not to."

"Good. The fewer people who know the better."

"I am close to some people that I'd like to tell." She longed to confide in someone, share her scary hours with someone who would listen, and care.

No answer.

"Did you hear me?" she asked.

"It's best not to tell anyone, Emily."

"Keeping secrets can be difficult." She thought of Seth, and Grady and Liz. How she'd like to sit down and spill it all out.

"We'd prefer you didn't reveal your connection to us."

She shut her eyes and willed herself to breathe slowly. "What about a U.S. senator?"

Rosetti laughed. "For God's sake, Emily, a politician is the very worst person to keep a secret."

"But he was Nate's friend."

"We trust no one until proven innocent."

"You can't believe he was involved with Nate's death!" She'd stopped being polite, didn't bother hiding her irritation.

"I didn't say that. I am reminding you, we have an

agreement and secrecy is part of it."

Her lips tightened to keep from arguing with this hard-ass agent.

"Emily? Meet me tomorrow at one o'clock at the drug store at the end of your street."

"They're watching my house." Her control broke at last, bringing a spate of tears and sniffles at the end of this emotional roller coaster she rode.

"Meet me, and I'll have a chance to observe what happens when you leave your house." He paused. "Tomorrow. One o'clock."

She agreed reluctantly and then put down the phone. When she had decided to work with the FBI, she'd understood some days would be difficult. She wished Mike Riley were here. Working with a Peace Seeker was far better than this agent who had a steel rod up his back.

After setting the phone back in its charger, she picked up the Penny Bear that Liz had given her for consolation after Nate's death and sat in the rocking chair, cuddling the soft brown bear, and crying quietly. Tears flowed down her cheeks. Of course, she still mourned Nate. *Give yourself a hug for your progress.* In less than a year, she'd come a long way. Why did Nate have to die? She refused to believe it was his time to leave this life, as Ann Marie had suggested. *Nate, please. Why did you leave?* When no response came, she buried her face in the Penny Bear and considered her future.

Conflict resolution without war. That was the Peace Seekers' goal for this century. They were ordinary people working toward what might an impossible goal. She would do what she could for the cause. The thought reassured her. She dried her eyes and tried to forgive the weakness. Gratitude was needed. There was much for which to be grateful.

Keep a grateful heart, Cassie.
She wasn't sure if it was Nate's voice or her thought.

It was her afternoon for Kung Fu. According to her trainer's advice, she alternated her workout habits. Kung Fu one day followed by a day of stretching and rest. Then aerobic exercise followed by more stretching and rest. She practiced Kung Fu three days a week, but thought about it constantly. Meditation became an every day discipline. Clearing the mind of all idle chatter brought her closer to the power of the universe.

Her workouts went well. She gained confidence with every session. Today Mai Li added offensive maneuvers to the defensive poses they had worked on earlier. Cassie wondered if they would ever be used on a real opponent, as Agent Rosetti had suggested. She hoped not, but she worked hard on developing the *machismo* needed to attack the eyes or throat.

On the walk home from training, she stopped at a local grocery store that survived in the city by furnishing quality food for working people and singles like Cassie who had no car and no need for large quantities. She bought enough fresh produce and other items to last until the next Kung Fu session. Even though she was careful not to buy too much, the groceries in the cloth bags weighed heavily on her arms.

During the afternoon, Grady's apartment above was quiet. Perhaps he was on an assignment for the paper, something he'd wanted for a long time. She fixed a salad with grilled chicken for dinner and ate at the high tavern table in the dining room. With elbows resting on the table, she thought of Grady's insistence on having it, and his offer to pay for the set. He was a sweet guy, who was down on his luck.

After dinner, she washed the dirty dishes and wiped the

kitchen counters. Then she wandered into the living room and peeked around the lace curtain. No one appeared to be watching from across the street, nor were there any suspicious shadows. Perhaps she had imagined it. No, the man had been watching. She'd followed him and the FBI had identified him.

While Cassie watched, Seth's limo pulled up to the curb. Her heart did a brief dance when he walked up the sidewalk. Something about him made her skin feel more alive. She drew a calming breath. He was a fellow Peace Seeker, that was it. Nothing more. She shook her head in amusement over the denial. This was the man she was going to marry.

She opened the door and went out to greet him. "Come in. This is a surprise, two days in a row."

He grinned. "Nothing like a little courting to excite a guy."

"Don't get too excited, the rules remain the same." She led the way inside.

"I never did believe in rules."

"Sit down." She gestured at the sofa, but he chose the rocker.

He loosened his tie and shrugged out of his suit coat. Cassie folded them neatly and draped them on the sofa back. Seth said, "I'd like you to come to the office tomorrow to meet my staff. Rumors spread fast in this city, and everyone wants to meet you."

Cassie sat on the sofa and sank into its deep cushions. "Has Vicki been talking?"

"Let's not focus on Vicki. She's a good manager, and I need her."

Cassie nodded. "At any rate, I can't make it tomorrow, I have an appointment."

His eyebrows rose. "With who?"

Rosetti had instructed her not to tell anyone. "It's just an appointment."

"Break it." There was something controlling in his voice, something conceited as though the command came direct from headquarters.

She hesitated, fighting her visceral reaction. "I wish I could, but it's important."

He stared, open mouthed, as if unaware of the anger he'd created. "That hurts."

She put a hand to her mouth. She knew pain and had no wish to inflict it on another. "I didn't realize how that would sound. Of course, you're important also. It's just that I really need to keep this appointment. It's not social."

Seth pinched his chin with his long fingers.

"Seth, don't be angry. I'd like to have more kindness between us."

He stirred in the rocker. "I'm not angry." He rubbed the back of his neck. "I'm trying to figure out what to do about you."

Cassie decided to lie. A little lie, between friends. "I'm working out at the gym in the morning." Which she was. "And it's my day for art class." Which it wasn't. She spread her hands. She wouldn't say more. She only wanted to spare his feelings. But it was a deception.

He seemed appeased, but then she realized he could read her mind if he wanted. She stiffened, waiting for the anger that might surface.

"Okay," he groused, "can you make it the day after tomorrow?"

"To your office? Sure. What time?"

"Come in the morning, about eleven o'clock. I'll take you to lunch afterward at the Senate Dining Room."

She smiled. "Heavy stuff, Seth."

His eyes glinted. "I want to show you off."

"Should I get my hair done?" This touch of humor was what she wanted in their relationship.

"Of course. And stay home tomorrow afternoon. I'll have Vicki bring over some dresses from the boutique where she shops."

The pleasant bubble burst. "I don't need Vicki to dress me."

"Don't fight me on this. I want you to look right." He tempered the order with a smile. "No deerskin jacket this time."

He'd never learn! How could they cope if Seth had no insight into her feelings? "I know you mean well, but do you understand why I don't want Vicki selecting my clothes?"

"I've got a good understanding. But she picks out all of mine. It doesn't bother me."

Cassie bit back a reply and glared. "She doesn't dress you, does she?"

He locked his hands behind his neck. "Would you care if she did?"

"Of course I'd care."

"Good." He got to his feet. "One more thing, I bought you something."

"It isn't my birthday."

"Better than that. I'll be right back." He left the front door open as he ran outside.

She sat quietly, puzzled by his quick departure. Through the bay window, she saw him remove a package from the back of the limo. A gift? That was odd. Seth hadn't given her anything before, not even much of his attention.

After returning, he shut the door behind him, and then grinned, holding the package toward her. "I thought you might want a nice purse to carry when you visit the office."

"How thoughtful. I didn't know there was anything wrong with the purse I usually carry."

"Nothing wrong with it unless you're dining at the Senate."

"Are you ashamed of me?"

"Not at all."

"You just don't like my clothes."

Seth shook his head. "Cassie, don't be annoyed." He pushed the boutique bag toward her. "Here take it. Everything I do isn't an insult."

She looked inside and saw the logo of a designer purse. She recognized the brand name as being expensive. She felt as if she were turning a corner and starting down a street from which she could never return.

"Go ahead open it," Seth urged.

She reluctantly drew the purse out of the plastic bag. "It's lovely." She had a similar one in her closet. Dare she tell him?

"Go on, open it."

She looked at the purse from every angle. "Thank you so much."

"Cassie, look inside and see what the lining is like."

"I know how the lining looks. I have one somewhat like it."

"Why haven't I seen it?"

"You haven't seen much of anything that I own, have you?" She hadn't realized until now how angry she was that after moving to DC to be near Seth—at his request—he had virtually ignored her. Actually, she had known, she just hadn't shared her feelings with him. Perhaps she'd thought if she didn't acknowledge her anger, it might go away.

He took the purse off the sofa where she had set it. "Open it." He held it out.

She started to protest, but something in his eyes caught her attention. What was going on?

"Open it," he said again.

Puzzled, she took the purse and stroked its creamy leather. "It's lovely."

"Open it." This time his eyes crinkled in a smile. "Please."

She opened the purse and looked inside. "Very nice."

He reached out in frustration. "Don't close it. Look inside."

She saw a small gray ring box in the bottom of the purse and lifted her gaze to his. "What is this?" Her heart stuttered, and then regained its rhythm.

"Take a look."

She handed the ring box to him. "Do it for me. Please."

He took it from her. "Are you ready for this?"

Tears formed under her lids. "I don't think so."

"Yes, you are. You'd better be ready. I am."

She swallowed. Seth lifted the top and exposed the startling beautiful diamond ring. Its large, oval center stone was surrounded by a circle of smaller diamonds. They were all set in a thick band of gold.

She gawked at him.

"That night at the embassy," Seth said, "I told you it was at the jewelers." He reached for her hand. "Here, let me put it on your finger."

She pulled her hand away.

"What?"

She swallowed again. "You know."

He looked at her with a question in his gaze.

She pointed a finger at the floor.

His laugh broke the silence. "If I do this, you'd better say yes." When she didn't answer, he folded one leg behind him and lowered himself on a knee.

"Cassie, sweetheart, will you do me the honor of marrying me?"

She thought she would faint. Never thought it would come to this, despite all their talking.

"Answer me so I can get up off this floor."

She opened her mouth, but no sound came out.

Say yes.

She looked behind her. No one was there.

Say yes.

"Well," he said, "are you going to say yes, or do I need to see a chiropractor?" He paused. "Cassie…?"

She nodded. "Yes." She thought she might cry, but didn't want to spoil the minute for him. He'd planned this. Bought the ring, bought the purse, let her discover it. "I didn't know you were so romantic." She stood, put out a hand and helped him to his feet. And then she melted into his arms.

When he released her, she sank onto the sofa and admired the ring. "It's lovely."

He sat beside her. "I was hoping you would like it."

She smiled affectionately. "Admit it, Seth. You *knew* I'd like it."

"You're right. I thought a lot about what you would like. Classic, yet outstanding. In good taste, but incredibly special. Just like you." He leaned over and kissed her.

Her lips trembled under his.

He said, "I've been thinking about the wedding, but I didn't want to make any firm plans without consulting you."

Her heart sang. "You're learning, aren't you?"

"Little by little. It doesn't matter what position a man holds. It's important to consider his woman's feelings." He shifted his weight. "Cassie, I want us to build a great marriage. Not just a good one. I'd like to have a strong marriage to come home to at night. I want you by my side, and I'm prepared to do whatever is necessary for your happiness."

She sighed. "I'm ready to do my part."

"What do you think about being married on Mackinac Island where we met?"

"Do you mean it?"

"How about Eudora's Victorian cottage? You didn't sell it, did you?"

"I'd love that!"

"Since I'm a senator, August is perfect timing. I can be in Michigan then. I can help with arrangements, Vicki can help also."

"A wedding on the island would be wonderful." She ignored his reference to Vicki. "Let's make it as green as possible. We can set a good example for the public."

"But we don't want to skimp," Seth said. "The larger the wedding, the more people employed, the more money put into the island's economy. Plus, I'd like to have national press coverage and maybe special magazine coverage. The publicity can't hurt."

"I'm not sure," she said. "I'm not used to being put on display."

"You'll get used to it."

She had her doubts.

"I'll help you, Cassie. You won't be there by yourself. I promise to stand by your side." He slid next to her on the sofa and embraced her.

He held her so tightly she could feel his heart beating against her breast. He was warm and soft, and hard at the same time. And he smelled of…cinnamon. Cinnamon toast, crisp and warm with a hint of sugar. Not Nate's scent. Not Grady's, but Seth's smell, masculine yet comforting. The spicy cinnamon filled a need within her. It came from her childhood.

"Cassie." He put his hand at the back of her neck and

tipped her face toward his. Then his thumb caressed her forehead, the area between her eyes, the third eye.

A need to get closer possessed her. She closed her eyes and let the feelings rush in. She sagged against Seth, and he pulled her across his chest.

He gently touched her forehead. "The third eye to the root chakra and back again," he murmured. His hand swept around from her forehead to the back of her neck, and then down her spine to its bottom and then back again.

Sensations rushed through her. She heard music and the room swirled. She thought of Nate but, in her mind, his image had Seth's features. She pressed against him, pushing him back against the sofa cushions.

"Cassie," he said. Her name was the last thing she heard before camel bells tinkled in her ears and a kaleidoscope of color filled her eyes. His hand continued its exploration of her spine from neck to bottom, and back again. His palm warmed her skin through her clothes, exciting the chakras, and sending vibrations streaking through her. A vision of tigers entered the room first, then a parade of bears, grunting, growling, and filling her ears with sound, and her body with shivers. She surrendered to burgeoning sexual arousal, abandoned her control and went weightless, soaring through the clouds.

"Cassie." He was more insistent this time. He stirred beneath her. "Can you move?"

She slowly opened her eyes. "What?" She pressed against him sensuously.

"You need to move."

She looked around, groggy from the pleasure she'd experienced. She lay on top of him, and they were folded into the corner of the sofa. "Celestial sex," she whispered into his ear. "It was wonderful. Wonderful." She closed her eyes to reality and tried to recover the intense orgasmic feelings.

"Move your knee."

She looked down. It was pressed into his belly. "Poor Seth." She shifted her weight and he moved her aside.

She sprawled against the other end of the sofa. "Why so grouchy? Didn't you enjoy it?"

He stood and rubbed his back. "I think I pulled a muscle."

She smothered a laugh. His frown was a warning. She stood and straightened her clothes. "I'm sorry. Can I get you an aspirin?" She looked at him with amusement as he lay crookedly on her sofa. "How could you hurt your back during celestial sex? Isn't it all in our minds?"

"I don't know about you, but the sensations are in my body, and I'm damned sore from your climbing all over me."

It was all she could do to hide her laughter. "Really? Maybe you're out of condition." She tsked. "You need to visit the gym. We can't ignore our bodies and stay healthy and active."

"You're full of yourself today, aren't you?"

She held out her left hand and looked at the ring sparkling on it. "I am, because for the first time I think this is going to work between us."

He grimaced. "I told you that you needed a little sex."

"You can't fool me with that attitude. I know you felt the same things I did."

He struggled to his feet. "What do you have to eat?" Cassie followed him into the kitchen where Seth opened the refrigerator. "Wine, cheese, and…" He picked up a carton and sniffed it. "Old Chinese takeout?" He shoved it back into the refrigerator and shut the door.

"I've homemade lasagna in the freezer."

"Now you're talking."

"It will take me a while to thaw it out and heat it."

"That's okay. I have all night."

She took the aspirin bottle out of the kitchen cabinet and handed him a tablet. "And I have muscle ointment in the bathroom. Do you want me to rub it on your back while the food is in the microwave?"

He studied her under lowered lids. "Sure. You can rub me."

"I'll get it."

He went ahead of her into the bathroom and started looking in her medicine cabinet.

"Seth, what are you doing?" She peered around him.

"Just looking."

"There's nothing in there to concern you."

"I wasn't looking for anything special." He closed the cabinet door.

"Out." She indicated he should move into the hall.

He blocked the doorway. "Are you going to put that stuff on my back?"

"I am, but in the bedroom. Go in and loosen your clothing. I have to check the lasagna."

When she returned, she found him lying on her rose-colored coverlet with his shirt off. "Where does it hurt?"

He grinned. "Here." He pointed to his lower back.

She looked at him with suspicion. "You need to undo your belt so I can reach down there."

"Easy, Cassie, you're playing with fire."

"You should be pretty helpless with your sore back." She placed a dab of the soothing ointment on her fingers and rubbed his lower back. She'd never before touched his naked body, hadn't known his body hair glinted golden red against his skin. She drew a deep breath and continued applying the cream in small circles.

He grunted. "That feels great. When you're finished, lie down beside me."

She massaged his lower back until she felt his muscles relax under her hands, then put the cap on the tube, wiped her fingers on a tissue, and lay down, spooning in front of him.

He wrapped his arm around her waist, cupped his hands around her breasts and drew her closer. "My back feels better already. I'm glad we're together. You finally trust me."

"I do."

"We'll be married soon. In August. I can't wait."

"Neither can I." And she meant it.

He nuzzled her neck. "Is the food going to burn if you lie here for a while?"

"No, the microwave turns itself off."

"Then let's do it properly this time."

She stiffened, unsure of his intent.

"I didn't want to interrupt things in the living room, but the spasm in my back wouldn't let my mind follow yours."

He stroked her spine through her clothes, rubbed the spot at the nape of her neck and then gently massaged the area around her third eye. She stretched out her arms.

Seth rolled on top of her. She wrapped her arms around him, and with his weight pressing down on her, the music started, sensations coursed through her, camel bells tinkled and the room swirled in a cascade of colors. She thought she would die from sheer delight. Every cell quivered, every nerve fired. She gasped for breath. When she thought she couldn't stand the sensations any longer, she moaned and released a long breath with the chant of the universe's creative pleasure. "Ahhhhhh…"

Her breathing slowed, she opened her eyes. She floated with Seth just below the ceiling. She looked down at the couple embracing on her bed.

"Look at them," she whispered to Seth.

"Look at *us*. Aren't the mortals something special?" he said.

"Should we wake them?"

"Not yet, let's enjoy our weightlessness."

She looked at her arm. Where skin had once been, she saw a swirling mass of molecules spinning in place. "Seth? What's happening?"

"Your earthly body is down there." He pointed to the tangled arms and legs on the bed. "This is your celestial body."

She studied the luminous energy that was her arm. "It's beautiful. Why can't we see this body when we're…them?"

"Their sensory organs can't see celestial bodies. And it would frighten them if they could. They believe in their world, we believe in ours."

She looked out the French doors that led to the enclosed back courtyard.

Seth followed her gaze. "Do you want to go for a ride?"

"A ride?"

"Out there. At night, the earth is beautiful from above."

"How do we get there?"

"Through the doors. They're energy also."

"What about those two?" She nodded at the bodies embracing on the bed.

"They're tired. Let them sleep. We'll have an adventure."

She shuddered at the thought of leaving her body behind and with her fear, reality returned, and they fell to the bed.

She stirred under his arm. "Seth, are you awake."

He breathed deeply. "I am."

"I remember now," she said, "we were lovers in another lifetime."

Chapter Nineteen

When she awoke to the faint light of dawn, the first thing Cassie was aware of was the gold band with its huge center diamond on the third finger of her left hand. She lifted her hand to her face and studied the ring. It hadn't been a year yet since she accepted Eudora's invitation to the Mackinac Island Victorian cottage to help at a fundraiser in honor of the charismatic U.S. senate candidate.

Before she'd met Seth, she had daydreamed about being with him. Now her fantasy was becoming real. *Be careful what you wish for,* she remembered Eudora saying. Yet it wasn't Seth, but Nate Chambray, Seth's campaign manager, who had won Cassie's heart. They'd had a swift three-week romance last summer that had ended in tragedy.

Her breath caught in her throat. Nate had told Cassie from the beginning that she was pledged to Seth by an agreement made in a past lifetime. The three Peace Seeker friends had reincarnated in this time to help the citizens of the planet reach a higher purpose. Now their plans were coming true.

But this morning she had to do laundry, work out, and then meet Agent Rosetti at the drug store on Wisconsin Avenue—so much for world-changing activities.

At twelve forty-five, Cassie left the townhouse and walked toward the intersection of Wisconsin Avenue and O Street. Agent Rosetti had said he would be watching to see if anyone followed her.

She entered the store and headed to the paperback section, where she found a number of books at discount prices. The back cover blurb of a book by one of her favorite authors, Jamie Rush, caught her attention, and she considered purchasing it until she sensed a man beside her.

"Emily?"

She jumped and quickly glanced at the man. It was Rosetti.

He wore a dark suit and was fairly tall and muscular with nearly black hair. He offered a handshake. "Good to see you." She remembered his compelling dark eyes from the first time they had met.

Relieved, she shook his hand. His grip was pleasantly strong, his hand warm. "Please call me Cassie. It's my middle name."

"And you can call me Anthony." He stepped out of the way to let a shopper pass. "Is it okay to leave, or were you going to buy anything?"

She replaced the book in the rack. "Just looking."

"Good." He took her elbow and steered her toward the store's front door. "How about coffee at the Georgetown Cafe?"

At the popular restaurant down the street, Rosetti chose a quiet table in the rear.

"This is nice," she said just for something to say. She placed her purse on the floor between their two chairs.

Rosetti leaned down, took her purse, and moved it around a bit before he set it under his chair. "It will be safer there, out of the waiter's way."

She nodded, "All right," but wondered what that was all about.

He asked, "Have you been here before?"

She shook her head. "I don't go out much."

He looked as if he didn't believe her.

She smiled. "I know. I've heard it before. It's hard to believe, but it's true. I stay home a lot."

"Does your staying home have anything to do with your neighbor's murder?"

Sadness welled within her, and she blinked. "I suppose it has affected my behavior. This city doesn't feel safe anymore."

"You're wise to be careful."

She wondered if he'd followed through with his promise to see if anyone was stalking her. "Was I followed here?"

"There was no visible tail from your house to the drug-store. I was with you all the way."

"What a relief." She glanced around uneasily. "I never feel alone anymore." She brushed a strand of hair from her cheek.

Rosetti's eyes widened, and Cassie met his gaze. "Is something wrong?" she asked.

"Is that a ring?"

She flushed and spread her fingers in front of her. The large diamond sparkled under the overhead light. "It's new."

He leaned back in his chair. "Is this going to be a complication?"

She tried to rub the color from her cheek. "Not at all. It's just that…I'm engaged."

"Is that so?" he said dryly. "Is it…?"

"Senator Hawthorne," she finished his sentence. "We've been planning it for months, but now seemed like a good time."

"What is he going to say about your involvement with the

agency?"

"He doesn't know. You said not to tell anyone."

"I'm not sure." He scratched his head in apparent concern. "This engagement complicates things."

She stiffened defensively. "My working with you has nothing to do with him. This is my thing. If I have to choose, then I'll return the ring."

He held up a hand. "Hey, wait a minute. Don't go ballistic. Let me think." He looked at the waiter who approached to take their order. "Two regular coffees," he said with a questioning glance at Cassie.

She nodded her agreement.

After the waiter left, Rosetti drummed his fingertips on the table. "If something goes wrong, this might mean my job."

Her heart sank. "I don't want you to lose your job over me, and I certainly don't want anything to go wrong."

He sighed audibly and thought for a moment. Then he reached into his suit coat's inner pocket and pulled out a miniature purple pouch.

The waiter approached with the coffee. Rosetti concealed the pouch in his hand until they were served and the waiter had left. "I've been authorized by my supervisor to give this to you, so," he paused, "I'll go ahead as planned. If he thinks we need to change things, I'll let you know."

"Good."

He passed the cloth bag to her under the table. "Inside is what looks like an ordinary necklace, but the heart contains a miniature GPS transmitter. We'll be able to track your every move, every location, by satellite while you're wearing it. It's a backup for the cell phone, or in case its battery runs down."

She fingered the pouch and felt its weight. "I think I'll like having this."

"Wear it when you can, and if that's inconvenient, put it in your pocket if you're not using a purse. If you're in trouble, we can mobilize a task force, and we'll know exactly where you are. Not only that, but it identifies you to any police department, anywhere."

"Thanks, Anthony." She stumbled a little over his name. "I'll feel safer with this."

"My pleasure, Cassie." He leaned back and gave her a smile that chased the somber look from his face.

They drank their coffee, sociably discussing the merits of living in DC versus the Virginia or Maryland suburbs. Rosetti had a lot of knowledge about the area, and Cassie found him remarkably interesting as well as attractive.

When they left, she stood outside on the sidewalk with him and shook his hand before parting.

Rosetti leaned closer. "Remember, the GPS doesn't work unless you have it with you. Always take it with you when you go out, especially if you're alone."

Her heart warmed with his admonition. The man she'd considered cold and unfeeling had a softer side. "Thanks for everything, Anthony," she said. "I hope to see you again."

Rosetti barked a doubtful laugh. "Don't hope for that. You'll only see me if you're in trouble."

At home, Cassie went into the bedroom to change. She looked at the engagement ring on her finger. Seth. A ping of anxiety raced through her. To relax, she drew a deep breath and stood for a minute with her eyes closed. She needed to practice deep breathing and meditation for Kung Fu, and for her peace of mind also. Grady's footsteps above drew her out of reflection. She studied her ring. He must be told and now was as good a time as any.

She took her cell from her purse and punched in his number.

"Hi Grady, can I come up?" she said after he answered. "I've something to tell you." If she went to his place, then she could leave after she told him.

He hesitated. "I'll come down there."

"How about a walk instead?"

"That's great," he said with enthusiasm. "Ten minutes."

While changing into warm-up clothes, Cassie hoped he wouldn't be disappointed about the ring. That was probably asking for too much. It had been a mistake to become involved with Grady, but he was convenient and seemed as much in need of human companionship as she was. Plus, she had to admit it, she was attracted to him. She couldn't deny his effect on her emotions. Where had her Peace Seeker spiritual guides been when she'd let Grady get so close? *Correction!* When she'd practically dragged him to her bed.

Her cheeks warmed with the thought. Even now her body stirred with reaction just thinking about him and remembering the feel of his arms holding her, his warm flesh on her bare skin. She slipped into her walking shoes and jerked at the laces, tying them tightly. Oh, Grady, why was someone always hurt? Maybe she assumed too much. Grady might have been using her as a defense against loneliness as much as she had. He was no saint. However, a memory struck her, that night, there was something she'd noticed about him....

She stepped out her door and waited on the concrete front porch. Everything seemed peaceful and serene on this quiet residential street. She knew better. Someone was watching her. She fingered the necklace pouch that she'd put in her pocket.

The door behind her opened. "Hi, babes." Grady gave her

a big smile. "You're looking good."

"Feeling good, too." She went down the steps with Grady following.

"What's happening?" he asked.

"Let's walk first." They started down the sidewalk toward the C & O canal where they'd gone the other day.

When they reached the canal, they sat on a concrete bench. Cassie unzipped her jacket and let the crisp spring air cool her.

"Well, what's up?" Grady asked.

"I don't know how to tell you this, but it's happened, and you need to know. I'm engaged to Seth. We'll marry this summer in Michigan on Mackinac Island."

He grunted as if he'd been hit in the stomach. "That's a jolt."

"But not a surprise?"

"You're right about that. I knew, but I kept hoping that maybe there was a chance…that things could fall through."

"I'm sorry if I've disappointed you."

He put his hand on the back of her head. "Nothing you do could ever disappoint me. I'll always love you, even if as a brother."

She laughed. "I can always tell when you're bulling me."

His hand found hers and held it. "I'm serious. You can count on me. Call me if you need help." He looked at her left hand. "That's some rock."

"It was a surprise. Seth and I haven't been on the best of terms since I arrived."

"And then he found me with you."

Her cheeks immediately burned. "I'm sorry about that."

"There's no reason for regrets. I haven't any. Good lord, Cassie. It isn't as if we actually did anything!"

She thought about how they had taken off their clothes in

her bedroom, and his naked body against hers. She squirmed on the hard bench. "Let's change the subject."

"A summer wedding," he said. "Isn't that quick?"

"It's Seth's choice."

"Is he going to rule your life from now on?"

"I hope not. That's something I'll have to guard against. How are things with you?"

"They're looking up. Or they were, until this happened."

"Grady, don't go soft on me." She growled at him. "You've been away from the house a lot. Is the paper letting you write more?"

"Yeah, I'm covering the police beat, but they're giving me assignments that connect with that in some way. I'm covering murders and other crime that has public interest."

"It's good they finally trust you with articles."

"You know the condition of newspapers these days. They use a lot of stuff from wire services and not as much local reporting. But my job looks stable, and I've connections here. You know…"

"Your ex–father-in-law." She looked at him. "We both have elected officials in our lives."

He returned her stare. "Unfortunately."

So far their talk had been friendly. She hoped things weren't going to get unpleasant. "Let's go back to the house."

He stood. "I think I should say congratulations, or best wishes." He offered a hand and pulled her up.

"Let's jog back," Cassie said. "I need a workout."

The minute she was in her apartment, Cassie breathed a sigh of relief. Although she knew Grady was disappointed in her engagement, he remained her friend. Now she had to deal with Vicki from Seth's office, who was coming over this afternoon. The thought *cat lady* made her remember Ann Marie back at Peace Lake. She hadn't talked to her for a while.

She was eating a cup of yogurt with cherries on the bottom when her cell chimed.

"Liz," she exclaimed when she saw her cousin's name.

"Just checking up on you."

"I'm doing fine, and I've some good news." Cassie paused. "At least I hope you'll think it's good news. Seth gave me an engagement ring last night." She laughed with delight.

"You sound happy."

"I am. Can you tell?"

"I can almost see your smile," Liz said. "You haven't sounded this upbeat in a long time."

"Finally it's settled. I think indecision is more painful than making the wrong choice."

"Have faith. You can't make a bad choice. What's happening is what's supposed to happen."

"Thanks, Liz. I needed to hear that. I don't hear too many positive things about my marrying Seth."

"You'll probably gain more confidence in your decision as time goes by. And you'll be happy to hear, I've an opportunity for you to recharge your energy."

"Really? What?"

"I'm presenting a seminar on Cosmic Dancing in Winchester, Virginia. Winchester is about seventy miles west of DC in the Shenandoah Valley. I want you to come. You can share my hotel room."

"It sounds heavenly, Liz. I haven't seen you in ages, and you've been so helpful. I haven't thanked you for everything you've done."

"You would have to rent a car and drive over."

"That's not a problem. I don't mind not having a car here, but I do miss driving."

"Winchester is a lovely historic town. I know you'll enjoy touring it even if you don't attend the seminar."

"When is this happening?"

"Sooner than you might think, because I'm filling in for a workshop leader who had to cancel. It's this weekend. Can you manage that?"

"I'll be there. And Liz, I've more good news. I'll tell you when I see you."

"Great. I'll give you the address, and you can get a map online."

After she hung up, Cassie started up her CD player and danced around the apartment. She wondered what a class on Cosmic Dancing would be like and decided it would be a lot of fun as well as educational.

Even the thought of Vicki couldn't dampen her spirits. While showering, she sang at the top of her lungs. Then she dressed to another upbeat tune. Poor Vicki. As hard as the woman tried, she wouldn't win this one.

⊹ ⊹ ⊹

Vicki arrived at the townhouse that afternoon with a car trunk full of clothes. Cassie helped her carry them in. She was determined to be courteous. Armed with Seth's ring on her finger and the memory of celestial lovemaking in her heart, she could afford to be gracious.

Vicki said, "Seth wants you to keep as many outfits as you want and send him the bill."

Cassie's determination to be cordial cracked slightly. "He doesn't need to pay for my clothes."

"That's what he said. I'm only the messenger," Vicki looked

around. "Where's your bedroom?"

"Leave them here on the couch."

"No way. Seth instructed me to stay here while you try them on, and then advise you as to which ones look best."

Cassie's scalp tingled. "That's not necessary."

Vicki grabbed an armful of dresses and started walking toward the dining room. "Is the bedroom this way?"

Cassie stepped in front of her and put her arms out. "This is my house and my life. I'll decide what to keep or not keep." She took a calming breath. "Thank you for bringing the clothes, but you can leave now."

CHAPTER TWENTY

The next morning Cassie had returned from a walk with Grady, showered, and was putting the finishing touches on her makeup when the cell phone chimed. She ran into the kitchen and looked at the phone. *Detective Petter.* Maybe they'd made progress on finding Mrs. Williams's murderer. She shuddered as red filled her vision. After picking up the phone, she choked out a greeting.

"Ms. West," the detective said, "we have good news for you. We've arrested Mrs. Williams's son on murder charges."

"Her son!"

"We did a background check and discovered he'd been arrested a couple of years ago on a domestic violence charge. He roughed up his mother."

"She never said a word about it. But then, I didn't know her well."

"We brought him in for questioning and, after we offered a deal, he finally confessed. He hadn't planned to kill her. His business had gone down the tubes, and his house was in fore-closure. He was pressuring her for money. Apparently, he lost his head when she wouldn't help him out."

"But that's terrible. To kill your own mother." Tears threatened. This news was shocking. She'd never had a chance to know her birth mother or father and couldn't imagine killing one of them. "What a loss."

"Family violence is more pervasive than you might think. We usually look at family members first when there's a homicide at home."

"It's hard to believe, but I appreciate your telling me."

"I thought you'd want to know. Of course, it sometimes doesn't work out, and the accused withdraws his confession, but we're certain we've found Mrs. Williams's killer. It wasn't a case of random violence, or mistaken identity. You can relax now."

After Cassie put down the phone, she sank into her rocker and rested her head against its high back. It was over. The murderer had been arrested. The guilt she had been carrying with her since the murder dissipated. The front door Mrs. Williams had left unlocked for Cassie had not contributed to her death. Now she knew nothing would have influenced the outcome. This violence had been a family affair.

Seth's driver picked up Cassie before noon. She had to admit she looked pretty good in one of the outfits Vicki had brought over. It was a matte jersey, wrap-front dress with a swirling skirt, and its paprika color was outstanding. Around her shoulders, she draped its multi-colored paisley shawl in the same material. The outfit would make a statement and was appropriate for a senate lunch. Around her neck was the necklace with the gold heart and its GPS tracker. Her pre-programmed phone was in her purse. Talk about overkill.

She thought about asking where Seth would meet her, but

decided to relax and let the day unfold. She trusted him to take care of the arrangements. She also trusted the presence she felt beside her. When she had walked with Grady this morning, she'd sensed a spiritual presence. Was it Nate? She couldn't be certain.

As a new senator, Seth's office was in the Senate Annex. A couple of blocks from the building, his driver called him and said they would arrive in five minutes. Seth met the limo at the curb and helped her out. His smile looked sincere, but it was always hard to be certain.

"You look beautiful." He kissed her cheek.

"The clothes Vicki brought were perfect."

His eyes settled on the necklace. "Where did you get that heart?"

"Oh, this." She touched it with a fingertip. "I've had it a while." *For a day.*

"I'll have to buy you some new jewelry."

"That would be nice. By the way, thanks for helping with my wardrobe."

He grinned. "That's our goal from now on, Cassie. We'll help each other until the end." He put his hand around her elbow and walked her into the building.

She sensed the presence again, and wondered if it emitted from Seth. A glance over her shoulder showed no one else was close.

In his office a woman greeted them with a great show of welcome. "We had no idea the senator was getting married so soon," she gushed.

Neither had Cassie. But she returned the woman's greeting as warmly as possible.

Vicki stepped out of an inner office. "Here already? Welcome, Emily."

Cassie returned Vicki's greeting coolly. She couldn't help disliking the woman. Too many nuances swirled around her. Were Seth and she lovers? Or was Vicki putting on a show for Cassie's benefit? She was starting to suspect it was all a show. Seth didn't appear to have a guilty bone in his body. Nobody could fake innocence for this long.

"Follow me," Vicki said. "We'll meet the staff."

Cassie glanced at Seth, but he didn't seem offended by his manager's taking over the tour. She shrugged mentally. This woman had helped Seth through the last months of his campaign and now was his office manager. Accept it.

Vicki introduced her to everyone as Emily West, a name Cassie knew she needed to embrace as a part of her new life. Emily was different from Cassie. Emily would be a senator's wife and wouldn't wear deerskin-fringed jackets or have affairs with recovering alcoholics. She shivered.

A senate page stood and shook her hand. "Nice to meet you," Cassie murmured. "Nice to meet you," she said to the next person, and the next and the next.

Finally the introductions were over.

"I'd like you to see my office, Emily," Vicki said. "Seth, Senator Cooke wants you to call him. Something about lunch."

"Right. Cassie, go with Vicki. I'll be with you shortly." He turned away and asked an aide to call Senator Cooke.

Vicki led the way into her private office and closed the door behind them. "Did I hear Seth just call you Cassie?"

She nodded. "Cassie is my middle name. I prefer it to Emily."

Vicki gave her a scornful look. "How quaint."

"I suppose it is." Cassie strolled to the window and looked out. She'd learned a lot about non-violent resistance at Peace Lake. She would let Vicki vent for a while before setting her straight.

"You must be enjoying the excitement of being a senator's fiancée."

"I prefer the quieter life. But I'll adjust," she said without looking away from her view of the street below.

"That's what I wanted to talk to you about. Do you actually think you can fill Seth's needs?"

Cassie turned. "I'm capable of doing whatever is necessary."

"I suppose you think you can satisfy him sexually as well."

She wanted to laugh in this woman's face. If she thought Cassie was a pushover, she was mistaken. "Oh, that." She tossed Vicki a satisfied smirk. "Seth and I have no problem there and, in case you're fooling around with my future husband, you should know…there's no way you can win him from me. You might as well look elsewhere."

Seth opened the door and looked in. "Ready for lunch?"

"That and more," Cassie said smiling.

Vicki turned away, ignoring them.

"I'll be back in a couple of hours, Vicki," he said. "Thanks for your assistance." When Vicki didn't answer, Seth gave Cassie a look.

She shrugged and stepped out of the office.

When they were in the outside corridor, he asked, "What did you say to her?"

"Only what any jealous wife would say." She wrapped her arm around his waist and fell in step with him.

"A jealous wife?" he asked, but he was smiling. "What's this?" He touched her hand at his waist.

"Just a little loving."

He pressed his hand against her bottom.

"Seth," she whispered and tried to pull away.

"You started it."

She squirmed but he only tightened his hold. "Quit fighting me."

Cassie quieted and he removed his hand. He would have his way, she realized.

I will *have my way, so cooperate.*

She stiffened. Sub-vocal communication. Telepathic speech. She blanked her mind.

Seth firmly took her elbow and steered her up this corridor and down the next and from one building to another and into an elevator, until they arrived at the famed Senate Dining Room.

Cassie's heart pounded. The instant she stepped into the large room, her new life began. She looked at the huge engagement ring on her finger and then looked around the room where Washington's most powerful club dined.

The maître d' led them to a table. A distinguished gentleman rose when they approached. "Emily, meet Senator Cooke," Seth said.

She accepted the senator's offered hand and murmured greetings. From now on, a perpetual smile would be her normal expression. Her hand tingled under his touch, and his eyes were shockingly familiar.

"Emily, my pleasure," the senator said.

"He's one of us," Seth said quietly as they sat down.

After lunch, the limo returned Cassie to her townhouse. She checked her mailbox before going inside and found an envelope from the university. She took it into her apartment and, with trembling fingers, read the enclosed letter. "You have been accepted..." She threw the letter in the air and danced around the room. She was accepted for the fall semester. It had been very fast and very efficient: the studying for the LSAT at Peace Lake with their legal advisor, the application forms, transcripts, etc. She wondered briefly if Seth had something to do with her quick acceptance, but pushed that thought away. It mattered little. She was going to law school this fall. Seth needed to know immediately.

When the voice mail kicked in on his cell phone, she yelled out his name: "Seth, call me! I've been accepted to law school." *Yea for me, for you, for everyone who helped me.* "I'm so excited, and I know you'll be glad, too." At least she hoped he would be. The three years of study should be worth the effort. Three years. She'd have to handle law school and marriage to Seth. She shrugged. She could handle both.

She kicked off her stilettos and headed for the shower.

Her brain sloshed with a stew of names from Seth's office, with plans for the future, and the necessity of playing a new role as Senator Hawthorne's fiancée, Emily West. Thankfully, the details of the new identity arranged for her at Peace Lake were firmly entrenched in her memory. Most of them followed her actual life as closely as possible.

Was this identity change really necessary for her protection? Seth thought it was, but he also had no idea she was cooperating with the FBI to uncover the group responsible for Nate's death—and Eudora's and possibly another friend in Michigan. Thank God she'd learned she wasn't responsible for Mrs. Williams's demise. She hated deceiving Seth and worried, if he learned the truth, how he would react.

She stood under a soothing shower for a long time until her guilt dissolved.

Finally, with her hair dry and fully dressed she picked up her cell phone and found she had a message from Grady. She hesitated, not certain she should renew her friendship with him now that she was engaged. The golden halo she'd seen the night their love making had been interrupted flashed through her mind. She hadn't asked him about the halo. Had it been her imagination? She punched his number.

"How many hours did you spend in the shower?" he asked.

He always made her laugh. "Pervert."

"Hey, be careful. I'm a respected journalist and novelist. I've got a bite from an agent on my novel."

"Really!"

"Yeah, they like my Washington background and that I was married to a congressman's daughter."

"And your writing might be good."

"Do you think?" he asked.

"It's possible."

"Just possible?"

"I'm sure it is, but Grady..." She remembered Detective Petter's call. "I've good news—double good news. I've heard from the detectives. They've arrested Mrs. Williams's son for her murder."

"You're kidding. When?"

"I found out about it this morning."

"I wish you'd told me earlier. When did they arrest him?"

"I didn't ask."

"Damn! I should have known about his arrest. There's a story here I'm following. I've got to go, Cassie. I need to make some calls."

"No, wait," she said before he could hang up. "I've been accepted to law school for this fall!"

"Did you ever doubt it?"

"Certainly. It was never a given. But that's not all. I wanted to ask you about something. You know that night?" Oh lord, what was she getting into now? "That night when we undressed?"

she said in a rush.

"I remember." His tone was cold. "I'm surprised you're bringing it up."

She was contrite. "I know but," she pressed on, "that night, I thought I saw around your head...a golden halo."

"Like an aura?"

"Yes! That's it exactly."

"Cool." His voice was emotionless.

"I thought so. Do you have any idea what it means?"

"How would I know? You're the psychic."

Chapter Twenty-One

Cassie was ecstatic. Her cousin, Liz, was speaking at a Peace Seeker weekend retreat in Winchester, Virginia and Cassie was going to join her. It was only Friday morning and she wasn't leaving until later in the day, but she was already packed and ready to go. Her rental car waited at the curb.

She'd told Seth about the visit to Virginia after lunch the previous day, leaving the telling as late as possible so he couldn't protest her going, and giving herself time to rent the car and take care of other details. She had presented it as something she was doing, not open to argument.

She had to fill the day somehow. A drawing assignment was due on Monday. Perhaps this afternoon, she'd walk over to the Lauinger Library on O Street and browse through books of drawings. She'd compare them to her sketches and see if she could make any improvements in her work.

She heard Grady's footsteps coming down the stairs and rushed to the door. "Grady," she called.

He smiled at her.

"How's the story going?" she asked.

"They accepted it, and being an eyewitness at the death

scene gave me credibility." He eyed her. "What's happening with you?"

"That's why I stopped you. I'm going away for the weekend. I wanted you to know that I won't be back until Sunday evening."

"Thanks for letting me know. Is that your rental car out there? I thought I saw you putting things inside."

"It feels so good to be behind the wheel again."

"Are you going with the boyfriend?" he asked.

She laughed. "That was Seth's name for you."

"Yeah? I never had a chance, did I?"

"You were there for me when I needed someone. I'll never forget you."

He put a hand on her shoulder. "You helped me believe in myself again."

She hugged him. "Good friends, right?"

He nodded. "Where are you headed?"

She told him her plans and said there was a phone number on her table if he needed it for anything. "You've my key, right?"

"I've got your key, your number, and your back."

"I'm leaving soon. I'm stopping by the university library to browse for a while."

"That doesn't surprise me. You're absolutely the kind of person who would browse in a library for kicks."

"And you're the kind who sits at a computer all night and writes novels."

"Okay, it's a draw. We're both nerds. Have a good time this weekend."

"Thanks." She started back into her apartment.

"Cassie, wait a minute." He reached into his pocket and removed a white feather. "You forgot something." He handed it to her.

She cupped the feather in her hand and stared at it.

"For good luck."

She closed her hand around it. It was warm in her fist. "Grady?"

"Take care." He pulled the door open and walked outside.

After spending a couple of hours at the library and making some drawings in a sketch book, Cassie grew restless. She might as well leave for Virginia. She could stop on the way and have a light supper.

She should have left earlier, she thought. Traffic would be horrendous later, but Liz wasn't arriving at the retreat until seven o'clock that evening. She didn't want to arrive at the hotel before her, because Liz was the one who had booked the room.

Since it didn't matter, she decided to stay a little longer and spend the time looking up the U.S. Senate on the library's computer. She studied the different committees and reviewed what Seth might be doing in the future. But her tolerance for quiet work had left her.

Once outside on the sidewalk, she realized she'd turned the wrong way. She quickly retraced her steps and saw the man who had followed her that day on Wisconsin Avenue. At least, he resembled the one she'd seen. She grabbed the FBI phone from her pocket and snapped a quick picture of him before he could turn away.

"What?" he yelled, and came at her.

Frightened, she spun around and spied a curbside mailbox only steps away. Without thinking, she dropped the phone into the sanctuary of the U.S. Postal Service.

Cursing, the man reached for her. Cassie's training kicked in. She assumed the Crane stance, with her arms flapping like wings in front of his face. Startled, he stepped backward. When he came at her again, as she knew he would, she formed her hands into Crane beaks and aimed one at his eyes and the other at his solar plexus. He covered his face defensively, and then she kicked him in the groin with all the energy she possessed.

She whipped around and ran down the street toward the rental car. She looked back several times, but didn't see anyone behind her. When she reached the car, she was panting. It was ready to go, and so was she. She threw her purse on the front seat and climbed in. It would be good to get out of this city if only for a day or two.

She drove toward Virginia and never looked back. It was nearing rush hour, and the traffic was heavy. She thought she might have been wiser to leave the car where it was and run as fast as she could to a place of safety. However, that option was past, and she had no choice at this moment but to keep on driving.

She turned at M Street and then took the Francis Scott Key Bridge and followed US 29 into Virginia. The traffic slowly wound its way into Alexandria then merged with Jefferson Davis Highway, although it wasn't the route to Winchester. She drove around for a while to make certain she wasn't being followed.

Earlier in her stay in the district, she'd visited Mt. Vernon on a day trip around town with Grady. There was a small restaurant nearby where they'd eaten. She'd head that way. If she was being tailed, she didn't want to lead them to Liz in Winchester.

She thought about contacting Rosetti at the bureau and reached into her purse. What was she thinking? That was the phone she'd tossed into the mailbox.

Then she remembered Rosetti's number was saved on her personal cell. Shaking her head at her confusion, she selected his name and punched Send. The phone rang five times and then voice mail answered. Annoyance surged through her. Oh sure, when she needed him most, he wouldn't pick up!

She left her name and number and then, searching for support of some kind, she thought she might call 911 or, she thought again, she could call Detective Riley in Michigan. She could tell him what happened. He could notify the FBI hot line that she might be in trouble and explain about tossing the phone. Maybe an agent would pick it up from the postal service. Mike could advise her about calling 911. She probably shouldn't. Everything looked calm around here. What assistance did she need? None, at the present time.

As the traffic inched southward, she punched #2 on her personal cell.

"Mike Riley." His voice sounded calm, almost disinterested, but Cassie had already figured out that was a put on. Mike cared more about his job than anyone she'd met recently—a Peace Seeker trait.

"Mike, it's Cassie. I'm in a bit of a spot."

"Shoot."

She laughed nervously. "I'm sorry, but I left my gun at home."

He let out a snort. "Okay, then it's not an emergency?"

"Not really, but I did have a bit of a battle with one of the guys following me and—wait until you hear this—he tried to take my bureau phone from me. I threw it in a mail box."

"The Feds will love that. Where are you now?"

"I'm driving a rental car." She described the car and gave him the license tag number. "And I've passed over the Key Bridge into Virginia heading toward Mt. Vernon."

"Why?" His tone was concerned.

"I'm on my way to see a cousin in Winchester, but I didn't want to go directly there. At first, I thought I'd try losing myself in traffic, and I do mean traffic. Everyone must be leaving DC for the weekend."

"Do you think someone's following you?"

"I don't know." She cleared her throat to hide the shakiness she'd noticed in her voice. "What should I do? Should I call 911?"

"Don't do that just now. I'll contact the Feds and tell them to activate their GPS, and I'll tell them to call your cell number. I imagine they'll give you a location where you can be picked up."

"I don't want anyone picking me up. I'm meeting my cousin in Winchester. She'll be frantic if I don't show up."

"Then call her and cancel. We need to make sure you're safe. They'll set you up with another phone and arrange surveillance for the next few days to guarantee you're not in trouble."

"But Mike—"

"Listen up, Cassie. You're under orders now."

She hesitated. "Yes, sir." Respect, with a touch of ice.

"Any place around there where you prefer to meet them?"

"I'm headed down the parkway toward Mt. Vernon. Should I take the long way around to see if anyone follows?"

"Forget about any tails. This might be the break we're looking for. If someone follows you, the Feds will arrest them."

Her heart skipped a beat. "I'm headed for a small restaurant I know near Mt. Vernon. I can't remember its name."

"I'll contact the bureau now. They might call you back with different instructions, but for now do as I say."

She drew a quavering breath. "Thanks, Mike."

"Be careful, Cassie. I'll talk to you later." She heard the

concern in his voice and felt reassured. She was alone in the car, but soon she'd be monitored closely. A glance in the rear-view mirror showed nothing alarming behind her.

She drove for a while and the traffic thinned. As she entered a curve in the road, she saw the restaurant's sign ahead of her. A black car had been behind her for the last five minutes and it remained there, a respectable distance back. Behind it, she could see a white car. Mike had said not to take any evasive maneuvers, but she didn't like pulling into the restaurant parking lot. If either of the cars followed her in, it could block her way out.

She would drive until the next turn off and then make a U turn and come back. She could check then whether one of the cars stayed with her through the turn.

Her cell rang. Caller ID indicated a call from an unknown person. "Hello?"

"Agent Rosetti here, Cassie. We've got you on GPS. You missed your turn in."

She touched the golden heart at her neck that held the tracking device. They knew everything, these Feds. "Two cars are behind me, and I want to make sure I'm not boxed in." She put the phone on speaker.

"Is someone behind you now?"

She glanced in the mirror. "They're both following me, but way back."

"Keep going then."

"I thought I'd make a turn and circle back to the restaurant."

"That's okay, but don't try to lose them. If they're members of that group we're watching, we want to take them in."

"Check that." She smiled despite her rising anxiety. She hadn't been around enough agents to pick up their jargon, so she made up her own.

"Here's my turning spot, I'm making a 180 now and heading back toward the restaurant. It's starting to get dark, my headlights just came on, and..." She looked in the mirror. "The black car turned with me. He's following me." Her voice rose at the end.

"Stay cool."

"What should I do?"

"Whatever you do, keep moving. I don't want them to catch up with you now. We're only ten minutes away. I'll notify the local police."

Traffic cleared, and she gave her car more gas, urging it forward. To quiet her last doubts, she took the turn she thought would lead her toward the river. She slowed then and looked in the mirror. The black car followed.

The back of her neck prickled. If she were behind them, she could try to block their approach with her psychic powers—set up some sort of auric barrier. She needed to get behind them. Get in their minds. She'd practiced it at Peace Lake. Anne Marie had taught her to concentrate her powers to block any violence meant for her. But she needed to find a place to turn around.

She lost sight of the black car on a sharp curve. As the road straightened, she saw the sign of a riverside marina on the road's shoulder, and then the marina itself. Acting on intuition she killed her lights and pulled into the parking lot. Gratefully she saw it was shaped in a U, with two entrances. Darkness had fallen and perhaps the night would be her friend. Her pursuers sped past the parking lot where she waited. With her lights off, she pulled back onto the road. Now she was behind them.

She inched her car forward until she was fifty feet behind the black sedan. Full darkness had descended and it was a cloudy night. With her lights out, they may not know she was behind them. She stared at the driver of the car ahead, willing him to leave her alone. Slowly, in immeasurable increments, the car increased its speed and pulled away from her. She slowed until the car was out of sight.

She knew she didn't have more than minutes before they discovered she had lost them. When she saw a sign indicating a fork in the road, she turned onto a smaller road and immediately saw a parking lot. She made a quick turn, still with no headlights, and pulled into a parking place hidden from view by a group of large bushes. Trembling, she killed the engine and sat listening to her heartbeat. She didn't know how long it would take those who followed to realize they had lost her, but she had to make a decision. She could wait in the car for them to double back, or she could take off on foot to find a better hiding place.

She picked up her phone and called Rosetti. "I've lost my tail, but they're sure to return."

"Cassie, do what you think is best. If you think you're in danger, then start running. You have the tracer on you, don't you?"

She fingered the necklace. "It's here."

"Then get out of the car and keep moving. Whatever you have to do, don't let them catch you. Do it now."

"Roger." She'd heard that in a movie.

The black car rushed past the parking lot, going the other way. She didn't want them to turn around and search the area. She left her car, leaving it unlocked in case she needed to get into it in a hurry. She grabbed her purse and at the last minute turned and took her deerskin jacket out of the backseat. The night was chilly and she might need it.

Crouching low, she ran into the darkness. There were

houses on her left. To her right, a line of trees. She kept to the right, away from the houses and the road until she came to a wood chip path. It was completely dark now. She trotted down the path, stopping occasionally and listening for footsteps or voices behind her. Sooner or later, she'd have to get off the path, but she wanted distance between her and her pursuers.

Minutes later, she ran out of path, and out of land. She found herself standing next to a log fence guarding a low bluff that ended at the river's edge. At least there was no moon. The water looked as black as the trees she had just left.

Swinging her legs over the fence, she slid down the low embankment and ended up feet from the Potomac's edge. She figured they'd never think she would go into the water. She wouldn't, but she'd make it look as if she had.

To her left were some private docks. Then she saw black shapes pulled up on land at the water's edge. Canoes. The memory of another night in another place flashed through her mind—last summer before she'd trusted Nate—when she'd escaped from him in a canoe.

She didn't need to do that now. All she had to do was crouch here in the darkness under cover and wait for Agent Rosetti. She heard a car door slam in the distance and then the muffled noises of people picking their way down the path, their footsteps crunching on the path's chips.

She was safe now. Rosetti would find her using the GPS, unless the bad guys were tracking her also. If the voices she heard were people from the bureau, wouldn't they be calling her name?

Terror froze her. She didn't dare wait to find out. She crouched low and paused long enough to take a plastic pouch from her purse, empty out the granola snack, set her cell phone on vibrate, and seal it in the bag before returning the bag to her purse. Then she headed toward the canoes. She grabbed the nearest one, found it unsecured, and pulled it with all her strength into the water. Wading beside it, she quickly felt her feet leave the muddy river bottom.

She hung from its side with one arm and struggled to control the canoe's movements. She silently willed it farther away from the dock. It floated on a sluggish current toward the Chesapeake. Her efforts were concealed by the cloud-filled sky. The only light was the pale reflection off the clouds from the bright city lights.

Her purse hung from its strap around her neck. Chilled to the bone, with one hand clutching the canoe, she unsnapped the purse, found her wallet and shoved it into her jacket pocket. The leather fringe floated against her fingers. It was a duplicate of the jacket she'd worn the night last summer when she'd escaped successfully from Nate.

That night she'd fooled him into thinking she was dead by abandoning the canoe and trapping air inside her jacket, making it into a floatation device. Except now she was wearing a tracking button on her necklace. The FBI knew where she was. Were the men following her also tracking her?

She let go of the canoe momentarily and sank beneath the water as she struggled with her shoes and socks. She let them drop to the bottom then kicked to the top. Whack! Stunned by the jolt to her head, she sank again, wincing with pain, and tumbled helplessly in the black water.

Slowly, lungs burning with the need for air, she steadied herself and quietly breast stroked away from the shape looming above her. Her arms were heavy and tingling from the blow to her head against the canoe bottom. She broke through the water's surface and peered back at shore. Dark shapes approached the spot where she had entered the water.

The silence of the night convinced Cassie those searching for her were not FBI friends. They would be shouting for her by now—calling her name. Instead the shadows scurrying at the water's edge moved without noise.

She had no more use for the canoe, and it was too easily seen. Although dizzy from the blow to her head, she reached up and tipped the canoe until it filled with water, and then let it drift away downstream. With the canoe taken care of, she plumped her deerskin jacket with air and frog-kicked her way in the opposite direction.

She clutched her jacket and willed herself to ignore the pain in her head that crowded out other thoughts. She swam upstream and away from shore, letting the canoe drift away in the opposite direction with the sluggish current.

At the sound of men on shore, she kicked harder. Silent flashlight beams danced over the water, and she headed toward the middle of the river. As the lights swept over the dark river, she anticipated their advance and ducked under the water when the beams approached her. Her silver-blonde hair was wet, and she was confident it wouldn't reflect light from their flashlights. The natural ripples on the river masked her slight movements.

She closed her eyes briefly in an effort to clear her vision and wondered, just for a moment, if she'd seriously injured herself. Flashes of light burned against her eyelids, but that could be from the stress of being hunted.

Opening her eyes, she watched from a distance as a low dark shape set out from the shore. Panic struck as the dark shape materialized into a canoe headed directly at her. She turned away from it and frog-kicked as strongly as she could without splashing and without injuring herself further.

When she thought she'd put enough room between them,

she stopped moving and took the plastic pouch from her jacket pocket. This had better work. If not, she'd soon be fish bait. She rested the pouch on top of the deerskin and opened it using her teeth as well as her fingers. She removed her cell phone, shielding its light as much as possible. Her finger trembled as she pressed #2. At the sound of Mike's voice from Michigan, she whispered, "I'm out on the river in the water, straight out from the dock, but there's a canoe on its way after me."

"Rosetti is on the other line." Mike said. "I'll pass the word along."

She silently closed the phone and cradled it in her closed fist, being careful to keep it dry. All she could do now was wait, and silently push against the sluggish current.

She gently frog-kicked farther out to the middle of the river, heading toward Maryland. No doubt they were tracking the GPS necklace she wore.

The phone vibrated in her hand. She opened it and Mike's voice said "Cassie, drop the phone. Drop everything you have. Take off your shoes, clothes, everything. Let them sink. Trust me. The enemy must be tracking you, also. Do it now!" The phone went dead.

She closed it and dropped it into the water. Then she released the clasp of the necklace and threw it as far from her as she could. She pressed the air from her jacket, pushed it under the water, and swam away. A few yards from where she'd released the jacket, she looked toward the Virginia shore. The low dark form continued slowly toward her.

Her heart pounded fiercely, and she stopped swimming. She wasn't going to make it through this night. What could she do to save herself? Could she try moving ahead in time as she had when she was in Walloon Lake running from Nate? She'd escaped from him then. She could do that now. But at this instant, she wasn't sure what was ahead of her. If she died, if her body died, here in this frigid river, and if she moved ahead in time, she might never see this life again.

The risk was too great. And there was no use trying to return to the past. She knew from experience the past couldn't be changed. Time travel, or translocation, wouldn't work here. She had no alternative but to overcome her anxiety and fight her way out of this situation.

She quieted her mind. Maybe she could pick up the thoughts of her pursuers. But her heart pounded too loudly, her pulse beat in her ears, and her mind wouldn't give up its struggle to control the situation. She had to follow Mike's orders.

To remove her pants, she raised one knee and sank underwater. Next her sweater came off, and then her blouse. She let herself go under and pulled the clothing over her head and released it. Then her bra. She struggled with its clasp, finally freed herself from its embrace and let it sink to the bottom. She hesitated. He'd said everything. With reservations, she wiggled her panties over her toes and let them go.

After another life-giving breath, she reluctantly removed Eudora's diamond earrings and her black coral ring, and let them drop to the river's bottom. Her wallet had gone down with her jacket. She was completely naked except for her diamond engagement ring. She hadn't taken it off since Seth gave it to her. She wouldn't remove it now.

The canoe wasn't far away, but it pursued her with less purpose. The men's soft voices carried over the water. She couldn't make out the words, but she sensed their intent.

Keeping only her eyes above the water, she continued breast stroking her way upstream and toward the Maryland shore as best she could. After the first strokes, a feeling of freedom overtook her. The pain disappeared from her head and neck. Her arms felt stronger. She closed her eyes and let her instincts guide her away from those following. The cold water against her bare skin became her friend—its coolness invigorating and life giving.

She remembered as a teenager skinny-dipping at Mackinac Island. Those Northern waters had been colder than this Virginia estuary.

Her movements fell into a rhythm. Each silent stroke followed by a thrusting frog kick. As she reached far inside herself for a strength she hadn't known she possessed, time lost its meaning. Peace fell over her.

Are you there? she asked her special spiritual guide.

Cassie. I'm always with you.

She closed her eyes against the sting of the water and stopped struggling. Immediately, cold consumed her.

Don't give up! Keep moving. We're here for you.

We?

Nate's here also.

Warmth filled her.

Don't be afraid. We'll keep you afloat.

Then she heard voices shouting. Flashlights, more shouts, a shot. The pursuing canoe, as difficult to see in the black night as she was, continued on its path toward her. She lifted her head and saw light shining across the water.

"Cassie!" She heard a man's voice.

Yes, I'm listening.

"Cassie!"

The water embraced her. *Nate?*

"Cassie!"

Thank you, Nate.

With the last of her strength, she opened her eyes and

treaded water.

Two dark shapes, canoes, were headed into the river, each with a flashlight bobbing with the canoes' movements. They were heading downstream.

"Cassie!" She recognized Anthony Rosetti's voice.

"I'm here!" Her voice was little more than a croak. That wouldn't work. Okay, if they couldn't find her, she'd go to them.

Filled with a renewed source of inner strength, she swam toward the lights. No need to hide her movements now. She only needed to swim toward them. If the idiots would stop shouting for a moment, they would hear her stroking through the water.

"Here!" she shouted as best she could during a brief moment of quiet.

Everything hushed.

"Here, behind you!" She splashed her arms against the water's surface.

The lights spun in the darkness and caught her face, blinding her momentarily.

A hoarse laugh arose from her throat. She was on stage with all the flashlights on her. She waved both arms.

Oh, lord, here she was in the middle of this Virginia river with no clothes and at least two canoes headed her way.

A man reached down to grab her, and she couldn't stop laughing.

"I'm coming in with you," Rosetti said.

"No, I'm okay. Just lift me out of here."

He grabbed her under her arms then quickly backed off. "Wait, I'll get a jacket to cover you."

"Forget the jacket. I want out of this water." She put an elbow and a knee on the side of the canoe and started pulling herself up.

"Whoa! You'll tip it. Let us lift you over." Agent Rosetti looked over his shoulder. "Jack, steady the canoe."

Strong arms wrapped around her and pulled her aboard. She knelt at the bottom of the canoe and imagined her skin glistening in the sudden revealing sliver of moonlight shining through a split in the low clouds.

She threw back her head and laughed out of sheer joy of being alive.

Agent Rosetti placed a man's suit jacket around her shoulders. She slipped trembling arms into its sleeves.

She looked at the jacket and smiled at him. "Do you always wear a suit, Agent Rosetti?"

He grinned. "It's the uniform of the day, Ms. West." He briskly rubbed her back through the heavy cloth. "Especially when canoeing."

A surge of exhilaration passed through her. "I think I could swim the Atlantic tonight."

"Please, not on my shift."

"I only said I *thought* I could."

"It's adrenaline."

Teeth chattering, she nodded.

"It will leave you soon. I'll probably have to carry you to the car."

The rush of energy was already ebbing. "I want to thank you guys." *Thanks, Nate.* "Thanks for saving my life." She spoke to the other agent who paddled the canoe.

"It's our job."

She shivered. "Do they teach canoe paddling at the agency?"

"I learned during my misspent youth at Lake Champlain," the man at the rear said.

The other canoe drew closer. "Need any help?" a man called.

"No," Rosetti answered. "We're okay. Are the perps secured?"

"Tied up like garbage."

Their canoe softly bumped a dock, and Agent Rosetti looked at her. "We'll steady it, Cassie, while you climb out."

"Ah," she whispered, "Tony, would you happen to have any panties with you?"

He grinned. "Not tonight, sorry, Cass."

"Thought you might."

"Not my luck."

"Mine either."

He took her hand. "Tell you what, I'll get out and help you onto the dock."

She buttoned the suit coat. "I could use some more buttons here."

"You're doing great. Don't lose your nerve now. You're almost home."

"Did you find my clothes?"

"You don't need them."

"What about the men?"

"As we speak, they're in custody. You've been a great help." He moved his head close to hers. "I'm glad you weren't injured."

She didn't mention hitting her head. It might complicate things and postpone her return to her apartment. "Catching Nate's murderers was worth any risk." And dying was not the worst thing that could happen. She thought of the ethereal Inner Kingdom where souls met between lifetimes. She would see Nate again. She was certain of it.

Agent Rosetti pulled himself onto the dock. Cassie leaned

toward him and he grabbed her under her arms and lifted her from the canoe. She felt the rush of cool air against her bottom. Then he swept her up into his arms.

"You can't carry me all the way to the car."

"I can. Never doubt the FBI."

"Oh sure." She squirmed. "Anyway, put me down, my bottom's hanging out."

"It's dark. No one can see. Besides, we're all gentlemen. No one is looking."

"Oh, sure."

Chapter Twenty-Two

"You're where?" Liz sounded incredulous.

"I said I'm in a car with the FBI. I didn't want you to worry when I didn't show up at the hotel."

"Cassie, what happened?"

She looked at Rosetti who sat in the backseat with her. "I'll tell you later. For now I'm going home. I'm sorry, Liz." Tears wet her eyes. "I wanted to see you."

"Wait, Cassie, don't hang up. Don't forget the golden robe. Wear it this weekend."

She wiped her eyes with her fingers and waved away Rosetti's offer of a handkerchief. "I'm doing all of it," she told Liz, "the golden robe, and auric protection. I'll light a white candle. Liz, I owe you and the other Peace Seekers so much."

"Is Seth with you?"

"No, he thinks I'm with you for the weekend."

"Could you make it here tomorrow?" Liz asked.

"I doubt it. I'm exhausted, and I have a terrible headache. They wanted me to go to the hospital, but I'm going home instead."

"Will you be safe? Do you want me to come and stay?"

"No, I'll have FBI surveillance tonight, just in case. And, Liz, I know your work is important for others. Teach them what you know. I promise I'll be all right."

She hung up, shivered once, and handed the cell phone to Agent Rosetti. "I'll be happy when I have some clothes on."

"You should go to the hospital."

She wrapped the FBI's thermal blanket tightly around her. "I'll be all right when I get home. Just tell me all this was worth it. Did you learn anything?"

"We will. We suspect they're the lowest level of a cleverly built pyramid. They only know the contacts on the next level. I told you about the man at the top, but we have to fit the pieces together. If these guys talk, then we can move to the next level. Sooner or later we'll get them. We always do."

Cassie smiled. "That's what I've heard. It's too bad there are so many rotten people in the world."

"This guy is rich in a material way, but I wouldn't want to be him. He's the only son of an only son, and as soon as he came into his money, paranoia set in. He's highly frightened of groups he believes are out to change his world—take his money away. If it's the person I told you about, he's an American who created a sanctuary on a Canadian mountain, not too far from the Idaho border.

"That's sad."

Rosetti grinned. "Would you believe he's afraid of the federal government?"

She raised her eyebrows. "Really?"

"He thinks we're out to get him."

"Maybe he's not so crazy after all."

Rosetti shook his head, and his expression sobered. "He's crazy all right. You, of all people, should know that."

Cassie stood in the shower and let hot water flow over her. She had thought she would never be warm again, but gradually the warmth reached her fingertips. When that happened, she knew she was okay.

She'd accomplished what she set out to do—help catch Nate's killers. Of course, Rosetti wouldn't confirm the two men taken into custody were the ones who killed Nate, but she knew they were. Her memory of that night had returned. She clearly recalled the two men. They had been in her condo elevator. She would testify against them when, or if, the opportunity came.

Although Tony Rosetti and other agents had debriefed her thoroughly, she wanted to talk to someone. She needed to be held. Grady? He was right upstairs. He would come down in a minute if he knew she needed help. No. Grady was someone she would always love, but he was her past. Seth was her future.

She put on striped pajamas, then her white terry robe and heavy socks. She wrapped a towel around her wet hair.

She punched in the numbers on her landline. Both cells were lost forever. "Seth?" she said, when he answered.

"Are you with Liz?"

"No, I'm home. I didn't go to Virginia."

"You don't sound right. What's wrong?"

She fought to control tears. She could do this. She was strong.

"What's wrong, Cassie?" Seth's voice was filled with concern.

"I need you to come over." She swallowed her tears.

"I'll leave right now." He hesitated. "Tell me."

"We'll talk about it when you're here."

She heard him sigh. "Okay, sweetheart. See you in fifteen minutes."

She placed the phone on its base and shuffled into the living room. She pulled down the blinds over the bay window, picked up her Penny Bear and sank into the rocking chair. With her arms wrapped around the teddy, she folded into herself and stifled sobs while she rocked.

The past ten months flashed before her eyes in a life review. Meeting Nate, then losing him, Eudora's death on Mackinac Island, both caused by the same men who were in the pay of some powerful man or group who stood to gain the most from continued chaos and anarchy. She sobbed brokenly and then slowly gained control.

Ann Marie's smiling face passed before her eyes, Rupert and Lucille at Peace Lake, kind people all of them. Then Seth. And Grady, dear Grady. Her heart skipped, and she waited while it settled. Grady was her angel, she accepted it now. He'd watched over her and loved her in the way he knew best. Mrs. Williams. A new flood of tears. Her neighbor had also lost her life. And Cassie almost lost hers tonight. Thanks to Detective Mike Riley and Special Agent Tony Rosetti, she was alive and sitting in this rocker waiting for Seth.

She shivered. Her wet hair was draining the heat from her body and her head was pounding. Slowly, she climbed out of the chair and headed into the bathroom. The whirr of the hair dryer sounded loud in the tiny room. If Grady were home, he might hear the sound and wonder why she hadn't gone to Virginia.

As she dried her hair, she thought about Grady. A smile lightened her heart. How about having a personal angel? That must be why he'd given her the white feather. She was wrapped in thoughts of celestial beings when Seth's booming "hello" dragged her from her dreams.

She almost dropped the hair dryer. "I didn't hear you at

the door."

He smiled. "I rang. Good thing I have a key."

She turned the dryer off, set it down and rushed into his arms. As she clutched him, tears flooded her eyes.

"What's wrong, sweetheart?" he murmured into her ear.

"I can't begin to explain."

"Really?" He walked her into the living room and pulled her down on the sofa next to him. "Tell me."

Her hair straggled over her face and lay damply against her neck. "Don't be angry."

He rose and walked into the kitchen.

"Where are you going?" she asked frantically. "Don't leave."

He returned with a box of tissues from the kitchen counter. "Cassie, calm down. This isn't like you." He handed her the box.

"I know." She wiped her nose. "I'm a mess."

He sat beside her and cuddled her. "Tell me everything."

Twenty minutes later, he paced the living room. "I simply can't believe you would do such a thing."

Exhausted, she sighed. "Please, Seth. I told you that I didn't mean to hurt you by keeping it from you."

He waved his arms. "My wife, my intended wife, running around DC with the FBI, putting herself in imminent danger, swimming in the Potomac River in freezing weather—"

"It wasn't freezing." What would he say if she confessed to being naked?

"And I knew nothing about it." He threw himself into the rocker. "I can't believe it."

A smile curled the corners of her mouth. "Do you want a divorce?" Seth's indignant little boy tantrum helped her see the incongruity of her action. Had she actually done all that? Had she worn a GPS tracker? She laughed softly.

He gave her his full attention for the first time in the last twenty minutes. He folded his hands over his abdomen. "If we were married, I might consider a divorce, but it's too soon for that."

"What then?" she asked. "How can I make it up to you?"

He studied her. "I'll think of something. Are you through with the FBI?"

"Not quite."

His eyebrows rose.

"I might have to testify in court," she said.

He grunted.

"Seth, think about it. These are the men who murdered Nate." Her voice shook. "I helped catch them."

"Do you think Nate would have wanted you to risk your life?"

"He was with me in the water—"

"I'm sure he was."

"—and he was proud of me."

Seth hesitated. "I am also." He walked over to her and extended a hand.

She took his hand and let him pull her to her feet.

"Cassie, do you realize how extraordinary you are?"

She shook her head.

"Come here." He gathered her into a tender embrace.

"Seth, please forgive me." She nestled into the warm welcome of his arms and rested her pounding head on his shoulder.

"Of course. Just don't do it again."

"If I do, I'll tell you."

He held her away from him. "No. Promise me."

She pulled on a damp strand of hair and stepped away. "You understand, don't you," her voice rose, "this was something I had to do. I had to find these men. They, and whoever hired them, are the guilty ones, not me! My God, Seth, they killed Eudora, and then my Nate."

He stared at her until his expression softened. "Okay." He kissed the top of her head. "I understand. We'll never forget those who are gone. I promise their memories will always be part of our lives." He tilted her chin and looked into her eyes. "But this is our time now, and I'm claiming this dance."

She wrapped her arms around him, realizing once again how huge he was, how strong and warm and comforting, and... how completely male. Her heart beat in rhythm against his and she offered her lips.

She slept well that night and, except for a disturbing headache, awoke in the morning with an awesome sense of accomplishment. She felt whole and complete. She'd had the courage to give her all. She had actually done it! Somewhere she knew Nate was looking down and approving her actions. For the rest of her life, she would remember this moment and know she had the ability to accomplish anything she wanted. And why? Because she had overcome her fear and her concern about what others might think. Her heart filled with gratitude for those who had helped and believed in her, even though at times she hadn't believed in herself.

Nate had believed in her. Grady believed. Ann Marie, Liz, Detective Mike Riley, and Special Agent Anthony Rosetti. And Seth. Her heart stuttered when she thought of Seth.

No, he hadn't believed in her. He only considered her as window dressing for his career. She froze. Was that true? Her spirits sank when she thought of Seth's anger at discovering she'd concealed her work with the FBI. The man was a control freak. A control freak with incredible charisma. If she married him, she'd be under a microscope for the rest of her life. She'd be the politician's wife, the good wife, never sure of him, of what he was doing, or with whom he was doing it.

The realization hit her with the force of five Gs. It tore at her, weakened her legs, and wrenched her stomach. She knew she couldn't marry Seth. Not now, not in three years. Never! She sat on the edge of her bed trying to pull together images of their future. No matter how hard she tried, she couldn't fit Seth into the picture. It was time to consult her spirit guides. She'd do some meditative chanting before breakfast. She already knew what she had to do, but any support the universe gave her would be gratefully accepted.

After meditating, Cassie sat at the table in the dining room and made a list of what needed to be done to replace her ID and other personal items she had lost in the river. She had talked to Tony Rosetti and he was assigning an agent to bring new ID over to her. He was also giving her a newly programmed cell phone. He'd laughed when she apologized for losing the necklace. From what he said, she learned that the arrested men were talking in exchange for a lighter sentence. She had done her job and the Feds were appreciative. They wanted to continue monitoring her safety. Just in case.

She'd put the finishing touches on her list when the doorbell rang. Grady smiled at her when she opened the door. "Hi," he said. "I heard you showering and wondered why you'd come home."

"Something happened."

He looked toward the street. "Trouble with the car? Did you return it to the rental agency?"

"Something like that."

His long look made her nervous. Then he asked, "Is there

anything I can do to help?"

Sweet, angelic Grady.

When she refused his help, he stared at her. For a moment she thought she saw his aura again, but she blinked, and the golden light disappeared.

"You don't need my help do you?" he asked.

She shook her head.

"It wasn't the car, was it? Something else happened that you can't talk about."

She smiled at him. "Thanks for understanding."

He put a gentle hand on her shoulder. "Let me know if you need anything." He turned to leave.

"Wait," she said. "Thanks for the feather, but I lost it. I sure could use another one." She put out her hand.

He reached into his pocket and pulled out another white feather, kissed it, and handed it to her.

She closed her fist around it, and tears sprang into her eyes. "Thanks, Grady, for everything."

After she closed the door behind him, she pressed her forehead against the cool wood. The headache would not stop.

Her phone rang and she ran into the kitchen and lifted the receiver. "Hi, Liz," she returned her cousin's greeting. "Glad you had this number."

"Are you okay?"

"Grady just left and Seth is bringing dinner. I'm so happy you called."

"Why, is something wrong?"

"Not in the way you might think, but I've changed. When I woke this morning I realized I can't marry Seth. I spent some time meditating and chanting, and I have to tell him that I can't go through with this marriage."

"How strange! Not your insight, but during the workshop

today, I had a vision of your future. Seth wasn't in it."

Cassie leaned against the kitchen counter. "What do you mean, he wasn't with me?"

"My guides showed me a different future for you."

She clutched the counter. "My intuition told me the same thing! But reality always said, 'Marry him.' Nate's influence included." Then she remembered Ann Marie. Her mentor's guidance had been anything but encouraging toward Seth.

"All I can do," Liz said, "is tell you what my spiritual guides showed me. You need to make your own decision, but they said you should finish law school and seek your own destiny apart from him."

"It's going to be a difficult time for both of us, but I know I have the courage to tell him of my decision."

"Cassie, I see more for you than what you planned with Seth. I saw you speaking at an International Conference to world leaders, and he wasn't there with you."

"I don't know about that. All I know is that I'm happier than I've been for a long time. I'll talk to Seth tomorrow. Give me your blessing."

"You have it."

⊕　⊕　⊕

Even though Seth brought dinner over, Cassie waited until the next morning to tell him of her decision. She wanted to be certain she was doing the right thing. When he answered his cell, he told her that, although it was Sunday, he was at his office catching up on work. He agreed she could see him if she came right over. He'd tell security to expect her. When she entered Seth's office, she smiled at his assistant who was working on the computer. "Is he able to see me now?" Cassie asked.

"He's in his office. I'll show you the way."

She had dressed carefully for this meeting, wearing one of the dresses Vicki had selected. Even though she knew what she was doing was right, not only for her but for Seth as well, her heart beat faster.

He met her at the door to his inner office. "You never cease to surprise me."

Her mouth was dry. "I guess life is full of surprises." Quite a lead into what she had to say.

"I thought you'd be spending the day in bed following your little adventure Friday night." He put an arm around her and dropped a casual kiss on her forehead. "Sit down." He held a chair for her at his desk and then he sat in the executive swivel chair behind it. "From your tone over the phone, I take it this isn't a social visit."

"I only wish it were."

"Take your time. I've thirty minutes before my lunch appointment."

Her mouth opened and closed twice before he broke the silence.

"I suppose you have cold feet again?" He made a tent out of his fingers and had a grim look about his mouth.

"I wouldn't call it cold feet. I have to do something difficult, but I'm not frightened."

"You're going to tell me the wedding at Mackinac Island is off."

He already knew. He was, after all, a Peace Seeker. His telepathic talents matched or were greater than hers. "That's about it," she said.

"What's the reason this time?"

She swallowed. "I've found the courage somehow to follow my heart, to be a whole woman. I don't see that happening as your wife."

"Is it the landlord?"

"It's not another man, Seth. It's within me. There's something I have to do, and while I don't know what it is exactly, I know it isn't my destiny to be with you."

He sighed, leaned back, and stuck his thumbs in his pockets. "I've had doubts about you from the beginning. You seemed too weak to handle being a senator's wife, much less the country's first lady."

She held back tears. He'd touched her where she hurt the most, her supposed weakness, her insecurity. She took a deep breath. "I have strength within me to do whatever is necessary."

"No balls."

"What?"

"You heard me. You don't have the guts to follow through with what you start."

She rose slightly and then settled down in the chair. "I'm glad we've had this talk. I would have been miserable as your wife, and you wouldn't have liked it much either."

He shook his head. "I would have seen to it that you were happy."

"How can you say that when you hold such a low opinion of me?"

"Cassie, I love you. I've wanted you from the beginning and I still want you. But you're like sandpaper to me. Every time I get close, we argue. If you change your mind, you will be happy married to me. I promise. We'll have children and you'll have the family you've always wanted."

"We never talked about children. I thought they weren't part of the agenda."

"They're a necessary part of a president's persona."

She thought that one over. "You would use children to further your political career?" She stood. "I'm glad I learned this now instead of later."

He rose and walked around the desk. "Don't make a decision too quickly. Take your time to consider the consequences."

She removed his ring from her finger. "I don't need time. Here's your ring."

He refused to take it. When she reached to put it on the desk, he took her fist in his hand. "Think about what you're doing to the Peace Seekers' goal for us."

"I—"

"Wait, think about it. I've just announced our engagement to the world. Now a week later, you're returning the ring. How will that play out in the tabloids? What will that do to my reputation? People are certain to look for other problems."

Her mind spun with the implications of a newly elected senator's fiancée breaking the engagement. "Seth, I don't want to hurt you in any way, personally or politically."

"I never thought you did. You're a woman of high character. Otherwise, I'd never have considered marrying you."

Her hand with the ring in it was still covered by his larger hand.

She smiled. "High character? What about the night you found me with Grady?"

His eyes crinkled. "That was just spice."

"Spice?"

"To go with the sugar." He wrapped his arms around her.

The tension in her muscles eased. They were going to part friends, after all. She took a deep breath. "I am sorry it isn't working out for us."

"I know, and I would never want you to go against what you think is right." His breath was warm on her forehead. His ring was clutched in her hand. "But do me one last favor, Cassie? Please?"

She could feel his auric field blend with hers. They

were fellow travelers, after all. Time travelers, reincarnated Bodhisattvas. "I like it when you say 'please.'"

"I won't beg, but please do this last thing for me. Don't break our engagement until it's absolutely necessary. Do what you need to do, study law, travel, whatever it is. I'll support you in any way I can. And then when you come to a point where you feel it's time, or if I feel it's time, then we can part as friends without ill feelings."

He held her away from him by her shoulders. "What do you think? Will that work for you?"

His eyes captured her gaze. In them she saw truth, love, and decency. He was a Peace Seeker like her, a reincarnated soul returned to earth for another lifetime. He was love embodied. What less could she do?

She nodded. "That works for me."

He smiled, and she held out her hand with the ring in it. He slipped it on the third finger of her left hand.

"Should we shake on our bargain?" She held out her hand and he took it.

"No kiss?" he said.

She laughed. "No more kisses. You're too seductive." She looked at the ring on her finger. "This ring means nothing, Seth."

"It means that I'll be by your side helping you in any way I can. It also means that we can still work together for our Peace Seeker goals as colleagues, but not lovers."

He walked her to the outside corridor and left her at the door. She stood for a moment alone in the hall and listened, but she didn't hear Nate's voice.

Goodbye, Nate, my love. From now on I'm making my own decisions. Silence. She squared her shoulders and headed for the elevator that would take her to the lobby and from there toward the rest of her life.

The end